The Family of Hilda

By the same author:
History
Sisters, Saints and Queens
Travel
Diary of a South Coast Walk with a freedom pass
Children
Six Dragons on a Hill
The Chimney People

[Cover: image of stained glass by L Everretts in St Peters, Monkwearmouth]

Copyright © : Neil Edington 2020

This book is sold subject to the condition that it shall not, by way of trade or otherwise, be lent, resold, hired out, or otherwise circulated without the publisher's prior consent in any form of binding or cover other than that in which it is published and without a similar condition including this condition being imposed on the subsequent publisher.
The moral right of Neil Edington has been asserted.
ISBN:9798564747394
ISBN

Printed by kdp Amazon

Introduction

St Hilda, thanks to the writings of Bede, is rightly recognized as one of the most celebrated saints of the seventh century and is, not surprisingly, the subject of several historical novels. My justification for adding to the genre partly lies with the exciting archeological discoveries that have been, and are being, made, by the University of Reading at Lyminge in Kent. I have added a stay in Lyminge by Hilda, to cover her 'nobly in secular occupations' period described by Bede: thereby emphasizing her 'family links' with her aunt, Queen Ethelberga, the queen's daughter Eanfled, whose daughter Aelffled, was given into the care of Hilda at Hartlepool. The family is completed by the close links of Hilda with her elder sister, Hereswid.

In the area of Anglo-Saxon names, they have always seemed to be variable, continue to be 'updated', and will probably continue to do so. I therefore chose, by and large, to stick with those of the original translation into English of Bede's 'A History of the English Church and People' [HE].

HE is inevitably a principal source for the framework of the narrative. But I would like to thank the sisters of OHP, at Whitby, for their hospitality and use of their library. I have already acknowledged the work of the Reading archeologists at Lyminge, led by Dr Gabor Thomas, but I also am grateful for help at the Hartlepool Branch of Tees Archeology for direction and inevitably to the works of Professor Rosemary Cramp for several of the sites where Hilda was abbess. Professor Barbara Yorke was particularly helpful in advising me as to what I could and could not know as to the wives/partners of King Oswy and the various attributions of his children. Other sources of reference are listed in the bibliography.

The Revd Richard Bradshaw kindly gave me permission to use an image of Leonard Everretts' stained glass window of Hilda in St Peter's Church in Monkwearmouth as the cover for the book.

Roger Cline was generous enough to proofread my first draft, but all errors, inconsistencies, and misrepresentations must be the author's.

NE October 2020

The Family of Hilda

Introduction..3

The drama of Easter...........................10
The reign of Edwin.............................17
A marriage and an idyll's end..................27
The dispersal......................................50
A return to Kent..................................62
The visitors......................................78
Resolutions....................................107
Key changes....................................129
Transactions..................................145
A return 169
A shift in the Northern Kingdoms.............. 200
A new home............................ 217
A visitor from East Anglia.....................231
A meeting..250
A celebration & a change.......................261
Resolutions................................ ..278
Home to rest..................................298

Epilogue...315
Bibliography.....................................317

9

Northumbria North = Bernicia

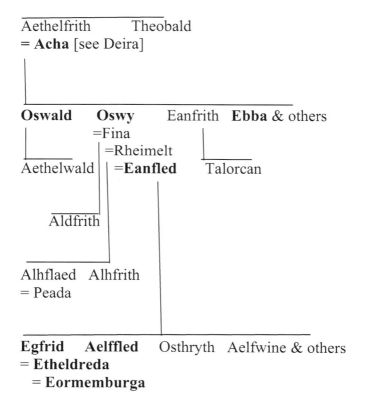

11

12

Northumbria South= Deira

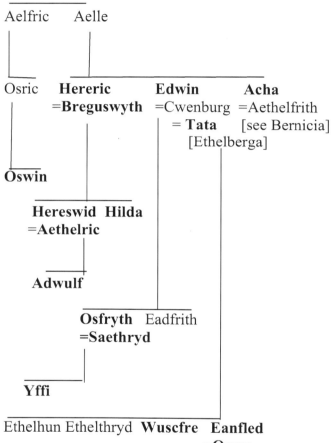

13

KENT

Ethelbert
=***Bertha***

Eadbald   ***Ethelberga [Tata]***
=***Ymme***   =***Edwin [see Deira]***

Eormenred   ***Erconbert***   ***Eanswith***
=Oslafa   =Sexburg

      Egbert   Ermenilda   Earcongota   Hlothere

Eormenburg   Aethelred   Aethelbert   ***Aebbe***

15

16

The drama of Easter

As birth days go, to be born on Easter day must count as being singular, not least for the fact that the by the next time your birthday coincides with this important festival you will be a young adult. In 626 there was the added complication that Easter in the north of England could be calculated according to the Celtic or to the Roman calendar, so that celebrations of the fasting and the festival often occurred several weeks apart; which could be divisive in a household.

But for Queen Ethelberga Easter was according to St Peter, and the birth of her daughter Eanfled on this Easter day was a relatively easy delivery as deliveries go, which was good news as she would have several more children.

What she and her midwives did not know, as she pushed to bring the little child into the world, was that in the main hall an assassination attempt was made on her husband, King Edwin. The poisoned dagger of the erstwhile guest, Eumer, had been meant to kill the King, but his faithful thegn, Lilla, unarmed, had thrown himself between his king and the assailant, thereby taking the brunt of the blow through his shoulder, deflecting it from his king. Even so the vigour of the thrust behind the long dagger went through Lilla to scratch the king's arm, carrying with it a trace of the poison smeared onto the blade. Lilla had fallen, bleeding from a severed artery; and already pale from the poison. Eumer hung poised for a moment, aware that his mission had been thwarted: awaiting the inevitable reprisal, his life, his home, all flashed before him. He pulled back the dagger and tried to strike again, fatally wounding the thegn Fordhere, before Bassus, tall and broad, in two strides took hold of him from behind and slashed his throat, discarding him to the ground to bleed out.

It all happened so rapidly that there was a stunned silence in the hall. Bassus, a trusted thegn, took the king's bleeding arm and poured the nearest vessel of ale on it to wash out the poison; staring at the king, he enlarged the scratch to help the blood flow out. Edwin grimaced and nodded,

"Prepare a reply: and look to the queen" was his fierce response. Bassus nodded, bowed and stood down as others came to bandage the king's arm.

In the stables the horses chewed on hay, unaware of the strife in the great hall. A late blackbird scavenged the enclosure of the geese, hoping for pickings of grain. The early moon had its steady, reflected light, masked and unmasked by fleeting clouds. The smoke from the fire of the hall curled out into the night and was buffeted by the south westerly gale.

19

Eanfled, the little, newborn princess, suckled at her mother's breast, snuggled in the warmth of the birthing tent, innocent to the turbulent world into which she had been born.

The two sisters, Hereswid and Hilda, sixteen and twelve years old, were divided. Hereswid had been deemed old enough to assist the queen in her struggles; the younger Hilda did help, but was kept busy carrying bowls of steaming water to and from the curtained enclosure; listening to the cries of anguish as Ethelberga pushed, and pushed again; then, hearing the unmistakable wail of the newborn baby, so that all the faces, inside and outside the tent, paused, and broke into smiles.

It was a little girl, a new princess; a new cousin to Hereswid and Hilda; even as an adopted sister in this royal household. For Edwin had rescued his nieces and adopted them into his family, while Ethelberga, being only twenty when she had moved northwards from Kent, had been delighted to accept them as much as younger sisters rather than daughters. All three were strangers to this northern court. The queen, in some ways, more so. For, while Edwin still had all the rituals of the Scandinavian Gods, she hailed from the Christian court of Kent. She had travelled north with the support of the tall, craggy Bishop Paulinus and his retinue who would at least minister to her and also educate her adopted sisters.

Paulinus, his thoughts and prayers much with Ethelberga and her birthing, had been at the

20

table of the long hall when the attempted assassination had occurred. Shocked out of his meditations, he made the sign of the cross over the dying assassin, shaking his head, with a desolate, murmured prayer of absolution; and stood in silent prayer for the King as the attendants applied herbs to his arm. 'Such blatant treachery: these heathen lands!' ran through his mind.

Then the faint cry of the newborn came into the hall; and he made the sign of the cross for a third time. This time with heartfelt thanks. He, assured that the king was in good hands, moved out of the long hall towards the candlelight spilling from the birthing tent. He found the young Hilda, with her hands clasped in happiness, peeping though the flap of the door, an empty bowl at her feet. He smiled and raised a questioning eyebrow.

"It is a little girl, Bishop; and the queen is well," answered Hilda, her own face quietly radiant; partly from the exertion of carrying steaming bowls of water. Paulinus nodded, half bowing his appreciation and thanks; noting the cool serenity of this child. She had attended the classes that he ran for the royal ladies, and she had benefited from the challenge of keeping up with her older sister. There were few privileges to this northern posting, he mused, but teaching Breguswid's daughters, Hereswid and Hilda, was one of the rewards.

It was Hereswid, the elder daughter, who briefly came to the door and pushed back the flap so that Paulinus could just see Ethelberga and her child on the linen and straw trestle; enough to bow and bestow a blessing on them both.

Edwin came in a few minutes later, his bandaged arm disguised by the wrappings of his cloak. He embraced his wife, affectionately known as Tata, lightly on her cheek, dropping on a knee to peer with joy at the little pink babe that was sucking contentedly at her breast. The queen put his pallor down to the excitement of the birth, still unaware of the dangers that had taken place in the long hall. Edwin had insisted that she should sleep soundly and that he would break the news in the morning.

He saw Paulinus in prayer outside the tent.

"You might have saved me from the stabbing," he said, somewhat ambiguously. A wry smile, and he continued,

"You will want to baptize my child, as Tata wishes?"

Paulinus nodded his head in affirmation.

"Then let it be so. But wait until I am returned from the south; and in better health."

He left to organize a reprisal for the betrayal; and the burial of his faithful Lilla and Fordhere. But not before he slept soundly, more weakened by the poison of the scratch than he cared to admit.

The night wind blew and the horses of the assassin and the royal household dozed together, unaware of the momentous events. Tata too slept

soundly, exhausted by her efforts, comforted by her nestling child.

In the mist of the morning, on the outskirts of the encampment at Goodmanham, they laid Lilla and Fordhere in their graves, dressed in battle dress, and with spear and shield by their sides. The gifts and horses of the southern party were given to their families; and extra hides of lands added to their estates.

Within a week a party of forty warriors filtered south in groups of ten: and the Wessex King Cuichelm and his thegns were put to the sword in the dark of the night.

By Pentecost they had returned home to find that all was well. The white May blossom was out on the thorn trees and the fresh breezes were heralding spring moving towards summer.

Edwin and his warriors were delighted to be reunited with their families. There were celebrations to be had as well as much administration to sort out. Six weeks of petitions lay at the door of the court, for not all had been quiet and peaceful in his absence. But they could wait until his daughter had been baptized; and he saw the pleasure that his acquiesence gave to his queen and the ladies of the court. Yet did he still hold back from committing himself and his thegns to this new faith. He engrossed himself in the squabbles of families; and pondered.

    The cattle were out grazing in the pastures, with the early flowers of the meadows bringing a spread of colours to the fresh green of the grasses. Lambs cavorted as soon as they found their wobbly legs, dashing to and fro from mother to field, from twin to unfettered freedom.

    For a while peace lay upon the kingdom.

The reign of Edwin

Edwin was tall and blue- eyed, with something of a red tinge in his beard: true Saxon colouring. Whereas Osfrith and Eadfrith, sons by his first wife, Cwenburg of Mercia, were more like her in colouring; both tall, but brown eyed and more swarthy than Edwin's paler skin. As young warriors they had their first outing in their visit to Wessex with their father; and had successfully returned unscathed. Osfrith the more delighted to return home to his wife and child: to find that his wife, Saethred, had pleaded that their son Yffi might be baptized with Eanfled on the safe return of the warriors.

And so it was. For Edwin was blessed that his sons by his first marriage were not only close as brothers and blessed in their marriages but delighted with Tata as their new stepmother, come sister.

They all retired to Yeavering to celebrate the baptism; and then feasted with pike and perch, with roast venison and wild boar. It had been Tata, encouraged by Paulinus, who had persuaded a group of her household to share in this declaration of faith. Edwin sat on the banks of the swirling River Glen, watching the procession as each candidate waded into the steadiy flowing river to be immersed and blessed by the imposing Paulinus, the lapping water scarcely covering his thighs, but making waist height in most of his supplicants. Immersed and ceremoniously dunked, they staggered out in their drenched robes, to be welcomed with an embrace on the bank by Tata; while Hilda and Hereswid, with linen towels, were by the tent where the dripping baptised might change into their new outfits. Edwin observed the joy it brought to them all; and mused. They had pegged out the foundations for a wooden church in York, but no more. It occurred to Edwin that he might do well to wait for the church to be constructed if he were to be baptized!

He rose and moved up to the Longhall where the spit was turning with the wild boar. They had some suckling piglets too. It would be a splendid feast he decided: even as the days were lengthening into the haze of midsummer.

It would be a further three years, with much pondering and careful observation before Edwin was persuaded to accept the faith of his wife, with the final clinching being the seemingly uncanny knowledge that Paulinus had of a singular moment that Edwin had many years ago. At his most despondent during his exile with the East Anglians an apparent stranger had appeared to him, consoling him with the prophetic promise that all would go well with him. The stranger had laid a hand upon his head, which seemed to seal it as a blessing; just as Paulinus did now. Whereby Edwin was finally persuaded to accept the faith of his wife; and the first baptism of Eanfled and Yffi was re-enacted, but this time in the minster at York, with the King himself entering the font, followed by a retinue of his thegns; and with remarkable enthusiasm by Coifi, his erstwhile priest of the pagan gods. Tata's heart was full; not least because Hilda and Hereswid also had followed Edwin into the baptistry. A truly royal procession! The queen now felt that her family was truly united.

All these young people looked back on these years with great affection. The stepbrothers, Osfrith and Eadfrith, preferring to remember the freedom of their outdoor training as warriors to the bookish training of their cousins, the sisters, Hereswid and Hilda. But Tata was as both a young mother and an older sister to them all. Of course, the young bore no responsibility at this age, so they knew little of the time that the king and queen spent in organizing and delegating, in peacemaking between factions, in anticipating divisions and diversions in the kingdom. Tata learned as much from her courtly dealings as she did from her scholarly studies, while the two younger sisters, apart from conversing in French with the queen, could use all their concentration on learning Latin and Greek, preparing skins for vellum, and pricking out texts for Cyanwith to fill with his unciform script.

The Northern Lands were also blessed by five years without a visitation of the plague; which had taken Cwenburg, the step brother's mother, when the two boys were small. So it was as if all the young royals grew up in an extensive, adopted family; where to be orphaned, partly or fully, was the norm.

Both King and Queen were thankful for their family's wellbeing; all too aware of how factions could and did destroy families.

For Edwin, when young and in exile, had been hounded by his brother in law, Aethelfrith, seeking to eliminate him as a contender for the throne of Deira; resolved only by an almighty battle in which Edwin, with the considerable help of Redwald, the Anglian king, and his son as allies, had triumphed. Edwin's sister, Acha, was thereby widowed by her own brother. Her marriage had been an enforced political liaison but had produced many sons and daughters. Edwin, bound through a shared childhood to Acha, had honoured his sister's rights and she had her northern lands on the banks of the river Tweed restored to her when Edwin had finally asserted his Kingship. Acha had kept her daughter Ebba with her for company on her estates, but she wisely had sent her sons to safety into the Scottish kingdom of Dalriada. From there her sons would sometimes spend time on the island of Iona, learning much from Columba's community of monks. She hoped that they might be safe there; for fratricide and male infanticide too often stained the summer pastures of these Royal Families.

Once a year, when the seas were calm, Acha would face the narrow crossing to Iona to join her sons, always accompanied by their sister, Ebba; and Ebba, even as a teenager, inclined more and more to be drawn to the religious way of life that she shared with the monks on the island, while she saw her blood brothers learning horsemanship, sword and javelin skills between their hours of scholarship and prayer. These trips also did coincide with Acha taking funding from her own lands to support the monk's community. They lived an unostentatious life, [she was sure that she would not have called it simple!], but there were always skins for parchment and inks that she could bring; for not many oaks grew on the island, so the ink of gall from the oak trees of her estates was much appreciated for their manuscripts: while cured wild boar was also a welcome change to the sons' menu. For while the island had sheep and deer, wild birds a plenty, even as plentiful as fish from the sea: yet there were no wild boar.

In these five years at Edwin and Tata's court Hilda and Hereswid grew closer, more skilled, educated, and as princesses, more eligible in the eyes of the King. None of this prevented them enjoying themselves. There were outings when they would escape the court and take their ponies into the hills.

A favourite spot had a small waterfall, which fell through the rocks to a silent pool. Three spindly rowan trees grew out from where the rocks had clustered but left crevices where the trees had rooted from seeds spread by the birds of the enclave. The slender trunks and branches rose up above the rounded rocks. It was if the three spindly trees were guardians of the pool, whose water was crystal clear and like a shaded mirror; until it was broken by the young bathers splashing water and spilling laughter, that was caught up and echoed round the dell. Tiring, the small group would retire to the bank to eat and drink refreshments of cold game and freshly baked bread. The bright turquoise dragon flies would then re-emerge from the reeds and take back the silence of the pool. Beetles and waterboatmen scudded across the water; young brown trout came out to fan their gills in the gentle eddies: and the afternoon dozed into small conversation.

It was on one of these outings that they had met Heiu, daughter of a local thegn, who used these summer pastures for his sheep. Heiu had added fresh berries to their picnic when they first stopped at her parents' holding to water their ponies; and she had joined them to visit the pool the second time that they passed by. An easy friendship sprang up away from the formality of the court, fed by her avid interest and quick perceptions when the sisters wrote on slates while they sat by the pool. They soon had her introduced to help at court. Her spinning and weaving were already accomplished, but it was her drawing and writing that were most admired as a natural aptitude.

So it was not long before Heiu also was part of the group that Romanus and Paulinus taught. Her parents were delighted at her move to the court, to see her talents appreciated and flowering: hoping that a marriage match might be made: not realizing that it was the charismatic Paulinus and the company of the two sisters which gave her more pleasure than the young turks and their games.

Hereswid also loved her studies but recognized that her younger sister was more gifted in her learning, even as Heiu was in her artistry. However, Edwin and Tata were very aware that this older niece was also appealingly eligible. When Tata had given birth to her first son, Ethelhun, it had been Hereswid, along with Hilda, who had looked after Eanfled, now mobile and into everything: but now Tata and Edwin encouraged Hereswid to think of her own future

By this time Edwin was the dominant King of the seven Saxon Kingdoms. Political marriages

31

were a means of strengthening his position; at least in theory, [for he all too well remembered that he had had to fight his own brother in law for his life!].

His own happy marriage to Tata ensured that relations with the Kentish Kingdom were solid, while he well knew that he owed his present security to the help that he had received from King Redwald of the Eastern Angles. It would be both advantageous and appropriate to reaffirm that pledge, he mused. This was particularly important now as Penda and Cadwollen, rulers of the Kingdoms of Mercia in middle England, were the ever-threatening thorn to his Kingship.

The Anglian Redwald had been as a father figure to Edwin, giving him refuge, even against considerable bribes, when his own brother- in- law was hunting him down. Even more than that, in the final battle, the King had lost his own son, Ragenhere, who had been as a brother to Edwin. Ragenhere's death had been a great blow to his parents, and to the Angles: the loss of their heir apparent. Edwin knew that the Eastern kingdom of Anglia was still in some disarray since Redwald's death. Redwald's next son, Eorpwald had been murdered by a henchman in a Longhall brawl, while the monastic Sigbert and cousin Ecgric were holding things together, but uneasily wary of the Mercians. There were no more heirs from

32

Redwald's family, and, on his cousin Ana's side of the Anglian royalty, only Athelric, the youngest, was still single: and eligible. So it was to this household that Edwin decided to send a sortie with a proposition.

He did first inquire of Hereswid, knowing that their mother Breguswith, having first fled back to her home in the eastern dales of the Pennines after her husband's murder, subsequently had spent time in East Anglia. She had been well received at Redwald's court, and had found a particular welcome, both from Redwald's queen and from Ana and Eredith.

Hereswid herself had fond, but distant childhood memories of this time. Unaware, at such a young age, of really comprehending her father's murder, her remembered dreams were of summers on the beach at Dunwich in East Anglia, with the excitement of nesting birds in the soft cliffs, of picnics once the sea pinks were out; of great migrations of sea birds, wigeon, teal, pink footed geese, and occasional small flocks of elegant black and white avocets: of the excitement and stimulation of living by the ever changing sea: her first experience of this magic. Life had seemed to have transformed into a long holiday for the young princess, blissfully unaware that this was exile. With Ana's daughter, Sexburg, she had been taught to spin and weave; and to read in a household that quietly observed their Christian faith in their daily lives: a formative influence on both the young sisters.

When Tata and Edwin discussed these matters with the eligible Hereswid , Edwin allowed Tata to lead the discussion. Hereswid's childhood memories disposed her favourably towards a return to East Anglia. But the thought of leaving Hilda, and Tata and her cousins here in the north, tugged at her heart. They now were her foundation, this was her family, particularly since it was in Anglia that their mother, Breguswith, had died. Her death had led to Edwin calling the young princesses northwards to make a home. She pondered, prayed, and discussed it at length with her younger sister.

However, Edwin and Tata decided to send an inquiry to the East Anglian Court.

Edric was a trusted thegn, and of wise enough years to be diplomatic. He took Cyanrith with him, who was young and agile enough with sword and spear; but in need of learning similar skills in diplomacy. Edric would be a good guide; while Cyanrith might be good company for the young Athelric, and might persuade him of Hereswid's attractions!

Hereswid awaited her future in some trepidation. She felt that she had little control over events again. It was in God's hands that she must trust.

A marriage and an idyll's end.

While the young folk remembered those five years of Edwin's rule with fondness, Tata counted them as years in which she grew wiser and older; not just through sharing Edwin's stresses of ruling his kingdom; but because she had the joy of two more births, a boy and a girl, Ethelhun and Ethelryd. But the sorrow that each of them had died within a short time of birth. Their deaths had given her the first taste of the deep sadness of bereavement where words seemed inadequate: a sadness that she remembered at the awakening of every day: where prayers were but some consolation.

But unspoken, small actions did help. She had the consolation that each of the infants had been baptized by Paulinus, and the even greater pleasure that Eanfled, her first born, flourished, with cousin Hilda being as her sister, and Hereswid now mostly in charge of them both. The three maidens also were often the source of the small actions of kindness. Hereswid would bring her a new soup that she had concocted from wild celeriac and fennel, spiced with a little stock from brown hare; or a newly worked piece of embroidery from Eanfled; while Hilda and Heiu would ask her to judge between sheets of manuscript. All these diverted her grief and helped her to cope.

Yet Tata was carrying child again, and her prayers were as much directed to a safe birth as to her lost children; perhaps a son for Edwin's sake: and the safety of the kingdom?

Meanwhile Edric and Cynarith were riding south, their intentions also to promote the safety of the northern kingdom. But their proposal was safety by a marriage proposal, thereby linking the East Anglian kingdom to Edwin's: strength in numbers.

They had their best horses and chose the overgrown Roman road from York, heading south to London. It was not much used by the travelling merchants for it was too exposed to brigands and robbers. But it was the most direct route for well-armed thegns on an important mission. They made good speed.

Nevertheless, it was a journey of more than two weeks, their journey breaking off for hospitality, readily given, on their way; both of them with their ears pinned back for gossip as to the activity of warriors from Middle England. It was rumoured that the Mercians were restless and in training again.

It was full spring when the pair of travellers arrived in the eastern kingdom. The winter corn was already sprouting its mid green, while the oxen were plodding ploughs through the rich black soil, ready for sowing the spring barley. The dancing catkin tails of the silver birches were joined by the fragile bursts of light green buds of leaves, and the air so fresh that it was almost drinkable. The spirits of the two messengers were inevitably lifted. If they could not now catch Athelric's attention for a northern fair maid they never would!

And so it was.

Ana and Eredith supported the Northumbrian's tributes as to the attractions of Hereswid; while Sigbert and Ecgric as co-rulers were both enthusiastic to strengthen links with the northern kingdom. They both feared that it was more a question of when rather than whether Penda would venture eastwards with his army. Let the princess come south with her dowry. She would be most welcome! To defend her honour would be an excuse for Edwin to join the Anglian forces against the might of the Mercians.

So, having feasted and received gifts of cloisonné brooches and gold torcs, the warriors began their return journey, taking the road north to

Lincoln this time, and crossing the river Humber at high tide in the small ferry, with their horses gallantly swimming behind them; showering their riders with the salt water as they shook themselves when they reached the far side, expressing their appreciation of the unsought swimming lesson.

Arriving at the court of Yeavering, Edwin was well pleased with the news of the acceptance.

Tata also; but she was full of understanding of the considerable change that would happen in Hereswid's life. Had not she herself been transported into another kingdom by these political manouevres? She had been blessed inasmuch as she did love Edwin; and bringing Paulinus and his retinue with her had been a great support. But it had been such a shift; her family support gone; so much responsibility; a colder climate!

But now she was again preoccupied. Her prayers had been answered. She had a son, Wuscfre, and her daughter Eanfled was delighted to hold and to nurse her younger brother; she and Hilda would take it in turns: both under the watchful eye of Hereswid.

Tata worried. She hovered so much over Wuscfre, his every cough or sneeze. Two infants dying before they were two years old left her on tenterhooks. She had much support from Saethred,

Osfrid's wife, who had also lost a child in the same outbreak of measles as Ethelhun. They would visit their small graves together, while Paulinus continually remembered them in the prayers of his masses. Child deaths were part of their way of life.

But the newborn Wuscfre was a vigorous lad and had his father's colouring. Edwin assured her that this son would be fine! Tata admired his optimism; and continued her prayers.

Tata pondered as to what support she might give to Hereswid. She wondered would Hilda wish to go with her sister to East Anglia? They had both become part of her family; yet she recognized the strong bond between them that their orphaning had only served to reinforce. She would miss them both greatly; as would her daughter Eanfled. But at least they would not need a Paulinus to go with them. For the faith was well established in East Anglia, with Sigbert more monk than King, while Ana and Eredith were an exemplary family in living their faith. And had not Sigbert invited Felix from Burgundy to be Bishop at Dunwich? No, she need not worry for their faith.

But she must put her mind to organizing a retinue for the young princess.

The cook interrupted her thoughts, asking for details of provision for dinner. Tata applied herself to daily administration.

At least Hereswid was now clear as to where her new life lay, and could begin to plan, even if in some trepidation. Much of her planning was shared with Hilda.

Hilda mused and prayed long. The Northumbrian Court felt like her family; but within that family Hereswid was the closest, her only real sister however close she felt to Eanfled. Both sisters had grown into eligible young princesses, sharing and competing at the same time in almost everything that that they did, recognizing their different gifts, yet in many ways it was as if they were joined at the hip.

Hilda sought the advice of Tata as to where her priorities lay. The queen inevitably discussed it with Edwin. Then Hilda discussed it with Paulinus, tall and austere as he was. He in turn was impressed with the clarity and consideration of her thought in one so young.

Finally, Hilda decided that she would ask permission of the King to accompany her sister to at least see Hereswid wed and established in her new life, after which she might return to be with Eanfled, Tata and her northern family. The King smiled wryly, the order of her priorities not wasted on him. He aquiesced, silently registering that the younger sister was quietly more self-assured than her elder sister. He wondered where he might, in due course, find a connection worthy of such a perceptive queen in the making. But he said nothing of this to her; although he did confide it later to Tata. The queen raised her eyebrows,

'I think that Hilda will make her own decision. To whatever she chooses she will hold true. Her loyalty is second to none.' She paused but added. ' Eanfled and I, would greatly miss her if she left the court.'

The King had nodded in agreement.

Edric and Cyanrith were both pleased to be asked to head the party that would escort the two sisters to Anglia, with a date to coincide with the winter feast of Michaelmas and of Baermoth when geese and livestock were culled for the winter months. It was a time when a great feast was always held; a timely opportunity to seal a betrothal.

Their journey was planned via the safer route of the River Humber and on to Lincoln in the kingdom of Lindsey, circumventing the Mercian lands, but using a specially enlarged raft to carry the party over the river in several trips.

■■■

The sisters had both left the hides of lands, restored to them by Edwin as their father's rightful inheritance, in the safe care of their aunt Acha; knowing that the tithed income would be well managed in her keeping. Their parting from Tata and Eanfled had indeed been a tearful one, with lockets of hair stitched into the back of brooches, amidst pledges that it was not a final parting: that they would meet again as soon as it was possible. But for Hereswid it was the last time that she would see them; and that she would have such freedom. She would forever treasure treasure the memories of those years with Hilda, Heiu, and Eanfled, under the perceptive kindness of Tata and Edwin.

The wedding was celebrated on a misty October day, full of great smoking fires. Hereswid was a comely bride, in white linen, with a golden torc round her neck and her hair decked with a garland of the blue autumn gentians from the woods. Bishop Felix came from his monastery to officiate at the ceremony and enjoyed this happy occasion enough to stay for the celebrations. Athelric, the handsome young groom, had all his family there. His brother Ana bringing his wife Eredith and their two daughters, Sexburgh and Ethelburga; two more princesses in the making.

From Eredith's condition it looked as if their family might soon be increased yet again.

The celebrations lasted long into the night; feasting and dancing, and the recitation of the stories of their forefathers, all merging into the dying embers of the night fire. The bride and groom retired and Hilda was pleased to receive the invitation to stay with Ana and his family for a few days. The household of Ana was new to her, yet akin to Tata's household in its dispositions.

Hilda stayed with her sister for two years. It was against a restless background of increasing tensions between the kingdoms of Mercia and Anglia. The land- bound middle kingdom of Mercia coveted an outlet to the sea and to France, to the continent of Europe. For many of the treasured artefacts of glass and silver came in via the eastern ports, to say nothing of the rich harvests of fish from the seas, and the easy harvest of the migrating seabirds, northwards in the spring, southwards in the autumn.

Hilda and Hereswid were largely oblivious to this tension. Athelric had his lands not far south of Dunwich, including the ruins of two Roman Villas which were of most value to his estates in as much as the Romans had cleared much of the wooded land for corn, and even for a small

44

vineyard. Athelric had built his own longhall, while many of his thegns chose to erect tents or houses of turf and wattle nearby. But Hereswid had managed to persuade him to allow her to convert the ruins of one of the Roman villas into a chapel since it faced east and west and had a porch to the south, and had possibly even been a chapel in its Roman days. Both sisters looked forward to Felix consecrating this conversion; and to one of his monks coming to celebrate a mass once a month. But Hilda would use it more often for her recollections and prayers as Paulinus had taught her. She prevailed to establish another room in the ruins of the villa where she might continue to prepare skins and one where she could actually continue to write. She did have to persevere to have both rooms re roofed with thatch rather than the fallen tiles. But, this done, the visit of the monk from Dunwich would always coincide with a visit to this room, often with sheets of manuscript from his monastery to be copied, and others to be returned.

So, in the first year the sisters were much diverted in setting up a household and a chapel, while after eighteen months a vigorously kicking lad arrived, loudly proclaiming his entry into the world. Aethelric felt his life was as good as it could be. The crops were good, the livestock thriving; and his son they called Adwulf after his uncle. Aethelric prayed that he might be as good a warrior as his uncle. It gave him an extra zest and enthusiasm in training his own thegns. He found that he threw the spear an extra ten yards; and ordered a new sword.

Now Hilda was much caught up in the household duties, especially when the baby Adwulf came along. But she also did find time to visit the monastery that Felix had established in Dunwich at king Sigbert's request. She also heard from Ana of an Irish monk and his followers who, with permission from Sigbert, had formed a community amongst the coastal ruins of the Roman fort at Burgh. She heard how they built their round huts from balanced stones rather than the wooden or turf huts that the Saxons built: and they shaved their heads across their skulls. How strange, Hilda pondered! However, it was Fursa their leader that drew Ana and Sigbert there. He had not the books and scholarship of Felix at Dunwich, with his French education, but Fursa did have the reputation of a prophet and a seer. Ana relayed to Hilda that the Celtic monks led an even more austere way of life than the Benedictine monks at Dunwich. Hilda longed to go and visit them herself, but Felix counselled that it would be unseemly. So she obeyed; and pondered more. What was the basis of this simpler life? The monks at Dunwich seemed austere enough. Even in her time in the north she had heard much spoken of the Celtic monks on the Island of Iona. How her aunt Acha's sons often spent time there. But, again, she had never managed to visit them.

As she saw Hereswid and Athelric become established as a family unit, it bore down on Hilda that she had promised her Northumbrian family that she would return. She did miss Tata and Eanfled. She discussed it with Hereswid, who reluctantly agreed, so, anticipating that her sister would make her way north again, began to accrue gifts that her sister might take back with her.

While the thegn Edric had returned home after the wedding, the young Cyanrith had stayed on and helped to set up the new household; enjoying the hunting on Aethelric's estate; helping with the roofing of the chapel and the scriptorium, training with Aethelric's thegns. But, while he might have dallied here and there with his favours, he had not settled. So when he heard that Hilda was much inclined to return to Edwin's court he was delighted at the prospect. He needed little persuasion to be her escort for the return journey. They would go by all the safe byways that the merchants followed as soon as the spring weather came.

■■

Hilda promised Hereswid, saying that she would take back charge of their lands so that she could report back to her. Hereswid had smiled wryly, and a little sadly. It was a thinly disguised excuse to return to Northumbria and its familiar court. Acha had looked after their estates well enough.

But it was true that Hereswid's life was now much taken up with her new household and the lands and people that she and Athelric had to manage. Even so, although it would be the first time in their lives that they would be parted, Hereswid could see that Hilda was striking out for her own independence, a trait that she had always had. Hereswid mused,

'So be it. You know that I will miss you,' she paused, 'and you will take my love with you towards Tata and Eanfled; and Heiu. And my gratitude to Edwin, and Paulinus and Romanus, for all that they have done for us both.'

She wondered where her younger sister's life would lie, recognizing a more forceful character than herself.

Hereswid left them to plan their return journey.

Cyanrith changed his plans. He thought that if they travelled as a small party they could make better speed by sail. Hlothere, one of the other young thegns, could ride with them some of the way and bring back their horses to Dunwich. There followed much debate between the travellers as to how far they should go by sea. Might they leave via the Great Ouse at Wootton and slip across to Boston via the river Witham? Or should they be bolder and go further north on their horses to Hunstanton, cross to Seathorne, and then sail further up the coast to land in Deira, their home fiefdom, at Withernsea? Of course, there was always the danger of pirates on the high seas, but the prevalent south westerly winds and a fast boat should outrun them if they were travelling light?

The desire for a speedy return won the argument, even though Hereswid, Athelric, and Ana cautioned for the shorter journey by sea.

When the February snow had begun to thaw, when primroses and celandines had begun to push green leaf tips through last year's dead grass, their flowers still nascent buds beneath the earth, Hilda and Cyanrith rode to Dersingham and, leaving their horses with Hlothere, sailed across to enter the River Haven, thence up to the small cluster of deserted Roman villas, but finding hospitality in the Saxon wooden houses at Skidham. Here was an eastern trading port served by the tides where they could buy fresh mounts to take them northwards.

Cyanrith chose a lively chesnut. A good sixteen and a half hands, very suitable for escorting a Northumbrian princess he thought. Hilda selected a steady grey mare, and between them they had a bay mule to carry their relatively light baggage.

They consulted with the local merchants and in the morning mist made good headway to Hagworthingham to cross at the ford there. It was here that they stopped to let their mounts drink and they themselves decided to sample the bread and meat that they had purchased in Skidham. They tethered the horses, allowing them to graze a little, when they were approached by two shabby travellers who held out their hands in supplication; whereby it became obvious that they were lepers, their hands with stunted fingers. Cyanrith rose to shoo them off brusquely. Hilda rose too, but to restrain him. She had heard of lepers but had never actually seen any. She knew well enough that often they were kept apart as unwanted mendicants, for they were thought to spread their disease. She scooped up their bread and meat and took it to them.

"We have no real need of this. Please take it," she offered, placing the food in their stunted hands. Cyanrith was so taken aback, quite nonplussed. How dangerous; and his food too! But he held his peace.

The two lepers bowed their heads, muttered thanks, and scuttled off. Hilda stood watching them go and pondered. They seemed so forlorn. It had not been difficult to give them their food. She turned to see Cyanrith staring at her quizzically.

"Come on, the horses are rested and refreshed. Let us see if we cannot make Linwood or Rasen for the evening. We will be a lighter load!" she offered.

Cyanrith grinned and shook his head. She was one on her own he thought: she certainly was one on her own!

The horses and the mule heaved a sigh and recalibrated themselves to another stretch of the journey.

And so it was that they arrived at Rasen for the evening; hungry, but in good spirits. And their good spirits sustained them to Hunstanton, where a letter with the stamp of Sigbert, along with a bag of coins, persuaded the young sailor Seldon to borrow his father's boat to make the journey northwards.

They had waited for the wildness of the spring tides to settle; even so the wind still blew freshly in early April.

No more than showers drenched their first days crossing to Seathorne where they were welcomed by relatives of Seldon's family, fellow fishermen; and they rejoiced at the rapid progress and their choice to sail. Both passengers ate well, having coped with their first day at sea.

But the second day saw rougher weather and their enthusiasm to return to Deira was modified by bouts of sea sickness where both began to long for the steady rhythm of a horse's canter rather than the desperate lurching of the small boat. White knuckles gripped the planking on which they sat, as well as holding tightly the ropes which strapped in their belongings. They hardly dared to raise their eyes to watch Seldon wrestling with the tiller of the shallow keeled boat. He tied Cyanrith's thighs loosely to the mast to secure him yet give him enough movement to adjust the sails in accordance with his instructions. Cyanrith gritted his teeth to try and follow his instructions, unashamedly crawling on his knees and hanging on to the mast with one hand as much as he could, while Hilda, similarly hanging on, tried to keep scooping out the salty waves that would lash them, breach the sides of the boat, soaking both them and their belongings. Time seemed to go on for ever with this assault, and yet be without time. Did anything else exist? Would they survive to safely arrive in Deira?

However, the strong winds also meant that they made good time, so that when the winds abated somewhat in the afternoon they could relax a little and think of Withernsea and home; not just of surviving. Neither said anything about their bold decision to choose the long journey home by sail.

Finally the small boat was safely beached on the long run of sands at Withernsea, disturbing a small flock of short-beaked turnstones, grubbing in the tide line of shingle and seaweed, before flying north for their summer nesting. The low soft cliffs were an easy scramble for the sailors, even if Hilda and Cyanrith still felt as if the shallow cliffs were still moving with the swell of waves. But by the time that they reached the hamlet a straight line of walking was a very welcome, and sustainable procedure.

They stayed two nights in Withernsea, as much to recover their land legs and stomachs as to find horses that would take them northwards. They also had a late spring day and night fires to dry out their baggage and their clothes. But twenty-four hours of spring weather is its own tonic, so that they were up early the following day. Seldon took his leave of them as a servant of the realm, rather than his yesterday's role of life-saving captain. Hilda gave him a silver ring for his daughter in Hunstanton. It had been meant for Eanfled from Hereswid. But it was all that Hilda had to give at that moment; and she felt sure she might find another on her way home; and that Hereswid would forgive her.

That tip of Deira, north of the river Humber, was as flat as Anglia had been, so they made good time, enjoying the fresh green foliage and welcoming flowers of early April. But both their hearts rose even as the coast began to rise into cliffs, each of them urging their mounts into a stronger canter to tackle the challenge. They paused to rest their steeds when they had reached the dizzying heights where the chalk cliffs were full of wheeling birds, cavorting and dancing in the eddying winds, mostly with a partner incubating an egg on the tiniest of shelves on the cliff face, or even an early chick peeping from under its mother's breast.
The travellers breathed in the cacophony and exhilaration of the cries and flight of the birds, which seemed to celebrate the unspoken excitement of the party's to their homeland. They urged their horses on. They were back in Deira: their own kingdom; their own landscape. Their steeds seemed to share the celebration of romping their way up and down the forested hills of the rolling countryside.

■■

54

It was nearly a week later before they reached Edwin and Tata at Yeavering, for they had at least to stop at Whitby where Hilda thought they would find a silversmith who would make her rings to replace those that she had already given away. The welcome that their return precipitated at the court far eclipsed the gifts of rings. But their brief stay in the valley at Whitby was a welcome break, even giving them time to stroll along the beach, with the tide out. The flat sands stretched, seemingly endlessly, to where a small flock of black capped terns defended their nests, where sandy beach turned into pebble. As she walked back Hilda had looked up at the cliffs, admiring the ruins of the Roman lighthouse, musing that there must be fine views from those stony crags. Perhaps on another visit she might have time to go and investigate? The image stuck in her mind.

But they had pushed on and were soon at Yeavering.

Having formerly presented themselves to Edwin and Tata, the young ladies Heiu, Eanfled and Hilda withdrew to the weaving house to catch up. Cyanfrith, having seen to the horses, was instantly out with his fellow thegns; then disappeared to be reunited with his family. Edwin promising a day's hunting for a wild boar that they may have a proper celebration as soon as possible.

■■■■■■■■■■■■■■■■■■■■■■■■■■■■■■■■■■■■■ ■■

While the ladies were overjoyed to be reunited, each of them noticed changes in the other. Tata remembered Hilda as a teenager who was following her sister, to support her and be with her in a new life. The Hilda that had returned had changed into a self-possessed young lady; distinctly a metamorphosis. This, as a first impression, was subsequently confirmed as they caught up with her learning and conversation. She had a new aura of quiet self-confidence which, while full of joy and warmth, was married to a detached objectivity.

Hilda, for her part, thought that Tata looked thinner and somewhat drained, although still caring and quick in all her thoughts and movements.

Eanfled had grown into a quite determined child who, having missed her adopted elder sister, hardly recognized this older transformation. But she was the first to wish to be with her in the following days.

Heiu had changed almost as much as Hilda. She had not travelled to another kingdom as Hilda had, but her mother had died and her father was not well; it had been an emotional journey for her at home. While her elder brothers had taken over running their hides of land, it had fallen to her to organize the family household for the best part of a year until she had trained Mistral to manage. So it had been these responsibilities that had molded her maturity, for one who was still a teenager.

 Hilda realized that memories of childhood were but memories; that the journey of her life seemed to have ever changing phases. She was so reassured to be back amongst her family. But it was a changed place. The young Wuscfre was walking and into everything. He was now the centre of attention as the possible heir apparent. While Eanfled was an ever- present elder sister to her brother, his real play- mate was his step-brother Yffi. Forever they would rough and tumble while Tata and his mother would spin and sew. The two, although queen and stepdaughter, where of a similar age and disposition, each with lost infants, so that they fell into a natural sisterhood, even as Saethred still deferred to Tata as queen.

 As she had promised her sister, as soon as the initial celebrations were over, Hilda made time to visit their estates, which bordered on those of her aunt Acha. Eanfled petitioned to come with her and the two of them took off to the western lands. Hilda found their territory to be in good order, due in no small measure to the fact that Acha had simply dealt with it all as an enlargement of her estates. Hilda was delighted to visit her and Ebba and to hear their stories of their visits to Iona to see her brothers,

Oswald and Oswy. Ebba's enthusiastic description of the community of Celtic monks attracted Hilda, while Eanfled listened intently. Ebba described a magical island set in the sea, with both misty and extraordinary light, full of wild birds, flying north, flying south; and seals and fish jumping out of the sea, chased by sea otters. How Eanfled wished that she could go too.

But it was Hilda who gave voice to Eanfled's thoughts.

'If I can escape the court I would love to come with you next time that you visit. That is if I may?' Hilda proposed.

Acha looked at this young niece anew. How she had transformed.

'Of course. We both would be glad of your company; and it sounds as if you have earned your sea legs in your journey home! I am sure that your cousins will be pleased to see you; and I think the community of brothers will not disappoint you.'

'Thank you,' Hilda paused. 'I was intrigued by the outward differences between the Roman and Celtic communities in Anglia; between Felix and Fursa. But both Sigbert and Ana seemed to move between them seamlessly, and always said that their shared vocations greatly outweighed their differences.'

Acha raised her eyebrows.

'Is that so? You are more travelled than your aunt! But I do look forward each year to my visit to Iona. Not just to catch up with my sons! Let us hope that the crossing is kind to us.'

This time that Hilda managed to spend with her aunt was more formative than the young princess recognized at the time. Acha was no longer central to the court; and pleased to keep it that way. She had survived, even enjoyed, a political marriage, managed to produce fine male heirs, and bright daughters. It was enough to retire to her estates.

Hilda's stay in Anglia had sharpened her awareness of the political moves between the seven kingdoms of Anglosaxon England, where princesses were often as pawns on an, at times, bloodied chess board. She now appreciated her aunt, not so much as a carefree haven from the business of the court, but as a source of wisdom.

It would stand her in good stead.

Hilda did manage a visit to the brothers on Iona, and she and cousin Ebba spent much time with the monks. The two princesses had their own tent to sleep in, and, by day, between the services, they would visit the other tents and help to make garments and linen for the brothers from the cloth that they had brought with them. But they also spent more time each day in the scriptorium, examining the texts that were being copied and the intricate designs that were being made of celtic knots and cartoon like representations of the animals of the island. On some of the feast days, if the weather was fine, they took picnics, and walked to the far end of the island, where they could see as far as the northern coast of Ireland. They would sit amongst the heather, while the bees buzzed with the industry of making honey for the brothers' mead. It was another world.

The joy of Hilda's return to Deira and Bernicia, and the news of her sister safely enjoying her motherhood, always had the distant cloud of the threat of the Mercians gathering their forces to threaten an invasion of either northern or eastern kingdoms; or perhaps both.

This cloud grew into a thunderstorm; forcing Edwin to summon his troops to move southwards to defend his kingdom at Hatfield.

His loyal thegn Bassus rode home, wounded and bloodied, with the news that the battle had been lost. He rode ahead of the news that the head of Edwin was on a pike at the gate of York; and that Cadwollan was marching North, laying waste to the countryside.

The idyll had finished.

The Dispersal.

Bassus counselled with Tata and Paulinus.
'We must get away at once, for the children's sake, as well as ours'
'It will be safer to go home than to try and hide in Dalriada.'
'The fishermen at Bamburgh will sail us southwards'
'Take as little as you can. Their boats are small.'
The conversation ran between the three of them, unanimously agreed.
Eanfled, Hilda and Heiu sat in the shadows, waiting. Eanfled slid her hand round Hilda's arm, and snuggled close. None of them said anything. They watched as Paulinus went off to collect his precious gold and silver, and his robes. Bassus and Tata sent for Saethred and her son Yffe. They knew that they had lost Osfrid, husband and father, in the

battle and that Yffe was as much a potential warrior heir as Wuscfre: two infant boys as vulnerable as lambs for slaughter. They must both escape. They must both be protected.

In the dim light of the dawn the small band trundled out in a hay wagon towards the coast.

'You most go to Acha as quickly as you can, both of you. I would that you could both come with us, but the boat will not take us all; and it is a long sail to Kent. I pray that we may all be spared. Come to us if you can; when all these troubles are over….when, when, when! God be with you both'. This from Tata to Heiu and Hilda with hugs and tears. Eanfled hugged and wept,

'Can I not stay with Hilda and Heiu, and go to aunt Acha? Please.'

'No, my dear, you must come with us. I cannot do without you and you will be safer with us; come now.'

Eanfled wept, running to Hilda,

'I don't want to go. Please promise that you will come to us, please?'

She clung to Hilda, who held her gently; but led her to her mother.

'Yes, I promise. I will come. But now you must go with your mother; and we will pray for your safe journey. All of us will pray.'

Hilda felt her own heart thumping, struggling to control her tears.

She and Heiu silently observed the large amount of luggage that Paulinus was taking, but said nothing. 'Did such luggage exceed life in its value?' remained unsaid between them. Obviously it did.

They waved them off, wondering if the travellers would arrive safely in Kent. Wondering if they would ever see them again. At least Tata's brother, Eadbald, was now King in the Kentish Kingdom. If the journey was successful the travellers should be safe there.

Heiu and Hilda stood still, too moved to wave, as the boat rode the seas, away into a small dot on the horizon. The gulls around the harbour soared high in the sky, their hard, mean calls filling the air as if echoing the sad feelings of those left behind. Or did the hard cries predicate the arrival of the invaders, who were already travelling northwards? A small group of black headed terns, mixed in amongst the gulls, added their plaintive falling call; kay-yar: kay yar. It was an abiding memory for those left behind.

The waves broke white over the bow of the boat with the passengers huddled in amongst their luggage more as ballast than as adventurers on the high seas. Now fugitives from their own kingdom.

Sigbert, the captain, cried out to them to lift their heads and see the pod of dolphins arcing in and out of the waves, escorting them out into the deeper waters.

'It is a good sign: we shall be safe if the dolphins are with us,' Sigbert grinned.

He and his son were used to having a hold full of nets, or, better, full of cod and mackerel, with herring in the right season. But this was a privileged treasure that he now was carrying. 'May their God and the dolphins speed a safe journey,' he thought to himself.

The palace at Yeavering was being stripped by those remaining. All valuables were taken out and hidden in the woods that went down towards the river. They knew that it would not be long before the troops of Cadwollan came to plunder. They marked their cattle and pigs and drove them towards the moorland and forests. The reputations of the Mercians were still told in the stories of the longhall. They would leave nothing untouched if they chose to come north.

Hilda and Heiu had two favourite fell ponies from their own estates that they kept at Bamborough. Their most important belongings were soon packed into bundles which sat behind their saddles. They headed off at a steady canter as soon as the longhall was cleared.

How could it be such a fine day when disaster was but a march away? The ponies picked up a sense of urgency, and that they had some distance to cover. This was no morning ride for exercise. They had a job to do, a goal to reach. They dug into the rhythm of their canter as Hilda and Heiu rode on in silence, each bound up in their own thoughts.

Heiu's anxiety was for her own family on their hides of land that they would ride through on the way to Acha. Heiu hoped that the news of the impending plunder would have already arrived; so was not surprised to find that the hamlet was already deserted, but for some of the old. They had chosen not to leave and persisted in trying to hide and disguise as much as possible, even if the houses were to be torched. The two young riders, having paused to stretch their legs and straightened their backs, rode on having briefly watered the ponies and readjusted their girths and their luggage. They were halfway to Lennel.

Hilda's musings, as she rode, were for her sister, hidden in Anglia. She worried about Hereswid and Aethelric, with Adwulf, their newborn son, her first nephew. How long before the

Mercians turned eastward to plunder the Anglians? How long: how long, to the rhythm of the canter. One hand strayed from the reins and fingered the cross that she wore beneath her cloak, silently praying,

'Lord in thy mercy.'

They found the compound of Acha's estate also to be in the process of shut down. Her daughter, Ebba, welcomed them and enlisted their help. There was enough food and bedding left for them to stay overnight and help with taking vessels, spinning wheels, spades and hoes, to be hidden in small caves or in quiet copses; digging holes for some precious articles, carefully replacing the turf. The previous desolations of war lay in most adult memories. The strategies were well practiced.

'You must go with Ebba to Iona until the pillaging is over. I will stay here. I want to be here to manage the recovery. I have seen it all before: and I am old and female,' Acha said with a wry smile, 'Even if they find me they will not value me as a hostage; and I am past child bearing age!'

Hilda, Heiu, and Ebba said nothing, but recognized her tough wisdom. They knew that she was loved and respected in her estates; and that she had chosen not to remarry after the death of Athelfrith. It had been enough; her husband killed by her brother's forces. Ebba had absorbed much from her, even as her sons had remained in exile in the kingdom of Dalriada, in the southern land of the Scots.

'There is a spare pony. Take these cow hides with you to make tents for yourselves, for you may be there several months. Oswald, Oswy and the good monks will help you to set up; and Ebba and I have prepared enough ink for a few sheets of their script. Take it now, for I know how they value it. Ebba will travel with you for the invaders would not spare her'.

They took their leave, absorbing and admiring the strong determination of their mother and aunt; leaving much unspoken. Would they meet again, they wondered?

They crossed the river Tweed and rode on again, receiving hospitality wherever they stopped, passing on the news of the impending disaster; waiting until they were nearer the coast to request tent poles for their stay on the island, knowing how precious wood was out on the island, but how abundant on the coast.

They did cross the narrow seas between the islands. First to Mull, with the ponies on a raft; then a days journey to cross the island of Mull. Finally, leaving their ponies behind in the care of a local

68

farmer, who also had his own boat, they made it across the narrow, but turbulent, band of water that separated this western isle.

It was a different world.

A sea eagle flew high above the harbour as if to herald their arrival, circling majestically. They waited for the sailor to affirm its importance.

'Why no, she's here regular. 'Tis strange if she's not around. Her mate will be t'other side of the island I reckon. Though they nest on Mull 'tis no distance for an eagle. Tis but a glide awa' for an eagle, if the wind be in the right direction,' was his cryptic reply.

It was a different world.

They left their baggage by the harbour and made for the shelter of the monastery enclosure. The guest house was still a long low tent at the edge of the enclosure, partly protected from the south westerly gales by a yard- high wall of turf.

Segenus, abbot and bishop of the community, came out to meet them, welcoming them to the community, and anxious to know what news they brought from the mainland, for they had brothers in various houses on the mainland. He smiled as they explained that they had brought material for tents of their own and suggested that they might put them to the east of the guest house where they would be more sheltered. The elderly abbot thought to himself,

'How perceptive of Acha to send these three young ladies well prepared; even with ink for the scriptorium: and three expert scribes!' He smiled and renewed his welcome. But he wondered about the threatening devastation on the mainland. Their brothers and their communities would be in their prayers, spoken and unspoken.

Two brothers were sent with a donkey to collect the travellers' baggage, and two other monks began to mark out where the visitor's accommodation might go. The brothers said that they might use their tent until the accommodation was arranged, and both of them buckled in to chisel out a crack in the rock where the central pole might go. Then it was time for Sext, the midday office.

So the days of the three young visitors became regulated round the daily hours of the monks. They did not always manage to rise for the early matins; but would hear the bell calling the monks and turn in their half sleep to mutter their own waking prayers.

It was a different world.

The magic of this island permeated their stay. How on a calm day it was like a balm to the soul; the sea and the sky an infinite, seamless, spread of blues, the air so vitally fresh that it seemed to sustain you on its own, giving you boundless energy. But equally the gales could lash in from the Atlantic for days and everything would try to hide from the battering wind and driving rain. Man and beast lay low. The sheep and goats would hamper down, hiding in dells and crannies. Hares flattened themselves against the ground, while the rabbits hoped their burrows would not flood. The few small cattle stood, stoically battling it out, steadily chewing cud, backs to the driving rain and wind. While for the brothers the offices of the day truly became their focus, and all duties concentrated on work in the buildings, in the kitchen, the scriptorium, and with the weaving.

For the three refugees the bustle of the court had indeed fallen away. It was a simpler uncluttered life, although there was much to do keeping body and mind together. There were no extra people to provide food and clothing, warmth and washing. Ebba had visited and stayed before with Acha, so she was delighted to ease Hilda and Heiu into their new roles. In this they gradually became part of the community, following the example of their blood brothers, cousins, Oswald and Oswy.

However, the young ladies were allowed their days of freedom. On fine days they would take baskets along with a simple picnic, to venture to the south of the island, seeing the sun shimmer on the sea, making bright diamonds in a shiver of silver light that danced and entranced. Their baskets they would fill with berries, blueberries, raspberries, blackberries, each in their season; and herbs for cooking and infusions, for medicines and lotions.

It was on one of these outings, when they had reached the cliffs of the southern most point and were seated, with baskets full of herbs and berries, to eat their sheep's cheese and bread, flavoured with a small taste of the berries that they had picked for the brothers, that they noticed a lone figure, half way down the cliff. It was Heiu who spotted him; but Hilda who said,

'I think it is Aidan. I heard that he has been on retreat. I never thought that it would be here'. She paused, 'We might move? We might disturb him.'

They gathered up their things and moved a little to the east, out of sight and sound of the solitary monk; but where the sun still shone, reflecting silver on the sea.

Even so the image of the lone figure and his meditations stayed with them all, even as they conferred in whispers.

On the mainland the villages and holdings were plundered and burnt by the marauding

Mercians. Those who had been stubborn enough to remain were slaughtered without distinction. Acha, concealed with a few members of her close household in the forest at the foot of the Cheviot hills, waited in a group of small caves, their entrances concealed by night. They rightly thought that the invaders would not stay long, for the warriors themselves became vulnerable by night. Their horses could disappear. There were not the food stores that they had hoped for. There were no pickings of weapons or jewelry They would try the next hamlet.

Elsewhere there were pockets of resistance, with losses on both sides. But there were not enough young men left to organize into an organized band of warriors.

Oswald and Oswy had cut short their stay on Iona shortly after the three young ladies had arrived on Iona, making a choppy crossing back to their training ground in Dalriata. There was no point in making a rushed return to their Northumbrian kingdom. But they needed to begin to build an army.

The sons of Acha and Aethelfrith were now the rightful heirs to the kingdom of Northumbria, both Bernicia and Deira. For Edwin's two older sons had been killed: Osfrid in battle alongside his father; while Eadfrid, having retreated to Deira and made a treaty with Cadwollen, had been treacherously murdered in a betrayal. True, Edwin's line was still present in the infant sons of Tata and Saethred, but they were distant in Kent, and of no age to be serious contenders for the throne. There was no other news of them. The Kingship was Oswald's for the taking.

Slowly his army, over months and into the new year, gathered in Dalriata, some of them young Scots, out to help with reparation or simply to seek adventure.

Hilda, Heiu, and Ebba spent a year on Iona; learning much about the Celtic ways of monasticism. Heiu knew not for several months that she too was orphaned in the pillaging; her parents' estate too early in the running line of the Mercian destruction, their attempts at hiding caught out, and the details of their deaths spared her ears. Both her other brothers had died in battle with Edwin. Now she too was without blood family; grieving, but sustained by the monks of Iona and the friendship of Hilda and Ebba.

■■■■■■■■■■■■■■■■■■■■■■■■■■■■■■■■■■■■■■■

A Return to Kent

The southwards journey of the royal party to Kent had not been uneventful.

At first the queen and her retinue had stopped by night in hidden bays.

Bassus, who had managed to sleep fitfully on the boat by day, stayed awake through the hours of darkness, alert to any movement in the shadows of the full moon. His precious flock slept. Their luggage had included a flimsy tent, which provided cover for Tata and Saethred and the three children, although the young Eanfled chuntered about sleeping with the boys; while the boys wanted to stay on watch with Bassus: and so they did for a while. But were carried fast asleep within the hour and quietly hidden in the safety of the tent.

Paulinus curled his lip and wrapped his robes around him. Needs must; and a rock was his pillow under the shade of a thorn tree, drastically shaped by the prevailing coastal winds. He recalled the austere lives of the Desert Fathers as he murmured in his fitful sleeping.

The prevailing south westerly winds had made the going slow. The boat constantly tacked to and fro. Sigbert and Sigfred were sailing in waters whose coastline and tides were unknown to them. So they did but keep the coast in sight and sailed well out at sea to give them room for their manoeuvres, hoping to thereby avoid hidden sandbanks or rocks.

After three days hard sailing, [or was it four, Tata felt that it had been a week], they sailed past Hunstanton on the north coast of Anglia and headed further south for Dunwich. They thought that the East Anglians might be a safe port of call before they tackled the rest of the journey to Kent. At least they might stay with Hereswid and Alchrid for a few days: hopefully giving days without seasickness for Saethred and Eanfled.

Their unannounced arrival was rapidly assimilated. Once their grim news had been conveyed to the court of Sigbert and Ecgric, Paulinus sought Felix in his monastery, while Tata and the children, escorted by Bassus, made for the estates of Hereswid and Aethelric, where they were made most welcome. Two suckling pigs, three geese, and an inadvertent crane were rapidly prepared for a feast. Fresh beds were made up with linen sheets. They were even able to wash and borrow a change of clothes for Tata and Saethred.

■■

'It is as a return to paradise. I must not think too much of the rest of the journey.' Tata offered. Then, turning to Hereswid, 'But you look so well. Marriage and motherhood so suit you,' she continued, lifting the young Adwulf into her arms.

They had broken the dreadful news of Edwin's death; and the pillaging. Hereswid's first concern had been for Hilda.

'I would that I could have brought her with us,' came from Tata followed by a pause.

'Had we thought we could have organized another boat. But it was such chaos. I so feared for the children; my wits were not at their best,' she hestitated, but continued,

'If anybody has the wit to weather these events it is aunt Acha. I prayed God speed them to her at Lennel. Acha has preserved her sons through all these troubled times.' She went on. 'Eanfled pleaded to go with them, my dutiful daughter,' smiling wryly and stroking her daughter's hair.

'But she will come to us, mother. She said she would,' came from Eanfled's upturned face. The two mothers half smiled at the innocence of childhood.

'I would that it might be so. I think that I miss her as much as you; and Heiu. They are both much in our prayers. As is Romanus, who also has promised to make his own way to join us.' This of her chaplain who had travelled north with her from Kent so long ago.

'I would rather have Hilda than Romanus,' offered Eanfled.

Tata continued to stroke her hair, 'That is because Romanus keeps you to your lessons while Hilda is your friend I think.'

'No, Hilda also taught me many things; and it was fun. I miss her,' came from Eanfled.

Tata and and Hereswid exchanged secret smiles. The wisdom of children?

Their stay in Anglia was but a few days; but long remembered by them all. Days of sunshine after days of disaster.

They were aware that Sigbert and Ecgric, mainly the latter, were intent on training their Anglian forces. For they equally feared that Cadwollen and Penda would turn their forces eastwards once they had their fill of plundering Northumbria. Penda's desire to be the next ruler of the seven kingdoms was well known: at whatever price.

Finally, Hereswid and Aethelric bid the Northumbrian exiles a fond farewell. They insisted on providing a second boat to accompany them on the last leg of their journey in order that they may travel in more comfort; and safety. As Frisa, captain

78

of the second boat, was a local man, he knew the ins and outs of the Anglian south coast; and how to head across the Thames estuary to Reculver where the way through to Canterbury was navigable through the Wantsum marshes. So Sigbert and Sigfrid felt much relieved. They sailed close to the local boat, within shouting and signaling distance, making good speed.

There was a consensus of opinion that when they reached the old Roman ruins at Reculver they would be safe; home in Kent: or so they hoped and prayed.

They stayed two nights on the Kentish coast, enormously grateful to their sailor crews; but decided to complete the rest of the journey to Canterbury with horses. Gratefully, the travelling exiles took their leave of the sailors.

Messengers were dispatched to Canterbury to tell Tata's brother, the King, of their pending arrival. Meanwhile they enjoyed the strange flat scenery of the marshes with its great skyscapes, only too thankful that there was no longer any rocking of a boat with which to contend.

The marsh marigolds sported their range of small golden cups, nestled in heart shaped leaves, and the wind blew keenly in the shades of surging sedges, the palest green through to darkest sage, contrasting with the pale fawns of last years crop.

The boys vied to ride pillion with Bassus on the new horses but were still young enough to obey their mothers and ride with them. Eanfled began to feel her independence and trotted well on her own piebald pony, who was equally independent in that she was easily distracted by lush vegetation, so that the young princess would tug hard on the reins and give her a good smack to catch up with the rest of the travellers. She still grazed whenever she could.

The path alongside the Wantsum channel was easily followed, but it was advisable to keep it to the south, for it was a mysterious quagmire, however colourful, either side. It was somewhat easier once they met the old Roman road that ran in straight stretches towards Canterbury. They had but covered a few miles when they met the welcoming party coming to meet them. Eadbald and Tata had not met for more than ten years. How each of them had changed: each quietly observing that the bloom of youth had morphed into the care of middle age, more gracefully born by Tata; more weightily by the king. But there was warmth in each of their embraces. Eadbald saw something he remembered of his sister in her daughter, even in the way she walked when she had dismounted and tethered her pony. She bowed, as her mother had told her she must, and Eadbald already thought of future liaisons for a graceful young princess. But for now she was more distracted by her wandering pony.

They regrouped, remounted, and soon were within the city of Canterbury. It had grown since Tata left. There was a bigger church and monastic enclosure: the longhall had also been extended; and there were tents and turf buildings everywhere, even some stone buildings reworked from the roman villas. Eadbald and his French Queen Ymme had cleared one of these adapted villas to accommodate the travellers and they were left to sort themselves out before a formal welcome in the longhall. There was much to catching up to be done.

While the adults conferred, the young folk, cousins who had never met, bonded more quickly and easily. They had no political issues to discuss. Ymme and Eadbald's children were young adults, two sons and a daughter, Erconbert, Eomenred, and Eanswith. But they were happy to take care of the three children that Tata had brought with her; and it gave them an excuse to leave the formal meeting.

Eanswith took Eanfled to find some fresh clothes and to show her the collection of writing that she was making, while the boys went to see where the horses were stabled.

The two young ladies entered a square building which had a roman stone foundation with

81

wood timbers supporting a thatch. Inside Eanfled saw a diminutive figure, plainly but elegantly dressed, who stopped her writing and looked up, her face breaking the wrinkles into a quizzical smile.

'So this is the granddaughter that I have never seen?', as much a statement as a question.

'Grandma, this is Eanfled, Tata's eldest daughter. The boys are with Erconbert and Eomenred,' Eanswith replied. 'Eanfled this is your Grandma who taught me to write properly.'

'Come, let me see you clearly' Bertha, the old queen, extended her arms.

'How like your mother you are. It is as if we have all gone back twenty years. Come, give me a hug; and welcome to your proper home!' They hugged.

'Everybody says how I look like my mother,' said Eanfled with something of a matter of fact sigh.

'Well you should be pleased. She is a beautiful woman: or was when I saw her ten years ago.' She saw Eanfled looking at the writing. 'And do you write as well as your mother?'.

'Hereswid and Hilda taught me to write. But Hereswid is married, and Hilda could not come with us because there was not room in the boat. And Romanus taught me too. I hope that Hilda and

82

Romanus will join us here too; as soon as possible,'
all spilled out from Eanfled.

Bertha smiled; a self- possessed young lady
in the making, with clear priorities, she thought to
herself. Like her mother in more than her looks!

'Well when Eanswith has you sorted you
might come and help me with this writing. Would
you like that? My eyesight is not so good now. I
could do with a good pair of sharp eyes.'

'Thankyou grandma, yes. I would like that.'

'Let us leave grandma in peace for now.
There will be plenty of time when you are settled.
Let me take you to find some more clothes and to
show you the tent that we have had made for your
stay here.' This from Eanswith who could see that
Eanfled would bring new joy to her grandmother,
who she knew to be frailer and more arthritic than
she looked sitting at her table. Queen Bertha smiled.
Her other granddaughter Eanswith was turning into
a determined diplomat herself and had been a keen
pupil in her learning. She sighed quietly. One never
knew what lay ahead: and she sighed again, pursing
her lips a little as she turned back to her writing,
wondering whether she dare use a little of the
precious blue ink in this decoration that she was
planning.

'I thought that I might find you all here,'
came from a silhouette in the doorway. It was the

young Sexburg from East Anglia, here as she was being courted by prince Erconbert. Turning to Eanfled she proffered,

'I have some garments that you might like to try,' and they left the old queen in peace.

Tata and Eadbald, brother and sister, had retired to a small room at the back of the palace that Eadbald had inherited from his father.

'It is so good to have you safely back Tata. So ghastly about Edwin. We all are on tenterhooks as to where the Mercians will strike next.' Eadbald started and, after a moment's break, continued,

'My mother has lands above Folkestone which must be yours by right. She has no need of them now. Much of her income goes to the small convent there as well as to the monastery here in Canterbury. We might discuss it with her as soon as you are settled.'

Tata nodded, 'I remember the land around the spring at Lyminge from my childhood. There was a small hamlet there. I think that we went there as children with Bertha when father was off hunting. Do you remember it?'

'I remember the hunting being pretty good down there. Plenty of deer in the woods; and hares on the pastures. The dogs loved it.'

■■

Tata smiled, somewhat wanly, delighted to be back, but now suddenly a feeling of exhaustion was catching up.

'Paulinus has gone to see Honorius at the monastery. But I might ask him about reviving the community there if everything works out; and it is acceptable,' she half mused to herself.

There was a pause: the realization that after all these years apart their lives were very different: and yet the foundation of these differences had always been there, even in their childhood days and their visits to the coast.

Eadbald rose.

'Let us hope that it will be so. Let us make it so. You are most welcome and well returned,' he reiterated.

'May it be God's will: even as we have been safely delivered,' Tata murmured.

Eadbald forestalled commenting more on the death of her beloved Edwin. He could see the exhaustion of the journey was catching up with his sister.

They retired to prepare for the evening's festivities in the main hall.

In the monastery at Canterbury Paulinus and Honorius were in consultation. It was fortunate that the guest house was empty when he arrived so that he was able to spread himself and his belongings. As soon as he had washed, rested, and changed he unwrapped the chalices and cross that he had managed to bring with him. He took them to Honorius.

'They are my gift to this monastery. You have a good house here.'

'They are beautiful things; a very generous gift. I think that they belong to you wherever your ministry takes you; which you must consider at your leisure now that you are safely with us,' was the archbishop's reply.

Paulinus sat with his head bowed.

'They are beautiful. But I would that they were used here in Canterbury. The queen did finance them, and she is here in Canterbury, so it seems fitting that they should stay with her. Besides, they are a constant reminder to me that my ministry in the north has failed. We are in exile, and the pagan Cadwollan devastates the northern lands. I fear that I failed to set up any sort of lasting community. I fear for the safety of those good souls that I left behind. These fine things do but remind me of my fine failure.'

Honorius nodded., shaking his head quizzically.

'You judge yourself too harshly Paulinus. You are tired. You need to rest and seek a spell of tranquility; and the spell of recovery may well bring a healing'.

The archbishop paused, 'I hear good reports of James, whom you left behind? He knows the land and the people well. These sad, unseemly things have occurred before. They are repulsive and devastating. But seed survives and new shoots grow: often where we least expect it. For now, rest; and make no hasty decisions. There are good things afoot here and matters that I would like to discuss with you further when you are more yourself and have the time to quietly consider them. You have long been in our prayers,' another pause, 'It is very good to have you back with us.'

And the meeting was at an end; Paulinus somewhat consoled.

It was several days later, feeling much restored, that Paulinus heard from Tata that she hoped to retire to the estate at Lyminge and, with the permission and support of Bertha, was leaning towards consolidating a religious community there. Already she had a wooden church and a house of her own, with a small community of sisters and families who tended the fields and the buildings. Tata felt that it was a true blessing of a homecoming to retire to her mother's house. Tata had decided to consult with Paulinus, to seek his advice and help.

Her discussions seemed a consoling answer to his present mood.

It was reassuring for him to return to an established structure in this kingdom of Kent. Something that he felt he had failed to make in the North. Moreover, here in Kent, Eanswith, the king's young daughter also was pressing her father to let her form a convent outside the fortress at Folkestone, only a few miles distant from Lyminge.

Seeds were indeed sprouting in unexpected places, here in Kent.

Albeit that King Eadbald would have preferred his daughter to marry into the kingdom of Wessex; a much more useful political alliance in his eyes. But Eanswith had rejected his proposals. The King recognized in Eanswith a will as strong as his own; and she had her grandmother's support, as well as that of his wife and daughter in law!

'And how will you manage a household so young, my child?' he had asked.

'Grandma has sent for a sister from France who is experienced; and I have already three of my companions who wish to join me; and grandma says there are four widows who are also so disposed. Please say yes, father?'

'Well let us see.'

The King could well see that he had been out-manoeuvred by the ladies of the court. Eanswith was a precious as well as a precocious daughter. He also remembered all too well how he had been cured of his fits by the monks of Canterbury under Honorius. He was not going to invoke the risk of crossing the church again through impeding this willful daughter of his!

So it was that Tata moved her family and household from Canterbury to Lyminge and Eanswith began to visit both Folkestone and Lyminge.

For Tata and her entourage it was simply a case of crossing the Canterbury plain to Bekesbourne, a small hamlet sitting at the mouth of the wooded vale of Elham. Here the Nailbourne tributary ran cut into the marshes to join the main waterway of the Stour from Canterbury, meandering seawards through Sandwich and the roman ruins at Richborough. But it was the inland route and the gradual uphill incline through the vale that the party took, staying overnight in the hamlet at Elham, and then the final stretch rising up to the freshwater spring at Lyminge that had been the attraction for a hamlet over more centuries than anyone remembered.

Such was the physical journey. But sighs of relief for different perceptions were breathed by many of the small group.

■■■

Tata felt that she might at last be safe and in charge with her three children, counting Yffi as her stepson, even as Saethred, his mother, had become as a sister.

Bassus, ever loyal to Edwin's dying instruction to protect his queen, saw that there would be much game to be had in the woods; and that there was a definite need to get men organized in building a new dwelling for his queen.

The two young princes settled in very quickly, rapidly building their own tents in a copse near the spring. But Eanfled lingered, older than the two boys. She had Hilda still in her mind and in her prayers. She so missed her elder cousin: so sad that she had to be left behind. Would she ever come to them here? It had seemed a journey that went on forever. But here in Kent Eanswith, the same age as Hilda, took Eanfled under her wing and invited her to visit and stay with her when she visited Folkestone, mapping out in the grassland where she hoped her father would let her start a small community. How the mapping might sprout into buildings and people?

Meanwhile, a month later, Paulinus was much recovered in health and in a better state of mind when the archbishop came to call on him.

■■■■■■■■■■■■■■■■■■■■■■■■■■■■■■■■■■■■■■■

'It is good to see you much improved' Honorius began, 'I have news both good and bad. The sad news is that Romanus of Rochester has been lost at sea,' he paused.

'I had sent him with important letters and other matters to visit Rome, to consult with the Holy Father.'

Another pause.

'It is a great loss to us. The wreckage has been found and none have been saved.'

He paused yet again, obviously moved by the loss. He recovered himself with a sigh. 'It has left a vacancy at Rochester. It is important that the house there is maintained, even as Eormenred, the King's brother, oversees the eastern kingdom of Kent. You might be well suited and inclined to lead that house?' He paused. Paulinus had but raised his eyebrows.

'Let us give it due consideration in our prayers. You might like to visit. It is an easy ride in two or three days'. Honorius gave a wry smile, 'and the monks are expecting you', he added.

Paulinus returned the wry smile.

So it was that Paulinus went to and remained in Rochester. But his gold and silver chalice, financed by queen Tata, went neither to Lyminge, nor Rochester. They stayed in Canterbury as bishop and queen had requested: the least that they could offer for their safe return to and for the sanctuaries that they were each finding in Kent.

Visitors.

It was to be a good eighteen months before a weary figure on a stout roan pony, accompanied by a pale cleric, looking uncomfortable on a thinnish bay mule, along with the young warrior, Aldhelm, on a sprightly chestnut steed, rode into the enclosure at Lyminge.

The new residents were still mainly living in tents and turf huts while the wood frame of the new longhall was rising and even being thatched at one end, with Bassus up there supervising the thatchers. Smoke rose from various fires; mainly for cooking, but also from a new forge that had been an early addition to the new community, along with a turf building where they could smoke fish and gammon for the winter months.

Geese and pigs seemed to wander freely, while ponies and donkeys hopped a little with their front legs hobbled to limit their wandering. It was a gently bustling hive of activity.

But visitors were rare, and there was a general pause as the travellers were spotted, first by Bassus from his roof top view. He slid adroitly down the ladder, snatching a spear leaning against the door post since he saw that the male visitor was armed.

As he approached the three riders, the figure on the roan pony threw back her hood: and Bassus lowered his spear and forgot to kneel.

'Why, 'tis my lady Hilda, if I'm not mistaken?' and then he knelt.

Rising he followed, 'And can this be young Aldhelm grown into a young soldier?'

Aldhelm smiled, secretly proud at being recognized by his erstwhile hero Bassus.

'It is Bassus, and you are not changed; and I charged with bringing my lady Hilda to you, as she had promised.' A pause. 'We are long weary and methinks my lady would rest upon your hospitality.'

But this was overtaken by Tata approaching, having put aside her weaving when she was aware that all work had stopped. She approached with open arms, shaking her head in disbelief, helping Hilda to dismount, embracing her gently.

'It is you: you who we left behind,' she paused, a little overcome.

'I cannot tell you how good it is to see you, to have you here. There is not a day that Eanfled does not speak of you and remind me of my folly! Come. Bassus, please take the pony and tend to her companions.' For Tata had not recognized the young Aldhelm grown into a warrior.

She turned to the cleric, frowning with a puzzled look, 'And is this Romanus who we also had to leave behind. You are quite grey.' She paused again.

'I think that you show that we have all seen too much; but perhaps you more than we have, here in the safety of our homeland,' she paused for a third time.

'Come, we have much to do to welcome our guests; our dear, dear family restored to us. It is indeed a time for celebration.'

Hilda was exhausted, but much relieved. She saw that the few years apart had not only aged Romanus, but also had touched Tata, even as she had gained an air of maturity; of being in charge and independent; but if anything, a little thinner; and was she hiding a cough?

The builders of the new longhall were diverted for the day to put together a hazel framework, then infill it with wicker work that they had prepared as room dividers for the new longhall. In time the wicker work might be plastered and limed, but for now they would simply be draped with hides to give Hilda protection for a place of her own. Her roof also temporarily diverted the thatchers from the main building. So Hilda was home and dry in a place of her own by the end of the day. She slept more soundly on her bed of covered bracken than she had for many a night: and was more than delighted when Eanfled brought her a bowl of water fresh from the spring early the next morning: even before they both went to the first service of the convent. For it was heading for midsummer, with the days seemingly lazy and endless, even in the face of much work to be done.

Eanfled had moved from childhood to adolescence in these eighteen months; and it was longer since Hilda had last seen her. Hilda sighed to herself, determining that she would cherish their time together. Intuitively she felt it would not be long before the King would be looking for a suitable suitor: that is, suitable for his political aspirations, and the safety of his kingdom. Hilda splashed a little of the water on her face. For now she could ask for nothing more. She must, with an uplifted heart, celebrate all the joys of a beautiful summer's day in an idyllic setting: even if it was a building site. It was the beginning of a new chapter. A whole day of catching up with Eanfled and Tata lay between the services of the small convent.

It was over several days of catching up that Hilda related her escapades in arriving in Kent. She, had survived on Iona while Cadwollan's mob pillaged and laid waste to Northumbria. She had waited for her cousin Oswald to amass sufficient warriors from Dalriata, many of them Northumbrians in exile, waiting to recover ownership of their countryside.

While the Mercians could, and had, destroyed, they could not hold the northern lands, particularly as the indigenous Northumbrians were well trained in hiding and in guerilla warfare. Over three months the invaders realized that they had reaped as much instant wealth as they could and were losing men at an increasingly alarming rate. Additionally, their own men missed their homeland. They began to retreat.

A sigh of relief had gone through the two kingdoms of Bernicia and Deira. But they waited another full month before Oswald began to take back the land. He was declared and welcomed as the new King of Northumbria by the people of the land. With this news percolating through to Iona, Hilda, with Ebba and Heiu, had rapidly returned to her aunt Acha. They spent the winter at Lennel, helping to restore order at their estate. Heiu, having left Iona with them, stayed for a short time in Acha's hospitality. But then felt that it was time to return to her hides family lands to see what might be recovered; fearing the worst. Acha insisted that Basah, her second in command, must accompany Heiu, and gave him leave for three months to help her recover her lands. For Acha knew that both Heiu's parents had been killed by the marauding Mercians, while her brothers had died by Edwin's side in battle. This tragic news Acha gently broke to Heiu. They saw her visibly seem to shrink as she heard it.

Hilda and Ebba were quite heartbroken to share her sad news and to see Heiu go. Their time in Iona had bound the three of them closely; even as sisters of an age.

But Hilda and Ebba were delighted to hear that Oswald had lost no time in bringing a monk from the Iona Community to Northumbria to re - establish their faith in the kingdom. Corman had been chosen and requested the island of Lindisfarne as a similar island haven to Iona: the isolation, the sky and the sea, light on water, the migrating birds and the abundance of wildlife. All these he knew as a tested foundation for life's pattern, celebrating the glory of God. However, Corman's very manner and his lack of skill in the local language fell short of winning the people of the Deira, much of it due to his inability to speak their native tongue. He complained that he needed not only the place, but the right people. He had set about finding twelve young men to build and populate this special place: even as he also was asked to attend Oswald's court; and even as he chose to attempt to visit his people on foot. For Oswald had requested that Segenus, bishop of Iona, might promote Corman to the status of a fellow bishop to minister to all of his kingdom: no small task for a somewhat fiery fellow long used to the isolated rituals of a closed community on Iona.

The transposition had turned out to be too much for Corman and within eighteen months he had petitioned to return to Iona. It had been to everybody's advantage that he was replaced by the gentler Aidan, of a much more patient disposition: and long respected by Oswald on his many visits to Iona. Aidan had succeeded and prioritized selecting his twelve young novices, two brothers, Cedd and Chad, and orphaned Eata, were among the chosen few. Building proceeded on the eastern island with this new young influx.

All this Hilda had heard while she was staying with her aunt Acha. But through the winter months she was party to Ebba petitioning her mother and her brother, now King, that there might also be a new convent in the kingdom. Her mother was sympathetic, her brother, King Oswald, equally so.

'I think that we need all the prayers that we can raise; even as much as warriors!' was his affirmation.

■■■

Hilda had been sorely tempted to join Ebba in her proposal for a convent at Coldingham on the eastern coast, far north of Aidan at Lindisfarne. Ebba felt sure that Aidan might somehow find time to visit her and help with the instruction of her small group? But Aidan had advised that they should wait upon this calling for a year or so, suggesting that Ebba might first spend time with the monks at Lindisfarne. There she might rejoin Heiu who, having sorted out her lands, and appointed Sigbert as overseer, had decided that her home estate bore too many sad memories. So, she had decided to enter Lindisfarne as a supplicant, living close to the guest house. Ebba, delighted to join Heiu again, had bowed to Aidan's guidance; while Acha saw her once exiled family being restored.

Hilda had been moved to review her own situation. Her thoughts had turned not only to her sister Hereswid in Anglia, but also to Tata and Eanfled in Kent. It was to the latter that she had made a promise. The falling call of the soaring terns still echoed in her dreams, echoing the departing pleading of her young cousin on that final day when the royal family had fled by boat from the onslaught of the plundering Mercians.

So, she had visited the hides of land that she and Hereswid still owned, not far south of Acha's estate, and spent the spring and summer reviving

100

and reorganizing the fabric of the communities. But her prayers and thoughts were elsewhere. Her natural abilities for organising, listening, delegating, supporting, seeing to the heart of a problem, flourished in this six months. She was more than grateful for having Adrian to leave in charge of their estates. It was he who had managed to hide most of the important tools before the Mercians came; to scatter their livestock into copses and onto the moors, dispersing the villagers in the forest, even burning down some of their buildings to make it look as if the place had been already pillaged, thus enticing the invaders to ride on to the next lot of looting: a strategy that had spared them more havoc and less rebuilding.

Hilda had sought both Oswald's and Aidan's advice over the autumn months. She had spent October with Ebba and Heiu at Lindsifarne in the guest accommodation. But still her promises to Eanfled and Tata pulled in her heart.

She had made a promise.

Aidan, hearing her confession and seeing her determination, variously advised that she should seek to fulfill this promise, through which she might find where her true vocation lay. At this stage he felt that she lacked the clarity of vocation that both Heiu and Ebba had. Oswald, on hearing of her proposed journey south, insisted that she should take the young Aldhelm with her, for they would have to avoid the dangers of the wild as well as of Mercia.

They had planned to ride to the Humber, the southernmost tip of Deira, and sail to East Anglia where they knew they would be safely received, retracing the journey that Hilda had made some years ago.

The beach at Withernsea, at the tip of the east coast, brought back memories of what seemed a different life. Then she had arrived with Cyanrith, both of them young and full of optimism, Hilda delighting in the knowledge of her sister, married and established in her new kingdom, while she and Cyanrith were returning, full of hope and joy at being returned to the pleasures of Edwin's court in Yeavering.

How much wiser, and sadder, she was now.

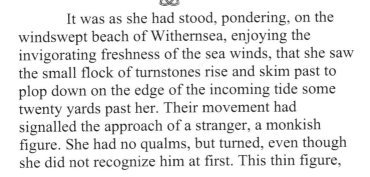

It was as she had stood, pondering, on the windswept beach of Withernsea, enjoying the invigorating freshness of the sea winds, that she saw the small flock of turnstones rise and skim past to plop down on the edge of the incoming tide some twenty yards past her. Their movement had signalled the approach of a stranger, a monkish figure. She had no qualms, but turned, even though she did not recognize him at first. This thin figure,

102

with a grey cropped tonsure, disguised her
memories of the young Romanus who had been the
companion and advisor to Tata when she had first
made the journey north to be Edwin's bride and
queen. Then he had been plumpish and dark haired.
The present slimmed down Romanus bowed, and
Hilda inclined her head and moved to clasp his
hand; but then did not, she simply smiled.

'It is brother Romanus, is it not? So very
welcome. So very welcome.'

She paused.

'I think that you must wish to return to Kent:
even as I feel called to keep a promise?'

'You read me well; as you always did, even
as a child, my lady.'

Hilda smiled wanly.

'Good Romanus, you taught me much. I am
forever in your debt. Although writing and reading,
sadly, are not my present occupations.' She turned
back towards the hamlet.

'Aldhelm and I will sail in two days' time to
Anglia, where I shall seek to see Hereswid and
Aethelric. Then we shall by pony and a ferry
crossing to Kent, God willing: and if Aldhelm has
done all his homework.' She mused to herself that it
was Cyanrith who had advised him on the route that
the three of them had made some years ago.

She continued aloud,

∎∎

'But I think that we both have stories to tell?'

So, it was in the hamlet of Withernsea that they had begun to exchange their stories over the two days of waiting to set sail. How Romanus had abandoned his priestly garb on the news of Edwin's death, followed by the hasty departure of Paulinus with the queen and children. Yet Romanus had kept his pendant crucifix hidden under his borrowed peasant's garb. For he knew that the Mercians were no respecters of the cloth. Yet in his new disguise he could meld as well as move more freely.

Alcuin, a young local shepherd, a sometimes attender of the church, had scattered his flock of sheep so that the Mercians might not feed on it, nor needlessly slaughter it. He undertook to guide Romanus through the hills and forests, living off what they could catch and picking the wild berries of the autumn; drinking from springs, and sleeping in bracken tents, the ferns covering an instant framework of broken boughs. In the following days Romanus had learnt much about eking a living from the land, while sometimes he would take out the one small book he had in his small pack and point out to Alcuin the different letters that made words: and Alcuin in his turn marvelled, finding the words soothing when Romanus prayed them.

■■■■■■■■■■■■■■■■■■■■■■■■■■■■■■■■■■■■■■■

They had headed south, down the spine of the Pennines, home ground for the shepherd, for it was where Alcuin regularly spent his summers with his flock. He could read the lie of the land like the back of his weather worn hand. Alcuin running hither and thither like a mountain goat, carefully anticipating an all clear before signaling to Romanus who laboriously clambered in his footsteps, stumbling and out of breath initially, but, within a week, slimmer and more surefooted. Caves and copses now varied their overnight shelter

They had come down from the moors at Swaledale, keeping in view of the river but avoiding the main path; often travelling by moonlight and sleeping fitfully in the day, fairly sure that the Mercians would have already plundered and moved on, but not so sure whether any of the invaders had begun to return to their homes. The two travellers circumvented the burnt ruins of Richmond and moved towards the old stone ruins of the Roman station at Catterick. Nearby they sought the beginnings, or remains, of James' monastery, not knowing what they might find; nor whom. But they had travelled in hope and on rumours.

They found that the half-built buildings had been partially scorched, but as there had been few riches, they had been rapidly abandoned.

■■

105

James and his six young novices had, some years ago, in the time of Paulinus, started to clear the land around the fledgling buildings. But now open spaces were not safe places to camp, so overnight Romanus and Alcuin had stuck to the protection of the woodland and a makeshift cover of hazel staves, having first indulged in a welcome bathe in the fast flowing waters.

They wondered where the brothers were, for, mercifully, there were no signs of corpses on the local site; nor of fresh graves.

'Trust James to be ahead of the game,' Romanus had muttered to himself.

Hilda had smiled at this point, remembering James working with Paulinus. It seemed a memory from another age. How marvellous that such a quiet devoted man had survived amidst this turmoil; and even started a foundation. But perhaps no surprise she mused on reflection?

Her reflection had been accurate. For Romanus went on to tell Hilda of how, thinking they were well hidden, he had woken to find Alcuin chatting to a young brother and hungrily gnawing at a leg of cold rabbit. It had not taken him long to join them and to learn that all the novices were hidden in the woods with many of the villagers; that they were intent on staying there until they had seen the invaders returning on their retreat. James and the elders of the village had seen all this happen before; their strategy was well practiced.

As yet they had attempted no restoration of the buildings, thereby maintaining an appearance of desolation and, hopefully, avoiding further desecration by the retreating troops. They would even let their fields go fallow for a season. Tightened belts were better than graveyards! The retreating forces would never search the woods for they knew too well that they would lose out to the guerilla warfare, lose out to the disadvantage of local knowledge.

So, a slimmed-down Romanus had survived, and his teaching skills had been much appreciated in the time that he had spent helping James regrow the monastery. How true the archbishop's perception had been that seeds would remain and grow!

Hilda had listened patiently and understood Romanus' call back to Kent without questioning. She counted her blessings that she had escaped, via her aunt, to spend time on Iona with both Heiu and Ebba. What a formative sanctuary that had been and, after so much destruction, the regeneration promised in King Oswald and Bishop Aidan was like the return of spring after a long hard winter.

Yet she knew that her pledge to Eanfled and Tata still held her. Thus her journey to Kent.

So the three of them had set sail from Withernsea, leaving Deira and heading south for Dunwich. Once there Romanus spent time in Felix's monastery, following in Paulinus' footsteps, while Hilda had spent a week with Hereswid and Aethelric in East Anglia, finding her young nephew, Adwulf, running around trying to brandish a small spear that tripped him up as often as it went in the direction intended. But still he kept trying to the delight of his father and the raised eyebrows of his mother and the benevolent smiles from his visiting aunt.

More seriously Hereswid confirmed that they were all in suspense as to what Penda, in Mercia, would do next. Sigbert, Aethelric's older cousin, held an uneasy kingship in Anglia, his calling more inclined to the monastery than to the throne. But fortunately, he was close to his cousin Ecgric, Athelric's older brother, who bore most of the responsibility for organizing and training the thegn warriors of Anglia. Hereswid confided that her husband was away much of the time training with them. Hilda could but nod her head, eyes downcast.

■■■

'It seems never to end. Why cannot they learn to live in peace, together? It is my daily prayer that the seven kingdoms may live in peace. But I fear that the kings of the seven kingdoms do not hear it. If only they had a smattering of charity towards each other.' She sighed.

'But even the seven wise virgins knew the sense in being prepared,' Hereswid countered. Hilda nodded ruefully. She was not going to argue with her sister. Hilda changed tack.

'You know that you can come to us in Kent if the worst happens. I am sure that Tata and Eanfled; and Saethred, will be delighted for us all to be together again, as we were in Edwin's day'. She repressed another sigh, and they both fell silent.

It was Hereswid who spoke again,

'I treasure those memories too. Only now do we see what a privilege we had under uncle Edwin; even as orphans. And I have been so fortunate here with Aethelric and the blessing of Adwulf.' She paused, but continued,

'Eredith and her daughters at Dunwich also have been a great consolation. She is from France and they seem to be so much more stable there, respecting the religious communities, even when the kingdoms squabble! I am much drawn to them.' Another pause.

'But enough of that! Let us celebrate your being here and your reunion with Eanfled and Tata: and Saethred: for I hear that she is there with her son?

Hilda ignored her question, looking distantly over her shoulder, with her calm grey eyes.

'It is always well to have our lamps prepared, Hereswid. For who knows where we might be called to carry them.'

This a statement rather than a question. She continued,

'But this time together is a special celebration to make and to remember: and to carry to Kent.'

And so it was that she carried those good wishes and fond memories to the ladies of Kent, at Lyminge. The travellers had arrived at Lyminge two weeks later. Aldhelm had executed Cyanrith's instructions to the letter.

Their time at Lyminge began as a time of flowering; a rare interval of creativity and tranquility.

Aldhelm was only too pleased to stay on to help Bassus and his team to work at building the longhall on the pattern of the one that they had known so well in Edwin's day at Yeavering.

■■■■■■■■■■■■■■■■■■■■■■■■■■■■■■■■■■■■■■■

110

Romanus was delighted to be allowed to join Paulinus at Rochester and to renew his shared passion for the scriptures and the rituals of monastic life. The security now doubly appreciated after his various travels.

Hilda found a whole new circle of like-minded sisters in addition to the treasure of being reunited with Eanfled and Tata. Of course, Tata stood as head of the estates of Lyminge, but they all respected and deferred to Bertha when she managed to come to stay, frail as she now was. For it was she who had started this small community, with its tiny church above the head of the spring. Tata's new longhall was well away from this church and from the smaller hall that Bertha had built years ago. But soon there was a new complex of tents and huts surrounding the two halls; a bustling hive of industry, contrasting with the peace and quiet of the small convent.

Hilda hovered between the two establishments and requested of Tata that she might take over the scriptorium, since Bertha was so rarely with them these days. So doing also gave her an excuse for rare trips to Canterbury to work with and to borrow books from the monks. Her request delighted Tata, while Eanfled petitioned to help her, thereby recovering her unpractised skills initiated in the north. Hilda made adjustments to the scriptorium, with a leather flap for a window, to give them more daylight, whence Eanfled would come and sit by her side, making copies in her tray of beeswax with a finely honed chicken bone as an erstwhile quill.

Yet it was not long before the sisters in the convent asked whether Hilda might also instruct two of the sisters in the preparation of vellum and the collection of the oak galls for ink, before they learnt to scratch with quills or test their skills with chalk on slate. It was not long before they were pleading for colours and seeking how to make them, observing closely as precious parchments were pricked out before the actual writing started.

Bertha's heart was with them even if her presence was rare. She had written to Neustria in northern France, whence she came, that they might be spared an elder sister, well trained in the disciplines of convent life, to oversee this growing, fledgling flock at Lyminge. For Bertha felt her own energies were ebbing. The ageing queen did celebrate the incoming energies from the visits of Hilda, Eanswith, and Eanfled, even as she had welcomed Sexburg from Kent. She could not but observe that Hilda and Eanswith, although cousins, born in the same year and of similar inclinations, were of such different dispositions, which complimented each other as chalk and cheese.

Certainly, both of them were determined characters, and recognized that strength in each other as fellow spirits. Already in Hilda, with her considerable exposure to crises, there was an early maturity, always marked by a considered opinion, married to an unusual ability to see to the heart of the matter, even when it was not necessarily presented to her. Whereas Eanswith, who had spent all her years in the protected environment of Canterbury, had not had her impulsiveness modified, nor her innate abilities tested. So hers was still the joyous enthusiasm of somebody much younger. It was infectious, making Hilda smile, raise an eyebrow; and ponder. Hilda noted that the young princess seemed to have her father at her beck and call; making Hilda wonder how she would have coped with Hereric, her absent father, the ghost of her family, painted only by the memories of her mother and sister. Edwin and Paulinus had variously filled that father role for her: but at a distance.

Eanswith was only too ready to enthuse about her inclination to belong to, even run, a house that cared for orphaned children. 'Why was there not one?' She would ask. 'There is no need to have children of my own when there are so many children who need to be looked after.'

Hilda could but nod in agreement.

'It would seem to be a great gift; even as it would be a considerable commitment', she offered.

'You must come and visit the place that father has promised to me?'

'Yes, I would like that if Tata and Eanfled will let me go.'

Hilda had wished there was the wisdom of Aidan to consult, to temper such young enthusiasm. Perhaps next time that she went to Canterbury she would seek the counsel of Archbishop Honorius; even venture to Rochester to ask the advice of Paulinus? Perhaps a letter would do.

In fact it was the arrival of sister Gertrude, an answer to Bertha's request for help, that settled the course of events. She had made the channel crossing from northern France in the autumn on a boat bringing wares to Canterbury. A few days staying with Bertha and Ymme were followed by consultations with the archbishop. This completed she was escorted up the valley and quietly welcomed by the convent at Lyminge.

Gertrude was quite large and of a middling disposition. She epitomized motherly care, rather underappreciated in her home convent. She would flourish at Lyminge. Tata welcomed her as a friend, and somebody who would take so much off her hands; not realizing, until it happened, how much she would appreciate the companionship of an older woman. It seemed no effort for Gertrude to quietly tell the headstrong Eanswith that she must spend at least a year with them in Lyminge while the buildings were made at Folkestone, which they might visit together from time to time. With the authority of the archbishop behind her, Eanswith fell in with Gertrude's advice, and everybody breathed a sigh of relief. Bertha decided that she might finally retire to the peace of the convent at Chelles, which Gertrude had left. She had a strange longing for her homeland after all these years of exile. It was curious how the fluency and manners of the French Gertrude had finally made that obvious to her. As with Tata, Gertrude had revealed an unidentified, unspoken feeling in Bertha. The old queen began to make her preparations.

The routine of the life at Lyminge was broken by the news that the King would come to hunt the boar; even as he also might visit his sister and his daughter. Tata asked Bassus to make arrangements for the chase since he now knew the lie of the land and the way of the woods. There were certainly boar and venison to be had and in the kitchens Frida was an expert at collecting herbs from the meadows. Even the longhall was at a stage where it was habitable for a summer feast.

The morning began with the rising mist leaving the bright jewels of dew on the meadows running down to the gurgling spring where minnows and newts hid in the side pools. Sandalled feet were unwittingly cooled and washed as they made their way down to collect water from the source. Smoke began to curl from several fires, with the lime kiln being left as embers on this holiday.

Eadbald arrived on a fine bay gelding, accompanied by Erconbert, his favourite son, on a spirited chesnut. Three other thegns made up their hunting party, while in Lyminge Bassus and Aldhelm had coerced two of the most experienced herdsmen to join the party, since it was they who really knew which local tracks to follow, and where they might close down the fleeing boar. For the king had come prepared with spears and hounds; three lean lurchers with noses as sharp as their eyesight.

'They would be better for hares on the Downs,' muttered one of the local herdsmen. He and his fellow herdsmen rode working ponies and one of them had a mongrel that did have a good nose; along with the experience not to tackle boar or stag on his own but to try and hold it at bay and await the reinforcement of the hunters.

The visitors were greeted by Tata, the hunt toasted with ale, and they were off and away in good spirits. Throughout the day the peace of the

116

spreading hamlet was interrupted with the near and distant echoing cries of the men and their dogs from various copses, the sounds reverberating round the valley in an eerie manner. The villagers waited, making preparations for their return, which was made with some bravura. A stag and a boar strung on poles between the herdsmen's ponies, while Aldhelm did have a brace of hares on each side of his grey mare: the lurchers had earned their keep: and there would be feasting for all.

It was the boar, bristles burnt off, and slowly roasted on a spit that fed the company. The stag had been gutted and left to hang in a well-protected hut, round which the dogs salivated, tails between their legs. Ale was quaffed by the hunters in generous quantity and the royal party related stories of other outings.

'Do you remember the twenty- four pointer that your sons took in the woods outside Rochester?' The oldest thegn had started. Tata, carefully seated with Hilda and Eanswith, and attend by Frida, noticed a fleeting shadow of a frown on the King's face. She knew him well enough. It was missed by most of the male company, but she guessed that it was the mention of his eldest son, Eormenred. She had heard that father and son were no longer on such good terms; that although Eadbald had appointed him to run the eastern kingdom from Rochester, it had all the makings of a power struggle. Her intuition made her heart miss a beat. Eomenred had two infant sons, even as she did. She saw the glance that passed between Eadbald and Erconbert, father and second son; and she shivered: and she had come to Kent to seek a sanctuary for herself and her children. She busied herself with chatter to her niece, but Hilda had seen her start, even as she turned it to mask a suppressed cough, and Hilda wondered what she had missed.

It was only later when the hunting party had finally returned to Canterbury that Hilda dared to pursue the matter when she and Tata were both working on a hanging tapestry one evening before the light faded.

'Why did the story of the twenty-four point stag disturb you so at the feast, Tata?'

'You miss nothing do you Hilda.' Tata replied, hesitating before continuing.

'It was the reminder at the feast that one son was there, and one son was not: and that the absent son has two vulnerable infant sons, even as I have. I saw the look between Eadbald and Erconbert. That was what disturbed me. My years with dear Edwin taught me to read the furtive looks between men. I do begin to fear for Eormenred and his sons, even as he is bold and ambitious. I even begin to fear for my own two dear sons. Just when I really thought that we might be safe.' Tata pricked her finger and a drop of blood ran on to the tapestry.

'Now see how clumsy I have become.'

'It is but a drop. We will take it out with salt in a minute.'

There was an interval while Hilda sought a pinch of salt, at the same time each was engrossed with their own thoughts. Hilda reopened the conversation.

'I remember Hereswid saying, while she worried about the threats to their estates in Anglia, how much more stable life seemed to be in France.' She paused; they stitched for a while, then Hilda continued,

'Ymme and Gertrude may give you good advice; and I think that Bertha has it in her mind to return to her homeland. There would surely be no threat to two Kentish boys in Neustria? But you would miss them sorely?'

Tata nodded in agreement with the last part of Hilda's comments. But maintained her silence as to her niece's suggestion as to the safety of France.

Yet that was how it came about. A month later the ship that had brought Gertrude to Canterbury took the two boys, Wuscfre and Yffi to

Neustria. Saethred, mother to Yffi, decided that she would go with them to take care of them at King Dagobert's court. But sadly Bertha, hoping to see out her final years in France, had fallen ill, and rapidly declined. She did but wish them a speedy journey and gave them her blessing.

'It seems that I am destined to stay here with my dear husband. I think that I shall rest by him in his grave at Canterbury. But pray for me in your new home. I shall be watching over you.'

So Tata, not only saw her sons depart, but had Bertha's funeral to organize. It was only then that she recognized how much support she had received from her mother; indeed, how her mother had provided her with this home at Lyminge.

Tata underestimated how much these different departures would cost her. As in Northumbria, which seemed a life time ago, Eanfled was again her main consolation; even as her daughter reluctantly admitted that she also missed the rumbustiousness of her younger brothers and, most definitely, the kind wisdom of her grandmother.

These departures coincided with Eanfled changing from an adolescent into a young lady. She spent even more time with the older Hilda and Eanswith. They, in turn, began to treat her more as their equal; a fellow princess. Tata observed this with some satisfaction, while her own inclinations led her to spend more time with Gertrude and Eanswith in the small convent at Lyminge; although she found the innocent, enthusiastic, energy of Eanswith sometimes wearing to her own present predicament, and would often escape to join Hilda in the scriptorium. Here it was quietly absorbing and intricate, work. Thereby a suitable distraction.

A year later saw the longhall at Lyminge completed, and very impressive it was. Bassus had connived with the carpenters to make pegs on some of the cross beams between the massive main posts. From these pegs he hung frames of woven reeds so that in the summer months they could be taken down and let the light stream in thereby making the whole space of the hall feel larger. The central parts of the floor had been laid with a special iron-enriched clay, packed down and polished until it shone a dull red. At either end the new palace had upper rooms where the queen and her family could retreat. The lathed walls were plastered and washed white with lime from the kiln, draped with the finished tapestries and other dyed linens, while twigs of rosemary, lavender, and marjoram were scattered on the floor by the doors to give off perfume when trampled. This an extravagance for the feasts they held to celebrate the completion of the palace.

Her brother, King Eadbald, declared that it outshone his palace at Canterbury and that he would have to come hunting more often. Ymme, his queen, said that it was worthy of her home in France, and that it showed all the grace of a woman's touch: at which Eadbald had roared with laughter.

Privately they were both pleased for Tata; although, in private, both commented that she looked thinner and somewhat strained. Eadbald also noted that his niece, Eanfled, definitely had the makings of a young princess who would be marriageable in another five or so years, having all the good looks of her mother and something of the red hair colouring from Edwin. Eadbald had accepted that he had lost his own daughter to her vocation, but Eanfled seemed not to be drawn to the celibate life. A most useful niece, he mused. He must indeed find the excuse to come here hunting more often.

Hilda observed and comprehended all this while helping Tata and Frida to organize the culinary aspect of the feast. She too was worried about Tata. But she busied herself with the cooking. They had pike and eels sent up from the marshes, and oysters from the coast. Then venison, slowly cooked in herbs, served with the tart stewed crab apples from the orchard and freshly cooked bread, rounded off with honeycomb and summer berries. Alfrid was in charge of the drinks, with the men generally consuming the home brewed ale, while Ymme had brought wine from the vineyards that she oversaw at Canterbury, rescued from the remains of the few Roman villas. Hilda and Tata stuck to cordial made from wild raspberries. The young Eanfled was allowed to experiment, sipping the wine a little; but quickly went back to the cordial; nevertheless enjoying the rest of the celebrations more than she might have, had she not tasted the wine.

It was another year that had passed. The crops had not been so good, a late spring followed by too much rain in the summer. The cattle and sheep were fat on the grass, but the yield of grain would be low and the harvest late. Nevertheless, most of the able bodied were out in the fields when a merchant came up from Canterbury with the news that the Mercians had invaded Anglia and slaughtered Sigbert along with the majority of his troops.

While this did not immediately threaten the safe haven of Kent, Hilda's heart had lurched at the news and the thought of her sister being widowed.

For surely Aethelric had been in the band of warriors: and her son, Hilda's nephew, perhaps now fatherless at such a young age? Just as she and Hereswid had been so many years ago.

Tata was with her when the news came and she saw Hilda tense but saying nothing. She went over and laid her hand on Hilda's arm, also saying nothing. Hilda had nodded, sadly and silently.

She felt a strong impulse to go to her sister. Who needed her most? Where did her loyalties now lie?

■ ■

Resolutions

After deliberations, prayers and consultations Hilda stayed at Lyminge. They heard that Ana was a puppet king under the Mercians in Anglia. Ana had been too ill to fight in the previous battle, but Penda knew him of old and deemed a native leader more likely to prevent guerilla warfare than an imposed Mercian ruler. The Mercians had learnt some lessons from their pillaging of the north!

Hilda's main persuader to stay in Lyminge had been Sexburg, daughter of Ana and Eredith, and married to Erconberht, heir to the Kentish Throne. Sexburg had argued that if Hereswid felt in any danger she would know that she could come with Adwulf to Hilda in Kent, or that she could easily sail across to Neustria to Sexburg's mother's home, since she knew how close the two families had become with adjacent estates in Anglia. Also, in these uncertain, warring, times, it was not a good time for anyone to make anything but compulsory journeys. It also was true that Hilda was a central figure of support for Tata now that Saethred and the

125

two boys had already gone to Dagobert's court in Neustria. Sexburg furthered her case, insisting that there was so much still for Hilda to do here. Did not Eanswith really need the balance of Hilda's common sense if she was to start her community at Folkestone? Being the same age, Hilda had as much influence on the determined Eanswith as the older Gertrude. While Hilda would always listen to Eanswith, she would separately discuss matters with the older nun, seeking ways to meld the two views.

Gertrude and Eanswith did soon take over the new buildings at Folkestone along with three younger novices and three widows who were ready to undertake the challenge of serving under the young princess. Gavin, who was already the priest serving at the king's coastal church of St Peter and St Paul at Folkestone, would celebrate mass for them even as Romanus had finally returned to Lyminge from Rochester to be reunited with Tata and to officiate at their small convent.

For the initial period Gertrude was nominally abbess at Folkestone, although everything was discussed fully with Eanswith, who listened patiently; for it was her wealth that financed the building. The new convent lay in the high fortress of Folkestone, which itself had been adapted from Roman foundations. The views from the cliffs were spectacular, but there was always a problem of carrying water up to the heady heights, with Eanswith delegating a donkey, carrying pots and panniers, to relieve the arduous task. She even undertook to include herself in the rota of leading the very patient donkey up and down the path to the spring on the lower coast. It could be done between the office of None and Vespers; and it did get her out of the convent from time to time. She would go down to the fishing village on the estuary, where she came across the ragged children working at repairing the nets. She took to taking freshly baked bread with her to give to the children while they helped her to fill the panniers with water. The waifs soon learnt to wait for her arrival and came flocking. Her inquiries revealed that many of them were orphans whose fathers had been lost at sea or to illness, and that they lived in makeshift tents on the edge of the village, catching rabbits, harvesting eggs from the seabirds, and scratching a living from those villagers who had more to spare.

Eanwswith discussed them with Gertrude; and with her parents.

'It always was my wish that we may look to these children. I see that they may be somewhat wild. But we could grow more flax and teach them to make the nets that they repair?' she offered.

'I think that they would have to be there as a school attached to the convent. For they will not fit into our hours: and you will have to limit the numbers or we shall be overrun,' was Gertrude's wise advice.

So it was that Eanswith chose ten children and found it was twelve as there were two with siblings who would not be parted. The children themselves took to making their own building and two volunteered to help milking the goats rather than with the building. The widowed sister Mildrith was put in charge of them with the help of the younger Astrid. Mildrith had children of her own, now grown up, so she was well experienced in the ways and wherefores of childhood. The new intake would not easily hoodwink Mildrith. Eanswith took time on three days of the week to tell them the stories that she knew from the scriptures, while Gertrude supervised prayers at the beginning and the end of each day. Two of the children found the discipline too much and returned to their foraging on the coast. But a mother from the village, who had six children, asked if they would take her middle two as she was struggling to cope, but would be greatly pleased to see them looked after by the sisters. So they were back to twelve children at the home on the cliff tops.

Gradually the new community settled. King Eadbald, visiting his fortress once a month, was quietly impressed by the quiet order that they achieved. Of course, he always went via his sister at Lyminge, with a days hunting with Bassus, and keeping his eye on Eanfled and Hilda, both of whom he thought of as potential political subjects for advantageous marriages. Hilda, who he knew to be a quiet influence on both Tata and Eanfled, seemed to keep him at a cool distance. But he thought that she would make a fine match for some northern prince in due course. His niece, Eanfled, seemed to grow in stature and comeliness so much each time he saw her, resembling her mother in so many ways. But this same mother said firmly that she was still much too young for matrimony, as well as that she needed her company now that the two boys had gone. Eadbald would simply raise his eyebrows; and tilt his head, giving nothing away.

It was when Eanswith was making the descent down the narrow path to collect water with the donkey and Geffrey, one of the younger boys, in attendance that he was distracted by seeing a herb that looked like the silver artemisia. An old sailor had told him that it was good for treating coughs, and as most of the school were down with coughs at the moment he pleaded with Mother Eanswith.

129

They safely tethered the donkey in order that they might carefully clamber up, only to find that it grew on the edge of a small freshwater pool.

'It is the cough cure herb, I'm sure?' queried Geffrey, not really being very sure.

'Yes, I think that it is. Let us carefully cut it to take it back so that Gervais may tell us more about it.' Eanswith paused as Geffrey got out his bone knife.

'But I think that this water is quite fresh and as a spring, although it soaks away again. It seems to run away.' She cupped her hands and sipped a little, splashing the rest on her arms.

'Geffrey, I think we have a new source of water! No daily need to travel up and down. Let us fill the donkey's pots here. What a blessing!'

Which was what they did, somewhat slowly and tediously. But they returned to the convent rejoicing. A new local source of water was a great relief to one and all. Although Geffery secretly was somewhat peeved. For he had enjoyed going down to the coast and seeing some of his friends again.

But Eanswith did continue to visit the village on the estuary once a week, to take food and clothing for the children of the nets.

Gertrude had been right to limit the numbers. For it became known that the nuns cared for children, so mothers would bring their sick children up to the convent to be cured. Fortunately, Mathild was even more expert than Mother Gertrude in the use of herbs; so, a separate small tent soon became the hospital of the convent. There were many successes that they could report, so their reputation for healing grew. But there were also some new burials in the softer soil of the inland fields. Some patients were taken from them; and the children learnt to remember them in their prayers, even as the sisters did.

The reputation of the new convent grew rapidly. Eanswith, consulting with Gertrude, had decided that they would concentrate the sisters' work on spinning, weaving, and needlework. Gertrude was only too pleased to accede to this as her own writing and literary skills were not her strength, while, with the children to care for, there was a continual need for fresh fabrics. But it did mean that what few books they had became even more precious. Tata had generously relinquished a copy of the office hours that had been made at Lyminge, brought to the coast by Hilda on one of her many visits. Hilda observing how well Gertrude and Eanswith complimented each other: sound advice moderating young enthusiasm. Archbishop Honorius did also gift books from his monastery at Canterbury, allowing Gavin a trip to collect them and to spend a few days with his former brothers in the monastery. Gavin's middle-aged life was certainly enriched by the convent of sisters so close to his own church at Folkestone. Two of the sisters even had promised him a new cassock.

Hilda was not the only princess to visit Folkestone. Aebbe, a cousin to Eanswith, daughter to Eormenred at Rochester, also brought precious manuscripts. This time they were from Paulinus and his scriptorium in his cathedral church with a monastery attached. Paulinus, now somewhat arthritic, had regained some of his charismatic preaching, which drew a devoted congregation on Sundays and feast days. Most of the local children were baptized at the monastery. Aebbe, from an early age, had learnt her latin, her reading and her writing, from the ageing abbot: and how that had reminded him of his previous life in the north, when the young ladies were Hilda, Hereswid and Heiu, with Eanfled, some years behind, but always making up fast ground. He gave thanks for rewards in his old age and for the privilege of seeing religious life flourishing in Kent. With serious arthritis it was rare that he would make the effort to visit Tata at Lyminge, yet when Honorius visited him he heard how the convent at Lyminge was growing: that now that Bassus had finished building

Tata a longhall palace she was considering the possibility of a new church for the convent above the head of the Nailbourne spring that supplied them so well. This church might be in memory of Bertha, in memory of Edwin, in memory of her lost infant children, and for the precious two, Wuscfre and Yffe, in the safety of French exile. The days sometimes seemed long for her without the two boys.

  But Aebbe and Eanswith made an immediate friendship at Folkestone, and the Rochester visitor stayed for a week or more, promising to revisit with more manuscripts if she could persuade Paulinus to let them go; even as she would happily work on them herself at home. She parted with some sadness. There was no such female company for her at Rochester.

  Hilda had not met Aebbe,but heard Eanswith's glowing reports and she admired the careful scripting and elaborate decoration of the new books that her sister princess had brought. It seemed that Rochester was indeed a new school of writing.

  However, Hilda had not heard of her sister Hereswid. She wondered how she had fared since Anglia had been so overrun. But in these worrying times it was better to assume that no news was good news?

The small blue butterflies fluttered, alighted, fed, and fluttered again. The white flowering nettles that the small blues were visiting were tranquil in the September sun. It was autumn and most of the harvest was in. The oxen were beginning to heave the ploughs that turned the stubble. But at the edge of the field the nettles grew. Hereswid viewed the comings and goings of the small blues, as she stood absorbing the peace of the day, wishing she could somehow capture the fragile, smudging delicacy of the blues on their wings in her tapestry. So much was in the movement, contrasting with the stillness of alighting; and so many shades of blue in the texture of their wings.

She was still in mourning for Aethelric, feeling that she probably would be for the rest of her days. Their son, Adwulf, was a great consolation; his innocent incomprehension that his father had simply gone away.

'But he will come back some day, mother. I know he will.'

Then half understanding that possibly he might not.

134

'I will look after you while he is away. We will do it together.'

But then looked quizzically at his mother.

'Yes, we will do it together. It is what he would want,' his mother had replied quietly, stroking his fair hair.

Adwulf was barely six, but suddenly catapulted into sharing carefully considered decisions by Hereswid, whereas before life had seemed to be simply doing what he was told to do; or, as he more often remembered, chastised for doing things he should not have done.

Even as Hereswid had heard of the defeat and the loss of her husband she had the support of Ana, now the puppet king, and his family. Ethelburga, Etheldreda and Witburga, his three younger daughters, were still with him and they took it in turns to come and stay with her. Ethelburga, the elder, even at a young age, was determined that she would in time go to the convent of Chelles, returning to her mother's homeland. While she was a great support to Hereswid it also helped to clarify Hereswid's thoughts that, for the moment, her responsibilities lay here with her son and Aethelric's estates. They were now her full-time occupation.

Under Ana's diplomatic kingship they were relatively safe from another war, even if there were high taxes to pay to their Mercian overlord. They must pray that the harvests continued to be good and that Adwulf might grow unhindered through his childhood in these difficult times. Six years of a happy marriage seemed such a short memory; how easy it had been to take it all for granted. How golden it all now seemed: and those long memorable years in their Northumbrian childhood with Hilda and Heiu under the loving care of Tata and Edwin?

She snapped back out of her reveries. The harvest had been good this year and Adwulf had grown a good six inches. There was much that she needed to do.

Heiu and Ebba, still at Lindisfarne on the north east coast, had heard of the fall of Anglia and also worried about and prayed for Hereswid and her family while they were both still attached to the guest house, each of them pressing Aidan to allow them to set up houses of their own. For they both had land and income from their estates to support foundations as they constantly reminded him. But Aidan counselled patience, while wondering if he might seek more help from Iona as all his twelve monks at Lindisfarne were scarcely more than novices.

■■

'Perhaps James at Ripon might have retained some older followers?' He mused to himself. But he did ask the young ladies where they might seek to establish their convents.

'We both spent time with you and your brothers on Iona, after Edwin's untimely death, and now some time on this island,' ventured Ebba.

'Should you approve, we seek a similar solitude on this our eastern coast,' continued Heiu.

'Ebba has land north of here at Coldingham ; and I have heard of the island of the Hart which lies nearer to Lindisfarne.' She paused.

'The King is well disposed,' Ebba added.

Aidan nodded and smiled.

'It is always good to be prepared in earthly matters. And I see that you have done your homework.' He paused. 'I have valued your time here; and the output from the scriptorium and the weaving will be greatly diminished when you leave. But we need those who are proven in the daily offices and called and sanctioned to celebrate the eucharist with you before we move. We must wait on all the pieces falling into place.'

One year later saw Heiu move southwards to begin a small community of sisters on the headland of Hart's Island, from where miles of golden beaches swept southwards to the northern boundary of the Tees estuary. Just as Lindisfarne was only an island when the tide was in, so Heretu, as Hart's island was known, had salt marshes separating it from the mainland. James had not had senior monks to spare, but Dravin came from Iona to minister to the sisters, and he shared accommodation with four lay brothers outside the convent. Fish and fowl were plentiful, while hefted sheep and a few cattle were purchased from the local hamlet on the estuary. It was a beginning.

Six months later Ebba, with Aidan's blessing, moved northwards to the prominent cliffs above Coldingham to form a double community with Justin from Iona bringing two more brothers with him. She had some considerable income from her own estates to help her build her convent, even as she was much encouraged by Oswald, her brother king, and by her ever-patient mother, Acha.

Paulinus in Rochester was much consoled to hear of these northern foundations; but did feel that much of them owed their origins to the community on the small western island of Iona; forgetting that initially he had baptized both of these young ladies, along with Edwin, in the scarcely finished church at York many years ago. Yet he now counted his blessings for the peace in Kent; even as the kindness of memory made much of Edwin and

138

Tata's days in Northumbria take on a golden haze.
Had the summers really been longer? The summer
here in Kent had seemed to fly past and the barley
was already reaped, with only the fields of flax and
oats still ripening.

It was as they were winnowing some of the
first barley that Bassus, who was now improving his
own house in Lyminge, saw strangers arriving. This
time the hooded figure was riding a mule, while a
young monk led a donkey carrying baggage,
plodding at a steady walking pace as a donkey does.
Bassus lent on his staff. A visit from the
religious was unusual, particularly unheralded. He
had to think back to the arrival of Gertrude for a
similar occasion: and this was no Gertrude. He
downed his axe and went to greet them.
The hood fell back and he struggled to
recognize Saethred. He dared to wonder; and hoped
not.
'You are welcome, my lady. You are most
welcome,' he muttered, continuing,
'The Queen is in the longhall, in her rooms.
I will take you.'
He led the mule round to the south door
where he helped her to dismount, observing that she
was too withdrawn to speak. She nodded her thanks.
He hesitated then went ahead to speak at the

139

partition that separated Tata's space from the main hall, addressing her from outside in sombre tones that might prepare her.

'My lady, you have a visitor,' pausing, 'that you might not have expected.'

Saethred had paused behind him, so he stood aside in order that Tata might see her daughter- in-law as she emerged from her quarters. The two women stood still on seeing each other; as if time stopped. Then Tata extended her hands and moved to take those of her trusted friend. Saethred held her hands close to her, lent her head on Tata's shoulder and silently wept. Bassus clasped his hands and looked hard down at the ground, wishing that he could not be there.

The two stood silently in their embrace for a while. Then Tata put an arm round her stepdaughter's waist and led her back into her chambers, sitting them both down on a bench by a small open window where she had been sewing with Hilda. Hilda rose, initially to greet Saethred, then seeing their demeanor, she gathered up her sewing and silently left.

'Tell me the worst. Tell me what has happened. I must know.' Tata said in a low voice.

Saethred shook her head, pulling herself together.

■■■■■■■■■■■■■■■■■■■■■■■■■■■■■■■■■■■■■■

140

'I had to come myself. I could stay there no longer.' She paused, 'It came with the soldiers coming back from Burgundy. So many of the children died. It was scarlet fever. Only two or three at first. Then everywhere that you looked there were no more children playing. It was as if a silence had fallen on us all. Some said it was a curse for our invasion. But I know not; only that I nursed them both and could do nothing. Wuscfre cried out for you, many times. That was as bad as anything: and their choking and gasping.' She broke into weeping again as she remembered it all.

There was no more to say. So they both sat silently.

Hilda had disappeared, without knowing, but fearing the worst, to prepare some valerian and some soup. She would leave them for a while.

As she cooked she strangely found herself humming a lullaby that her mother had sung to her so many years ago. At first she could not even remember the words, but the soothing tune she kept repeating to herself, rocking herself, rocking the memory of those two infant boys that she had held in her arms many years ago? She knew not why she sang it. Was it for herself and her memory of her mother; for her aunt and cousin, locked in their mourning; or was it for the two young princes, so innocently taken? Unknown to Hilda her voice carried to the two mourners and they were strangely consoled. The tune, oft repeated, brought back the words to Hilda.

> All will be well my love,
> As in my lap you lie,
> Soon you will sing a song to me,
> Then all will be well with me,
> When you shall sing a song to me.
> All will be well my love,
> As in my lap you lie.

But Hilda chose not to sing them.

The sad news, the death of their two infant sons that they were so desperately trying to protect, was to take the life out of Tata and Saethred for several months. They left the trappings of the palace and spent more time in the small chapel with the sisters of the convent. The regular services and the plainchant that Romanus had introduced seemed singularly consoling to their present disposition. Hilda and Eanfled took on the running of the longhall even as they both also frequently attended the services of the convent.

It was Bassus, his present project completed, who dared, a month or so later, to suggest that perhaps a larger chapel, than Tata had previously considered, should be instigated if his queen was

142

spending so much time there? Perhaps the queen might visit Paulinus at Rochester and discuss plans?

It had been the right move. Tata was brought back from her mourning to remember the gift of Bassus that Edwin had given her, how there had been no more loyal servant in her small fiefdom.

It was no surprise that Hilda asked to come to Rochester with her; and Tata mused on where the idea to rebuild the church had really come from. Was it really Bassus, or had Hilda had one of her perceptions and a word in the right ear?

Hilda added to her request that the visit was also an opportunity to borrow more manuscripts to copy, which did not deceive the queen and raised a wry smile, the first for many weeks.

'Hilda, your devotion to the scriptures knows no bounds. I cannot think of a more delightful companion, nor a fellow traveller who is more likely to remember all the details of the plans, or to keep us on track in our discussions for a new church!'

'Saethred and Eanfled are going to see Eanswith with her children at Folkestone. I think that Saethred is ready for that now.' She hesitated, 'We will ever mourn our losses; but we must mould our mourning. A suitable memorial to all that has gone before must be our present goal. I think that it is time that I stirred my old bones and that we ride to Rochester. Will you send somebody ahead to let Paulinus know? We might also stop off at Canterbury and discuss our plans, and predicament, with the good Archbishop?'

And so it was.

There had been a roman villa at Lyminge, even as there had been roman cities at both Canterbury and Rochester. In both, when rebuilding began, French stonemasons had been encouraged to make a living in Kent, resulting in hybrid buildings of stone and wood being developed. Visiting Canterbury, Tata heard and saw of the enthusiasm for the modern style; some even with windows and glass. In her initial enthusiasm for building her palace at Lyminge she had been able to persuade a talented apprentice from Faversham to come and make glass vessels for her table in the longhall. But he had now been looking to return home. Might this be a new project for him too? Perhaps glass windows in the new church?

Hilda had prepared precious manuscript that she might transcribe some plans and borrowed trays of beeswax in which she needled notes of measures to relate to Bassus.

'I hope these will do,' she confided to Tata. 'But I think that when we have had further discussions at home it might be easier for Bassus to come and stay here for a while? I am sure that there are issues of which we have not even thought ?'

'I agree, Hilda. Although I don't think that much escapes your beady eye. It is good to have you and your sharpness.'

The two women smiled, and Hilda nodded her head nonchalantly.

'It is a delightful project, Tata. I think that Bertha would be delighted.'

'Yes, it is a celebration as well as a memorial. Thank you.'

They rode back in better spirits, even as Honorius at Canterbury and Paulinus at Rochester had their spirits lifted by the visits of the two royal ladies.

The foundations of the new church were mapped out and digging, reusing roman masonry, quarrying new stones, marking trees for timber structures, all began in earnest. Bassus was in his element again, and keen to learn how wooden frames could be made for glass: light in the interiors in all weathers: what excitement! Tata and Hilda had discussed with both Paulinus and the archbishop as to whether they might allow a double monastery, as Romanus had a following of young men and widowers who might join him as well as some lay brothers who did much of the agricultural work on the surrounding land. With their agreement the plans had incorporated a long nave to the new chapel with a wooden screen to separate the sisters from the brothers, but a door so that Romanus could move between the two, while the screen had only three crosses above head height so that the music and the prayers could be shared.

Meanwhile Saethred was drawn to spending much of her time with Eanswith, Gertrude, and the small school of children at Folkestone. The bracing position on the cliffs seemed physically to blow new life into Saethred and the constant needs of both resident and visiting children gave her life a much needed wider perspective, even as the office hours gave her time for reflection. It seemed as a welcome resolution for her. It was no great surprise for the ladies at Lyminge to hear that Saethred had been officially received into the community of the sisters at Folkestone.

There followed four years of happiness and celebration. The new church at Lyminge was consecrated by Honorius, with Paulinus making the visit, slung between two mules, his arthritis too advanced to let him ride. Eadbald, Ymme and Eanswith all attended, with Gertrude and Saethred simply making a day trip for the dedication service.

■■

146

Eanswith was now formally abbess of her convent at Folkestone and Gertrude pleased to stand down and watch her protege grow in stature. The older nun was content to sit and spin and weave as her contribution to the convent and its children. They were crafts which she dearly loved and in which she and several of the sisters excelled.

The celebrations at Lyminge were not confined to the consecration of the chapel, but also to Tata becoming the abbess of Lyminge, with an additional small house built for her in the grounds of the convent, even with stained glass in the two windows. She happily shed the trappings of the grand longhall that all had admired. But not before long discussions with Hilda and Eanfled.

Both Hilda and Tata were very aware that Eanfled was rapidly coming of age and had that flush of beauty that come with the freshness of leaving the struggles of adolescence behind and entering a new phase of life. They could both see the King measuring her prospects each time he visited. For her part Eanfled discussed her wishes with Hilda as much as her mother, for Hilda still held the closeness of an elder sister, a role she had throughout her life.

'I see that it seems so right for mother to take orders and seek solace in this lovely place that she has created, and uncle has allowed. But I am not yet ready to follow such a calling. I feel that there is so much to do outside the convent that I would like to do. I think that I might, in due course, enjoy marriage and a family of my own, even as mother had. But not that just yet either. I do love the palace that has been built while we have been here. Do you think that you and I could run this with mother always being at hand for advice?' She smiled inquisitively at Hilda.

Hilda looked at her steadily.

'I think you are right. You must be as true to yourself as much as you are allowed. We are very fortunate to have the wealth that we have, for it does give your mother, and us, some freedoms. I will speak with Tata. I am sure that she will be pleased to relinquish some of the responsibility of running this place and I will be very happy to help in any way that I can. Your mother has the place well organized and I think that you have picked up many of her habits?' Hilda smiled.

An amicable transition ensued with Hilda a natural mediator between the convent and the longhall, between the queen and her daughter.

There were ups and downs in those early years but none so dramatic as those brought in by the turn of the decade.

Key Changes

The summer had been hot, but also dry, so while the harvest had been early it had also been rather meagre. The land felt scorched and the Nailbourne spring at Lyminge had been reduced to a trickle. The heat seemed to induce a lassitude in both man and beast, which was no preparation for the storms that were to break in the autumn. It was around the equinox, when the tides were at their highest, that the worst storms hit the coast and swept across the hinterland. The heavens opened and at Folkestone the spring in the cliffs now gushed. But the pouring rain did not hide the whistling of the wind in the trees, nor the shishing and snapping of leaves and branches as they were pounded and torn from their trees: the final eerie cracking as first one tree, then another, followed by a cascade of uprooting, falling, trees. The wild animals fled out of their forest or hid in their flooding burrows.

It was a time of devastation.

■■■

On the coast the chalk cliffs were repeatedly lashed. The limestone began to crumble, sliding from great heights into the turmoil of the fevered waves, taking with them part of the roman ruins and edging the new convent buildings at Folkestone perilously close to the edge.

It was in this tumultuous weather that a small french boat emerged from the storm and was helplessly driven into the harbour, the crew giving thanks that they had not been drowned in the torrid seas, that they had reached a safe harbour and dry land. The fishermen of the village had all braved the beating weather and gone out to try and anchor them safely to their moorings, fighting the gusting gale and the pelting rain. None of the Folkestone fisherman had even thought of going sailing themselves. None of the french crew had intended to sail across the channel! They had been picked up by the gale and gusted across the seas. Amongst the crew there were two young lads who had simply been taken on as training crew for a day's fishing. Seasick for most of the journey, hanging on to ropes at the bottom of the boat, they had to be lifted off the boat when it was finally beached. Even feet on the ground still left them fragile from their exhaustion. They were taken, as were the rest of the crew, into shelter and to sleep, into which they instantly collapsed.

151

The next morning had the freshness that follows the devasting sweep of a storm, while the sea, with the tide out, now had the flatness of a millpond. The sky a radiant eggshell blue and scarcely a whisper of the wind. The storm had blown itself out.

But the two boys woke with a fever. Osthryd, into whose hut they had been taken, immediately wondered if they ought not to be taken up to the convent where the sisters might take them into their care. Osthryd had her own family to manage and there was scarcely room for two extra invalids in her small hut.

So it was arranged.

Mathild took over nursing the two young lads, but became alarmed when, after two days, she saw that their fever had not broken and both of them had developed a hacking cough. She immediately told the rest of the children to stay away and went to report to Eanswith, who came and helped to try and sooth them.

But it was all too late. Several of the other children became feverish, shivering and unable to eat. Mathild looked in their mouths and saw the white patches. She knew what it was. She had lost her own children to diptheria. She moved swiftly, but without panic to tell Eanswith, only to find that

152

the young abbess already had a fever. She returned to Gertrude, who shook her head in dismay.

'Yes, I too have seen it and survived it, Mathild. It will run its course. I think that it came with the storm There is not much that we can do other than nurse and pray. I think there are no herbs that will cure. And the King is due a visit. We must get a message to him to stay away until the illness has run its course.'

But they were too late, for the King and the Queen arrived that afternoon and insisted on seeing their daughter. She begged them to keep their distance. Ymme insisted on taking over her nursing and Saethred joined her, taking it in turns to sit with her.

Within days the coughing and the white peeling lesions in the mouths of the children, choked and took their toll. Eight of the children died and the remaining four were weak and struggling: three of them survived, battling through the fever and the coughing. Mathild and Gertrude nursed and prayed.

But Eanswith also succumbed in the midst of her dying children; and the King, her father, only mourned her loss from his own bed. The choking coughing had the same consequences and Gervais offered his King the last rites. Ymme wept, inconsolably, a daughter and a husband lost within a week of each other; and so many children too.

The graveyard was filled. Gervais and some of the soldiers from the castle grew too familiar with hacking out graves through the shallow limestone soil away from the cliffs. The convent was in mourning; as was the Kingdom of Kent.

The news ran throughout Kent and onwards to the other kingdoms. In Canterbury Erconbert was declared King with Sexburg his queen; even with a court in mourning. In Lyminge there was the silence of not wishing to believe that disaster had struck again. They waited on more news. Who had survived? Had Saethred, Ymme, or Gertrude, or Mildred? What could they send them?

When no news came, Hilda had volunteered to load two of the donkeys with bread and a flask of live yeast along with spare linen, while she herself rode a steady grey mare. It was less than half a day's journey to Folkestone by horseback.

The sun shone periodically through scudding clouds. The weather now more settled and all the rich colours of autumn showing in the woodlands, the bright yellows of the birch and beech, the oaks still a fading green, but the pigs gratefully grunting and gorging on acorns. The shedding of the leaves let in more light. So there was that gentle luminous quality to a fine autumn day. Such beauty and tranquility in the journey when there was so much sadness in her heart. So much anxiety as to what she might find. It was a consolation that she knew the pleading of the psalm, 'Yea though I walk through the valley of the shadow of death, I will fear no evil: for Thou art with me'.

Yet as she rode, Hilda's mind was much on Eanswith. Why had she been taken so young? Had they seen a saint in their midst and not recognized her? That young, uncompromising, vision of a vocation, so blamelessly lived. Hilda had thought her young and impulsive, but was this not a reflection of her own careful consideration of any decision? With Eanswith it had always appeared to be so clear as to what she was to do. She remembered her infectious spontaneity, which had always made Hilda, who was the same age, feel as if she was a good ten years older; and rather staid. Now she would no longer hear that joyous enthusiasm which she realised was infectious, even as her instinct had been to temper it somewhat. Hilda wondered to herself. Did she begrudge the fact that Eanswith had been so able to convince her parents to help her in her vision?

'O ye of little faith,' she muttered to herself. But again found herself quietly singing to herself, remembering the good things that Eanswith had brought into her life. She must wait and see what was to be done that might keep that young vision alive.

The arrival of Hilda and her supplies were warmly welcomed. Saethred, Ymme, Gertrude and Mildred had all survived. Saethred had naturally taken charge of the day to day running of the convent, but at the end of that devastating month more help arrived. Another figure rode into the convent bringing more supplies. It was Aebbe from Rochester, who had come via Canterbury and received more supplies from Sexburg with a request to let her know what else might be needed.

The sisters at Folkestone began to regroup. They even went down to visit the village on the coast, hoping to find that here had been less damage there. But they found a scarcity of children. The infection had spread like wildfire and there were only two of the orphan net menders left. Saethred arranged for the fishermen to bring their damaged nets up to the convent, promising to train the remaining children and some of the sisters to repair them.

Many candles were lit; many prayers were offered.

156

Two months later Hilda decided that all was on an even keel and she was no longer needed. The young princess Aebbe had decided that she would remain at Folkestone; that this was her vocation, to follow in her cousin's footsteps, to try to maintain her work with the children. She had been discussing her calling with Paulinus in Rochester for some time while working in the scriptorium. This seemed to be a clear answer, here in Folkestone, on the cliffs rather than the estuary of the Medway. Here she was both needed, already known to the community, and felt it a privilege to follow in Eanswith's footsteps. Saethred and Gertrude were only too pleased to accede; and Aebbe brought the wealth of her estates with her! Archbishop Honorius came from Canterbury to celebrate her consecration as the new abbess and his blessing on the foundation.

Hilda rode back to Lyminge in sober mood. The trees now bare and silhouetted against a pale azure sky; the sun low and anaemic, the ground crisp and brittle with a light frost. The ploughed fields lay coated in a pale grey film, while the late afternoon sun shone on the thorns of the bramble and hawthorn. Spider's webs glistened, geometric, gossamer threads. The birds were mainly silent, so that the odd call was more plangent; but she saw a flock of finches pecking at the bright red berries of the thorn trees and the hips of the dog rose.

On this, bright, sunny day, it was one of the thorns that caught her attention, and which forever would hover in her mind. The path had turned a sudden corner towards the setting sun, and there was a flowering thorn tree on which the small flowers, on the bare branches, blew in the breeze. The tiny petals, all of them white, fluttered and fell, causing a minor cascade as if confetti, as if a blessing of snow. Hilda held up her hand, the fragile petals touching her skin as a caress, then falling to the ground. Her mare had stopped, glad of the rest, while the petals continued to fall on them both. They fell on Hilda's uplifted face where they made her feel as if she was gently weeping. She paused, as if she felt Eanswith with her. Then she kicked her mare on. The mare heaved a sigh; and they continued.

Hilda had heard stories of a special white flowering thorn, that might bear blossoms at any time of year; at Christmas, at Easter, or at Whitsuntide. Of how, the story ran, that it had sprung from the staff of Joseph of Arimethea when he had visited these lands long ago.

Was this a daughter from this sacred tree? Hilda wondered.

158

Tata and Eanfled were glad to welcome her back.

Bassus had pushed on with the building of the new church before the winter began to settle. The long footprint of the stone foundations lay in the trenches and the two masons were training the lay brothers to gather more flint from the hills to start building the walls when the weather would allow the binding of gravel, lime and sand to set. Tata and her sisters were spinning and weaving hangings and cloths for the new chancel but had stopped to make fabric for the few remaining children at Folkestone.

Eanfled had taken over the running of the palace while Hilda was away but welcomed her back warmly.

'I didn't realise quite how much you were doing for me until you had gone! I am more than pleased that you are back; and I think that mother will say the same.' She paused. 'Mother was very upset about uncle dying.'She paused again.

'Thank goodness the diptheria did not come here, and that we are all spared.' Hilda could but nod in agreement; and sighed.

The building, halted by the cold weather, left the men able to concentrate on thinning the woods, stocking up fuel for their winter fires and selecting sturdy poles for scaffolding, anticipating when the spring building might begin again. Then they were busy culling the stock for overwintering: busy smoking the meat from the livestock that were killed: busy curing the hides that were saved for foot wear and jackets: busy grinding the grain and storing it in large flagons, and making sure that they had plenty for brewing ale as well as baking bread through the winter months. Herbs and grasses were carefully dried. The one for cures, the other for bedding and fodder.

It was a winter that was kind to them all.

In Canterbury Erconbert and Sexburga celebrated their first born, a boy, and the Kingdom of Kent began a better chapter. But they heard rumours that Mercia was again building up its troops and that Northumbria was again threatened. They had scarcely had a decade under the benign rule of Oswald and the gift of Aidan at Lindisfarne. There had been but one attack of the plague in that time and all the royal family had been spared. But Penda of Mercia would be more devastating than the plague if he struck. The sisters at Lyminge prayed for peace and charity amongst the kingdoms: hoping against hope.

In the north the winter was not so kind. Heiu shivered in her hall of turf and hide, where the sisters lived while their more permanent housing was being built. The posts for the new building were sunk in the outcrop of rock that was Hart Isle. The infill wicker work, awaiting the mud plaster, was completed at one end of the building. But as yet there was no roof to keep out the winter weather. The winds blew unremittingly from Siberia, freezing their water supplies, so that they had a fulltime job with fires for thawing water for themselves and for their livestock. The hefted sheep huddled near to the huts. The summer had been wet in the northern lands and meant that they had heavier losses due to liver fluke so the sheep were not in a good state to carry their unborn lambs and face out the winter. But the wild deer did tough it out, and the occasional venison was a welcome addition to the convent's cuisine. However, as at Lindisfarne, the sea birds, resident and migrating, boosted their menu with both meat and eggs.

Heiu was putting a brave face on things. She had not fully realized how much work was involved in setting up and running a small independent house. Nor had she allowed for the fact that she was to develop a recurrent arthritis that seemed to appear particularly with the cold easterly winds. Aidan would make an effort to visit them every six weeks or so in these early days, very aware of the effort needed to hold a group together. The sisters were helped by a small group of lay brothers whom

Heiu was able to support from her own income. But the sisters were much involved in establishing the fabric of the convent. While the exposed position on the coast could be exhilarating it did mean that growing crops was a challenge. Much basic walling for shelter had to be constructed. The inner marsh land, separating the island, did make an ideal habitat for low growing willows, a ready source for wicker work, while the bark, beaten and soaked, yielded a soothing pain killer for Heiu's arthritis.

This was the grind of day to day survival. But, on a wider horizon, Heiu was equally aware of the unease in Oswald's kingdom. He was much loved and, while he more often visited his sister's convent at Coldingham, he did occasionally send them calf hides for their small scriptorium on Hart's Island. However, at the moment his greater preoccupation was, with the help of his brothers, training his thegns for battle. All his smiths and carpenters were diverted to making shields and swords, daggers, heads for spears and arrows. The yeomen archers would simply splice sharpened hardwoods into the tips of their arrows. Then some were expert at killing the right birds to hone their skills in making the flight of feathers for their arrows. Some archers carefully dipped the tips of their arrows into the berries of deadly nightshade so that wherever the arrow struck the outcome might be fatal. Horses were trained to charge in a line. Foot soldiers were disciplined to advance in a row with shields locked to defend against a hail of arrows falling from the sky.

But all this preparation was to be of no avail. Oswald fell at Oswestry: beheaded and the severed head hung on the gates at York. The northern countryside shuddered again. The Mercians retreated from their victory, having learnt the lesson of losing as much as they gained by ruthless plundering. Even so the two northern kingdoms, held together by Oswald, fell apart.

Bernicia separated from Deira.

Oswald's younger brother, Oswy, took up the northern kingdom of Bernicia, while his distant cousin Oswin claimed Deira as his rightful land. It was an uneasy juxtaposition. Ebba at Coldingham felt relatively at ease. She had her younger brother, Oswy, as her king. Heiu at Hart's Island remembered Oswy from Iona as being rather more scheming and impulsive than Oswald. For her it was Oswin of Deira who had the calm and stature of Oswald. But Heiu and her convent also just lay in the northern confines of Deira; she wondered if her supply from her hides of land would continue.

■■■

163

The ladies of Lyminge heard all this northern news via the travelling merchants. They worried, wondered, and prayed for peace.

Eanfled only had the happy memories of childhood of Northumbria, until her father's death and their rapid exit by sea: and of her separation from Hilda. Of course, the memories had been much tempered by the sadness of her mother losing her infant brothers and sisters. But she had been cared for by Hilda and Hereswid so that this kindness of childhood memory dimmed these sadnesses. The child Eanfled had known neither Oswald nor his brothers as they were in Dalriada, exiled from her father. So now, as a young and eligible princess, she absorbed the news and concentrated on organizing food in the palace for the next week.

Hilda held more complex memories of the two new kings. She mourned the loss of Oswald. She had admired him from the few times that she had spent time with him on Iona. She had always heard good reports of him from Acha. He had definitely been her aunt's favourite son. She wondered how Acha was faring? At least it was another of her sons who ruled her land. Hilda also remembered Oswin, as a distant cousin, and saw that there would be tension between the two northern kingdoms again. How she prayed for peace each day!

She also remembered Heiu and Ebba in her prayers, consoled that they had spent time with Aidan at Lindisfarne, and aware that they had finally broken away to try to establish their own houses. They were both dear to her. Hilda could not help but wonder if they had the clear, uncluttered, zeal that Hilda had seen in Eanswith. There was now no doubt in Hilda's mind as to the considerable undertaking that was involved in establishing a new house. She had such a direct experience with both Eanswith at Folkestone and now seeing Tata direct her energies to expanding the small house at Lyminge into something altogether more impressive. A double monastery for both men and women seemed something quite ambitious. There were the very obvious practical advantages for dividing the work needed to run a large house: but inevitably clear needs to avoid distractions between the sexes! Hilda would have loved to see how Ebba and Heiu were each faring. That unexpected year of retreat on Iona after Edwin's death had unwittingly bound all three of them together. Looking back it seemed like an exceptional year of privilege, when they were quite free of responsibilities, while at the same time they had learnt so much from the community there, both in reading and writing, in

165

attending the offices at all times: the mystery of the seasons on the wild island interweaving into the fabric of the liturgy: the one complementing the other: the freedom to wander safely in the wild beauty of the island: the light sparkling on the sea forever in their mind's eye: the quiet solemnity of services chanted by candlelight a repeated memory.

All of this coloured the present news for Hilda.

Tata was more engrossed in the running of her project at Lyminge. She had not known Oswald and his brothers either, although she had once met cousin Oswin, remembering him to be tall, handsome and of a courtly disposition. She thought that it would be unlikely that he would initiate offensive actions. He seemed to have an innate sense of fairness. Tata hope that Oswy, the younger brother was of a similar mind set, even as this was what precisely worried Hilda and Heiu. Tata did tend to half block her memories from the north. There was so much hidden sorrow there.

Tata and Hilda joined forces to inspect the progress with the building, inspecting the glass that was being smelted from sand and lime, with some being tinted with a touch of iron to tinge it green, while other batches had a smidge of sulphur to lend it a golden yellow. At least this making of the precious glass was not being held up by the winter months. Tata was also very aware of how Eanfled was maturing. Even as she was still but a teenager Tata could no longer deny that her daughter was emerging into an eligible princess. She had seen her brother thinking about his niece's prospects. Now Tata saw Erconbert, his son, chatting to her when he came down to continue his father's hunting! There was distinctly a new generation. Tata knew that she was beginning to feel her own age. She began to appreciate how Bertha must have felt, surviving through at least three generations. Tata remembered how she had been taken to Northumbria at not much more than her daughter's present age, admittedly with Paulinus and Romanus in tow. How long ago that seemed! It inevitably prompted the anxiety of the mother in her. This precious daughter was her only surviving child. Four lost children did live just below the surface of her thoughts on every day. What would this only daughter choose? What would the menfolk plan for her?

Transactions

The morning mist was thick enough to be a fog; clinging and damp, shrouding the land so that man and beast seemed to appear from nowhere, yet within a few steps disappeared again. The sun was hidden in form with the filtered light half-hearted. The inclement weather did not stop the building at Lyminge, but each of the men felt as if they were working in isolation, making solitary progress, occasionally calling out to each other when they needed something, or just to ask how things were going to ensure that their fellow workers were still there. They clung to the scaffolding more assiduously, with no real sense of how far they were from the ground. It was an eerie, muffled existence.

One effect of the pervasive damp and restricted vision was that people reached out to listen, as if that was the only sense that was not compromised by the weather. They could recognize the sound of their own horses and mules plodding, dragging timbers and masonry; but could they hear the steady sound of the rhythm of the canter of a

168

small group of approaching steeds? If so who would be travelling in this weather?

It turned out to be a group from Canterbury, headed by King Earconbert, but with some well-dressed strangers that neither Eanfled nor Hilda recognized; but Hilda recognized a motif on the cloak of one of the strangers that made her guess that they were from the Northern lands. She also noticed that, amongst all the relative finery, there was a smaller figure in the plain garb of a monk.

Grimelda, who was in charge of running the fabric of the longhall, came forward to take their cloaks, while Dermot took care of their horses. Grimelda told him, once the animals were tethered, to cross to the abbey to let Tata know of the new arrivals.

The visitors drank from the large copper caldron that hung by the door that was topped up from the spring several times a day. Formal greetings were made and Earconbert, still relatively young in his Kingship, pondered as to how he should open his propositions. Hilda felt her pulse quicken. It had taken a while for the faces to run though her mind, and through the years of memory. But she thought that she recognized the monk to be from Iona, from what seemed so many years ago in her life. Surely, he had been there with Aidan? But, of course, so much younger then. Was it Aidan who had sent him?

Her musing was broken by the entrance of Tata, somewhat thinner and stiffer than the King remembered her, but she was his aunt, even as Eanfled was his young cousin. He greeted the queen courteously. She moved instinctively to stand with Hilda and her daughter and assumed the authority of age.

'My lord you are as welcome as always,' she paused and looked round at his company, 'but I think that this is not your usual hunting party?' She turned to Eanfled, raising inquiring eyebrows.

'Are our guests staying?'

'Grimelda is arranging matters, mother. I think all is in hand, and Dermot will let Bassus know.'

Tata turned to the guests.

'I see that we have a brother amongst us. Perhaps a hunter of souls, for a change? I hope you will visit us in the abbey while you are here.'

The company smiled at the queen's dry humour.

'I would deem it a privilege to share the hours and the eucharist after so much travel.' The monk nodded; paused and began again. 'I bring greetings from Aidan, and from the king, my Lord Oswy.'

170

Earconbert saw that the opening moves had been made with no input from him, other than being present: so he softened the approach.

'Good aunt, we hear fine reports of the building of the abbey, adding to the magnificence of your present longhall, which has made us welcome on many an occasion. I hope that I might be permitted to inspect the progress and even attend a eucharist if our good brother Utta is allowed to celebrate, as he has already has in Canterbury.'

He continued,

'Sexburg sends her love to you all and she would be with us for this occasion, but she is, God willing, carrying our second child, and in that phase where she is much indisposed and advised to rest.'

'May she be well, may she be well; and our love and congratulations to you both on such joyful news.' Tata replied but then hesitated. 'But let us adjourn for a while and allow ourselves time to prepare for a suitable dining and meeting this evening. You are all most welcome, but you must know that there is much to do in the household for visitors unannounced.'

Tata so dispersed the group; but offered to escort her nephew to inspect the buildings via her new house in its grounds where she might discuss the things that she guessed that he had come to propose. Brother Utta was also invited to be privy to these discussions, since he had so simply hinted at them.

The sun was beginning to win out and the fog to give way as they traced their footsteps. The young King again noticed the relative frailty in his aunt's walking. She picked her way very carefully. There was no doubting that her mind was as sharp as ever, but also a definite physical frailty was emerging. The grass was wet and silvery, the path somewhat slippery from the inclement weather. Earconbert offered an arm to his aunt and it was taken with an appreciative nod.

'My feet are not as nimble as they were, Earconbert, nor my knees as flexible: but there is still much to do here. Your grandmother and father were kind to let me have this place. It is a great consolation to me.'

'They would both be delighted and impressed with what you have achieved here. It is a transformation; and we all love to come here from Canterbury. I know my father loved the hunting here.'

'I owe so much to Bassus in so many ways. He seems to thrive on organizing both the building and the hunting. Although I think I know which gets the priority when the company is right.' Aunt and nephew smiled.

'I do apologise for distracting him from the building when I come down. But I am sure that he returns to it well refreshed?'

'Well refreshed indeed,' was the reply he received. The retired queen had many memories of the duties of suppling mead to the thirsty hunters, dealing well with the banter, but retiring early when the hunting party became too bawdy.

The king entered his aunt's new house. He noted that she certainly had a good eye for charming comfort and was so up to date with glass in two small windows, allowing the faltering sun to throw beams of light across the table and benches, catching the woven colours of tapestries in the making, while the warm fire flickered in the hearth. The meanness of the day outside was left behind.

They settled as Gwyneth brought them each a glass beaker of mulled wine with which they warmed their hands as well as quenching their thirst. Tata nodded her thanks, which equally dismissed the servant from their conversations. The cook retired to tend to preparing lunch.

'And how is Aidan, Utta? I hear great things about him and it is my sadness that I have never met him. He served Oswald well as bishop, and looked after Heiu and Aebbe, who I do remember well.

You have much to tell me; even as I fear why you are here?'

Their conversation was broken by a commotion outside. Part of the scaffolding had collapsed and one of the builders was injured. Tata excused herself and went to find out who had been hurt. It was the older Sigbert who looked as if he had broken a leg.

'I think that he was too old for the scaffolding in this weather,' Tata chided Bassus.

'I agree ma'am, but he would insist on hodding as he has always done.'

'See if you can get a splint on it and take him to Mildred to look after him. Make sure that she provides for the family while he mends please,' she continued, 'I have the King with me. I think with news that I do not want to hear. So I shall have to leave you to organize things Bassus.'

He nodded and did not comment on the visitors. He had enough to worry about on the state of the buildings.

The King and Utta used Tata's temporary diversion to assess their strategy.

'I think that she has read us well. We should tread carefully. I think that she will reluctantly acquiesce,' Earconbert offered.

174

He was right. The queen had read that they came to seek the hand of her daughter for the Northern Province. She had raised an eyebrow when she heard that it was King Oswy of Bernicia who sought her daughter's hand.

'Is he not twice married and, anyway, a distant cousin to my daughter?' was the expected counterpoint that Earconbert and Utta had anticipated. Of course, they had discussed this with the archbishop in Canterbury and he had confirmed that there would be necessary adjustments to be made for the closeness of kinship in terms of reparation to the church. But the archbishop had been sympathetic to the wider political situation of the continuing threat to both kingdoms from the pagan Mercians. Honorius had also recognized the historical associations between Kent and Northumbria and that Eanfled would be but reinforcing those links that Tata herself had so significantly forged a generation ago.

'You scarcely need to remind me of my northern days with dear Edwin,' Tata continued in gentler tones.

'I pray for him here every day; and my lost infants. It has been a great consolation that Paulinus and Romanus were able to escape when disaster struck; and we fled.' She unknowingly ran her hand over her wedding ring as if to massage back the

175

happiness of her days in Northumbria. She diverted her gaze to the colours and light of the glass window.

'You must understand my apprehension for my only daughter repeating the journeys that I made those many years ago. It is not a mother's wish.' She hesitated.

'But she has come of age, and is as much guided by Hilda as by myself. I do not see her marrying into the Kentish kingdom, even though I know that she would like a family of her own. We must put it to her gently and give her time to make up her own mind. I will not stand in her way; but equally, I will be dismayed if I lose her.'

She looked at the couple before her with a sad look of resignation on her face. Earconbert suddenly saw that the frailty of his aunt was not just physical. He had always looked up to her with her heroic background of surviving, even celebrating, a northern journey and dramatically escaping with her boys, and going on to build this impressive estate in Lyminge. But he had previously only been an escort to his father on hunting trips, even as he still continued the forays in memory of the convivial hospitality and hunting. However, as he now was King the stage had changed and he was charged with different insights. Sexburg, his wife from the Anglian Kingdom, had advised him on the delicacy of this present mission. She and Earconbert had the privilege of a happy marriage, of a similar age, of a similar disposition. But, as Tata had pointed out, Oswy was considerably older and twice married, albeit twice widowed.

'How should we proceed aunt? Will you prepare the ground or do you wish Utta and I to formally discuss the matter with her?'

'I think it best if Hilda and I raise it with Eanfled first. Perhaps after None you could persuade Bassus to take the falcons out while I spend time with Eanfled and Hilda; and I might then even have time to catch up with Utta?' Tata smiled towards Utta who respectfully had remained silent through the discourse between King and the retired Queen, between nephew and aunt.

Earconbert took his aunt's words as much as an instruction as a question.

'So be it. Let us hope the falcons fly well in this foggy weather.'

Tata smiled gently.

'I think that the sun is breaking through. Enough for the sharp eyes of Bassus' falcons. Take care to wear the thick gloves and hold the birds high.'

'I will indeed,' Earconbert nodded his head. He knew that in her younger days Tata had flown her own falcons, taught by Bassus in Northumbria.

So it was that the office of None was said; the king and Bassus departed with the falcons, carrying their own refreshment on the back of their saddles.

Tata went down the slope to the long hall where she found Hilda and Eanfled, the one working on a manuscript, the other on the bodice of a new garment. They both looked up, ended their conversation, and put down their work, looking expectantly at Tata.

'So, what news mother? What have you been hatching now?' Eanfled began, somewhat impishly and lightly. Hilda held her peace, re - examining her manuscript. She had an intuition, confirmed by the serious expression of the queen, that she knew the subject matter of the discussions.

'Oswy and Aidan are concerned for the safety of their northern kingdoms. They seem to think that a marriage with Kent might strengthen their position; and the reputation of the attraction of a young kentish princess has travelled well,' began Tata, moving to sit down with them, shifting some of the fabrics that Eanfled had draped over the bench. There was a silence.

Eanfled looked at her needlework, considering the implications.

'Is this a proposal by proxy?' was almost murmured to herself, but audible to her mother and cousin. Another silence ensued.

'Is he not rather old; and twice married, with children by each wife. I would have more stepchildren than I would wish to bear. And is he not a blood relation of sorts? Why should I leave this place for him?' Eanfled continued, not looking up.

Tata looked at Hilda, who had but raised her eyebrows. Then Tata looked at Eanfled, while Hilda kept her silence.

'King Oswy does seek your hand in marriage, Eanfled. Aidan, via Utta, has cleared with the archbishop that if more foundations are given to the church then the distant family links will be overlooked,' Tata continued: Hilda pursed her mouth a little.

'We all know that the northern hospitality is second to none.' Tata continued.
'I think you must have memories of your childhood there with Hilda and Hereswid?' Here Tata paused.

'I, for my part, would miss you. I would miss you very much,' she echoed more softly. 'But you are of age and must make your own decision.' She turned to Hilda. 'What do you think Hilda?'

It was Hilda's turn to pause. She began,

179

'Marriage is one of the sacraments. It is not to be entered lightly; nor hastily. I think that you must consider it carefully Eanfled, rather than immediately.'

Another pause followed before Hillda continued.

'Oswy might not be the romantic prince that you had in mind, Eanfled. But he honours the church and his vows. And he is only a little over thirty, so scarcely older than I am,'she half laughed at herself. 'He has great wealth.' She mused as she looked at her half- finished manuscript.

'He is more mercurial than either his brother Oswald, or his cousin Oswin, who seems to rule Deira these days. It seems to be that the two present kings are not as at ease with each other as they might be.' She moved to put away her manuscript for the day as she continued,

'We all have some treasured memories of our time in the North. But none of us will forget the dire circumstances of your flight by boat from there to here. Here we have been blessed with sanctuary. While you have grown up and shown yourself capable and happy to be running this place while your mother builds across the brook.' Hilda returned to her seat, this time looking directly at Eanfled.

■■■■■■■■■■■■■■■■■■■■■■■■■■■■■■■■■■■■■

'Dear Eanswith, so young, had her clear calling to a religious vocation and to caring for orphans. She was an inspiration to us all. But there is a great need to try and keep peace between the kingdoms of this island. It is forever a challenge; and seeking that peace between nations can be just as great a calling; as well as bringing the comfort of a family that is well provided for. If that is where you feel drawn at this time. The threat of Penda hangs over all our kingdoms, seemingly forever.'

Hilda stoppered the last pot of ink on her small table.

'But no haste I think, Tata?' She turned to the Queen. 'I am sure that you will lead in the diplomacy with the king and Utta, who seems to carry the joyful transparency of Aidan with him,' Hilda concluded, deferring to the Queen.

Eanfled nodded her head, albeit more in assimilation than necessarily of acceptance. The three of them were so used to each other's company that no more needed to be said.

They retired to prepare for the evening's feast.

The same foggy weather prevailed on Lindisfarne, similarly limiting the building work that Aidan was trying to complete; or his young brothers were! They were at least more fortunate in

181

that the main buildings had been completed while Oswald had still been king; he lending them both help and funds to initially complete the chapel, the dormitory, with the kitchen and dining hall attached. They were now trying to make more permanent structures for visitors than the tented houses that Heiu, Aebbe and Hilda had lived in for their time on the island. These latter improvements for guests becoming more important as the monastery occasionally was visited both by Oswy or his cousin Oswin, the kings of the two kingdoms. It was the tall Oswin who seemed to absorb most from Aidan and the spirit of the community. Oswy came infrequently, and even then always seemed to be restless and anxious to get away again, never quite leaving behind the affairs of state. He also had the very present pressures that his sons were turning out to be a somewhat contentious handful. They were not yet of an age to challenge him, but like fledglings trying to fly, or fox cubs in mock play, there was instinctive competition in their activities. The gentler Oswin had but two daughters, so had but the prospect of advantageous marriages in due time, with every advantage that might bring, but without any threat to his own Kingship.

Aidan had already formed a well- loved community, even as he would spend a third of his time visiting parts of both the kingdoms, as he had when it was one kingdom under Oswald.

It was Oswy, on one of his visits, who had petitioned Aidan to ask for Eanfled's hand in marriage. Aidan had nodded without commitment but had agree to consider the possibility. The community would pray for guidance and a blessing on the outcome.

Aidan was grateful that the abbot of Iona had spared two brothers to help him in the early days. Dairid had been the more practical of the two, and pivotal for organizing the building and the farming. But Utta, mainly organizing the running of the household, between the religious offices of the day, had, seemingly, an extra transparent uncluttered spirituality that Aidan had felt privileged to nurture. So it had been Utta that he chose to send with Cedric on behalf of the king, accompanied by Aidan's notes to Tata, to Eanfled, and to Hilda: also with a vial of oil; for Aidan foresaw that one of their journeys might be beset with storms.

To Tata he wrote an appreciation of what she and Paulinus had achieved in bringing the faith to Northumbria; how tragic the circumstances of her exit; but how well remembered she and Edwin were by many still living in the kingdoms, both Deira and

Bernicia. How many had regarded that as a golden age. How delighted he was to hear of the news of the growth of her community at Lyminge through all this sadness. How he recognized the cost to her of her daughter following in her footsteps; but that she, above all others, might recognize the good that might come out of the agreement.

To Eanfled he echoed the value of the gifts that her mother had brought to Northumbria; commenting that Edwin had also been of mature years, and wiser for it, while Tata had been virtually the same age as Eanfled was now. He counselled that while Oswy was firm in his faith she might, as her mother had, bring her own spiritual mentors to help her in her adjustment to the northern way: just as the older Aethelbert had insisted that Paulinus should accompany her mother.

To Hilda he wrote bidding her well and of the good reports that he heard of her work in Kent. He also briefly wrote of the progress of Heiu and Ebba, each with their northern monasteries on the coast: how they both had succeeded in founding communities, but how Heiu was struggling with her own health. Even so they sent their love and their prayers to her; as did he and the community at Lindisfarne.

■■■

The three royal ladies read their missives; exchanged them; and smiled amongst themselves. It was only Hilda who had actually met Aidan, but all three agreed that he had astutely weighed them; their predicaments and their dispositions.

It was agreed, after some deliberation, that Eanfled, in due course, would travel north with Utta and Romanus as part of her household. She had turned to Hilda,

'You know that I would value your company in my household above all others,' leaving the invitation as half a question; and half knowing Hilda's reply.

'You know that I would gladly come. But I think that I cannot leave Tata alone at this time. It is enough that she loses you, even as she sees you retrace her footsteps. I shall stay with her. It is your time to fly!' She paused.

'But you know that we shall have you in our prayers every day: and here will always be a sanctuary.'

The winter months were a good time to spend preparing the trousseau and the gifts to be taken northwards. Also to send letters to Hereswid

that she might prepare to receive the party on its journey north, and might she prevail on Ana to prepare two boats to take the travellers to Withernsea, retracing what was becoming a well worn journey; but which neatly circumvented the dangers of Mercian territory.

The sisters in Folkestone wove plain, pale blue linen for Eanfled's wedding gown, embroidering the cuffs and the high neck with intertwining motifs of flowers and foliage in threads of white. The sisters and women folk in Lyminge made a matching stole, but also stitched together a cloak of fine leather that would keep out the rain, while the smith wrought a bold silver and gold torc for the king, with a more delicate one to match for the would be queen. Even the glassmaker saved some of his coloured beads for the new bride to be, and strung a fine necklace that would sparkle in any light, day or night. The cobbler stitched some bleached leather shoes from doe skin with a slight heel of walnut, [for Eanfled was as tall as she was slender, while the news was that Oswy was what is called 'sturdy' of build, and for his queen to tower over him might seem unseemly?]

Aldhelm had married and integrated himself into life at Lyminge. But, as yet, Astrid, his wife, had not borne him children, but she was a close friend of Eanfled. So they were persuaded to venture north to be part of Eanfled's new household, with the advantage that it was he who had escorted Hilda from Lindisfarne to Lyminge what seemed so many years ago. So he was familiar with the journey that they would make.

The spring months saw the days beginning to lengthen, while the woodlands were coated with small white anemones; bluebells nascent as emerging green clustered leaves, waiting for their turn to carpet the woodlands.

It was the bluebells and the white wild garlic who painted the trail that the royal party eventually made as they descended towards Canterbury to receive the blessing of the archbishop and acquire more gifts from Earconbert and Sexburg, along with the monks giving Romanus and Utta precious manuscripts for the new household.

Having crossed the Thames estuary it seemed no time until they arrived at Hereswid's estate to find that she had prepared to feast them from the successes of her estate, with suckling pig, jellied eels, and smoked herring, garnished with the fresh herbs of the spring meadows. Moreover, she had persuaded Ana to lend two of his longest boats to take the company northwards with all expediency. But Hereswid had not seen Eanfled since she was a child in Northumbria, nor had

Eanfled seen her nephew Adwulf, now shooting into the leginess of adolescence. So there was so much to admire and to exchange. To Hereswid it had the uncanny echo that Hilda had felt, of them as young children being taken on by Tata so many years ago when she had been as Eanfled was now, a young Kentish princess travelling, in some style, to the northern kingdoms.

The proposed short stay extended into a week of celebration.

The kingcups and irises were out and the leaves of the canopy of the trees had broken from their buds before the boats set sail at Dunwich. The party had thought that the high tides of the spring equinox were over by the time that the sails unfurled, but an unexpected south-easterly caught them out. The size of their boats was little defence against the size of the waves and the gusting of the wind tearing at their sails. The party feared for their lives, huddling in the ballast of the rocking ship with its shallow keel doing little to steady the rising and diving hull of the longboat. Eanfled clutched at the cross hanging round her neck, even as Utta and Romanus had their hands clasped in prayer. But all too soon they simply used their hands to cling on to the sides of the boat. It was then that Utta, whose pallor signalled an impending sea sickness, remembered the vial of oil that Aidan had given him. Bravely releasing his grip on the boat, with trembling hands he uncorked the vial and, with the cry of the hope of a blessing, he tipped the precious oil over the side of the boat: grateful that now he could cling again onto the side of the boat with both hands, the empty vial falling back into the bottom of the boat.

The waves subsided, the sun broke through the clouds. The empty vial, rocking at the bottom of the boat, was rescued by Eanfled, declaring it to be the most precious component of her trousseau. She would treasure it for many years to come!

Their arrival at Withernsea saw them emerge as a staggering, pale, but triumphant and thankful group. The rest of their journey northwards was but a succession of feasting with their spirits rising each day.

The longhall at Lyminge seemed strangely empty once the wedding party had departed. It was true that the spring brought its own sense of hope and the business of getting the crops sown. But there was no bustle of activity in the longhall, with both Tata and Hilda spending more time in the monastery. Hilda did divide her time between the longhall and the scriptorium, allowing Tata her

189

privacy in her abbey house. But, more often than not, Tata would invite her to join her with her tapestry. It did not escape Hilda's notice that the suppressed cough of the queen was becoming more frequent, nor that she had seen flecks of blood in Tata's handkerchief. She sighed to herself. It was indeed one of the reasons that she had stayed behind. How the pendulum had swung. Tata had always been the mainstay of the community; and was still: but physically she was distinctly fading. Hilda had words with Gwyneth, who confirmed that her mistress was indeed eating very little, even as she tried to hide it.

'Tis the dogs as do get the most of it; and she thinks I don't know,' Gwyneth confided in Hilda. So Hilda had words with Grimelda in the palace kitchen, ensuring that her talent for irresistible broths was focused on the delicacies that might tempt the queen. Hilda would carry them across to Gwyneth and quietly arrange that they were served to them both while they were working on the tapestry frames. With a smile, Tata would see them arrive.

'I could smell them before they arrived. I will persist with the tapestry while you tuck in, Hilda,' she tried.

■■■

'I would rather that you joined me. I cannot eat while the queen works.' Hilda paused but continued,

'Besides I think that your condition prescribes that you take better care of yourself,' she paused again. 'If you wish to hear of your first grandchild that is.'

Tata wove her needle into the tapestry and looked up across the room at Hilda.

'Did I not know you so well, I would say that you are trying to bully me; or to nurse me, or even treating me as a child,' this said with a gentle acquiescence.

'All of those, if I would dare: and if any of them might restore your health, Tata.'

The queen pursed her mouth and raised her eyebrows in resignation. She looked at the tapestry.

'The spring is with us. It does revive my spirits.' She took some of the broth and dipped in a little of the freshly baked bread that Gwyneth had provided.

'You are right. News of a grandchild would revive them even more. But I fear that I shall not see it, for I could never travel north again.'

She dipped in some more of the bread, somewhat wistfully.

'This soup is good. I think that it must be Grimelda's work?' Hilda nodded and they finished the food in silence, until they heard the bell ring for the hour of Sext.

The queen was right in her predictions. She faded gracefully and quickly with consumption: and without the news of a grandchild. But with the news that the marriage of her daughter had been a memorable celebration and that the new queen and her spouse seemed to be a lively combination.

Hilda was with Tata to her last. Saethred came from her Folkestone Abbey, Ymme came from the monastery at Canterbury, each to pay their respects as the Queen faded. All the communities were in prayer for the passing of their Queen. Earconbert and Sexburg had visited from Canterbury when she first took to her bed. But it was Hilda who monitored the visitors, feeling thankful that she could return some of the care that she had received from Tata throughout her life; even as her second mother.

Tata, knowing that she was dying, and having thanked a subdued Bassus, had sought to designate a successor to her convent and the estate at Lyminge. Naturally she discussed it with Hilda. Hilda had nodded.

'Tata, I read your inclination towards me. But I think that by tradition this must be Ymme's choice. She is now the widowed queen and is both of the right disposition and inclination. She has a husband and a daughter to remember here, even as the young family of Earconbert and Sexburg are thriving in Canterbury. It is a new generation. They will visit her here, even as they have visited you; and as you once visited Bertha. You know that Ymme has the experience to manage both the palace longhall and the convent, appreciating everything that you have achieved here. I have little doubt that the archbishop will approve.'

Tata had taken her hand, ignoring the last remarks.

'You mean everything that you, I, Bassus and my dear daughter have achieved here. It has been a good team and a blessing. Nor must we ever forget how much Bertha did before us. You are right, her spirit lives on here too.' She fingered her pendant cross.

'I shall be glad to be reunited with Edwin and my children. You will pray for us all Hilda?'

'Indeed, we all do and will.'

'And what will you do? Will you stay, or will you leave?'

'I know not at the moment, Tata,' Hilda shook her head. 'But with both you and Eanfled gone, and dear Eanswith departed, there is less to hold me here. I trust that you also will remember me in your prayers?'

Tata smiled acquiescence, even as she faded.

A return

A year passed.

Hilda, who was not generally given to depression, remembered it as one of her greyest years. She sat inside herself, observing the changes that Ymme inevitably brought to Lyminge. Hilda attended the hours of the monastery, consoling Gwyneth, Grimelda, and Bassus over the loss of their queen, putting in some hours to finish the tapestries that she and Tata had started, but spending most of her time in the scriptorium and borrowing more wax blocks of texts to transcribe from Canterbury.

But she felt a hollowness. It was as if she no longer belonged here, in a place that she had begun to accept as home. She began to acknowledge, as she perhaps had always known, that it was the people that made the place: that the place was secondary to the people. She also was more certain that she had the increasing realisation of the call to a vocation and to celibacy, so clearly seen in her cousin Eanswith. Hilda now recognized that Eanswith's short life had been more of an inspiration to her than she had acknowledged at the time. The inspiration had given Hilda the courage to seek more clearly her own calling, which, while she felt it would lie in taking vows, it would not be here, in Kent, that her future lay.

In her daily life, busy as it was, there was space in the times of silence when she would consider her way forward. Uncertain as to her direction, it was to her sister, Hereswid, in Anglia that she eventually thought that she might turn, perhaps remembering the stories that Bertha had told her, that Ymme continued to tell her, of the stability of the convents in France.

She decided that she would visit Hereswid. A visit to her elder sister felt long overdue; and it might help to clear her mind.

'May it be thy will, O Lord?' was her murmured prayer.

Ymme was sorry to hear of her decision to leave, even more so when Bassus decided that he would accompany her to East Anglia and then he would return to his family in Northumbria. The building of the fine new church in Lyminge with its long nave and glass windows was completed; and his Queen had died. He was finally released from the promise that he had made to Edwin to look after Tata. Also his own wife had died in childbirth with their second child some years earlier, and the infant had tragically followed its mother within a month. However, his first boy, Aldwin, was now of an age where he could travel and hunt as niftily as his father, albeit on a somewhat smaller steed. Hilda agreed that Aldwin would be good company for them both. They all needed a change of scenery.

The reunion with Hereswid was indeed a joyous one, with the unexpected event that Adwulf and Aldwin became inseparable from the time that they were introduced. Adwulf, a year older and the potential lord of the estates in Anglia, had the natural social advantage, but the good- natured Aldwin had the generous disposition from his father to enjoy the competition in whatever they were doing; hunting, training with shields, bows and arrows: even with their studies. Bassus began to wonder whether he would ever persuade his son to leave. There was no doubt that the change had lifted all their spirits.

Hilda and Hereswid had much on which to catch up. It was more than ten years since they had met. It was most noticeable to Hilda that Adwulf was now a young prince in the making and very much the apple of his mother's eye, even as she continued to run the estate with a firm, if sometimes stressed, hand.

The two sisters recalled their childhood: the murder of their father, the escape with their mother and the faithful Lilla. The two sisters recalled their first meeting with Tata. What a transformation that had been in their two lives. How, at that stage in their early lives, Hereswid had so protected Hilda, becoming mother to her younger sister; and how much they had both owed to the kindness of Tata, and of Edwin: and been in awe of the tall, gaunt Paulinus!

Hereswid, now in her own full motherhood, was so pleased and grateful that Hilda, by nursing the dying queen, had been able to repay in some way the considerable kindness that Tata had given them both throughout their childhood and adolescence. The two sisters were now of sufficient age and stature to recognize the fullness of the gift that parents can give to their children; even as they had been adopted as the King and Queen's children, and made part of their family.

As perhaps only sisters so close can, they discussed where they were going now in their lives. Was this another watershed for each of them? Hilda had already suggested to Ymme in Lyminge that she might seek a vocation, prompting the response,

'Hilda, you are more learned and, I think, a wiser head than I. This place would not have been what it is without you. I think that I could make you head of the novices and that you would be an exemplary model for each of them,' had been Ymme's reply, while archbishop Honorius had been very ready to bless her noviciate. But it had been a suitable role for her to devote all her time to caring for Tata.

Yet it had been Ymme, as the new abbess, sensing the restlessness after Tata's death and Eanfled's departure to Bernicia, who eventually had suggested that Hilda might think of travelling to France, to Chelles to take up her noviciate. Both Hereswid and Hilda had been brought up by Tata, tutored by Romanus and Paulinus, to be fluent in French and Latin, so there would be no problem of language. It was as if her visit to Anglia was a step towards France for Hilda. Hereswid also confessed that she would be tempted to join her once Adwulf was old enough to take over the reins; and, hopefully married. Hereswid had long relied on the friendship with King Ana and Eredith his queen. With Eredith also being French, her eldest daughter already at Chelles and her third daughter, Ethelburga, planning to go, the Frankish influence in Anglia had become almost as strong as it was in Kent. Indeed, it was probably only Eredith's tragic death in childbirth that had stopped her visiting her homeland. Even when Ana married again, Mathilda, his new wife, also came from Neustria, and the closeness of their friendship was blessed by naming their new daughter Hereswid. This young girl was also brought up singing all the French chansons;

199

and a sweet voice she had. All these things were recounted, recalled, discussed, mused upon over the weeks that Hilda stayed with her sister.

The tapestry of their lives was rethreading, a new pattern emerging.

It was while they were sitting spinning in the cool of a June evening, waiting for the sun to set and for the bell to ring for compline, meanwhile gently flicking off the biting midges, when they heard the dogs barking. Hereswid lay the threads of wool aside and sat pondering who might be approaching at this late hour. The barking stopped, so it must be somebody the dogs knew, or somebody who had a way with animals. Hereswid could see no horses or retinue, so she presumed that it was a traveller seeking rest, or a neighbor visiting? She knew that Adwulf would have gone out to the dogs and that he would deal with it. She resumed her spinning with Hilda.

It was not much later that Adwulf appeared in the doorway with a diminutive figure in a monk's habit, his hair tonsured in the celtic fashion.

'Aunt, you have a visitor,' was his announcement.

It was Hilda's turn to stop her spinning. She gazed at the small figure.

'Utta? Is it really you? You are most welcome. What news do you bring?' was Hilda's

200

immediate response. Hereswid, who had not met him before, asked,

'Has Adwulf offered you food?' Then, almost to herself,

'and indeed, what brings you here?'

Utta had grinned somewhat sheepishly, delighted to see Hilda again.

'I am becoming an itinerant monk; always travelling. But it is always at Aidan's bidding.' He paused and shifted his weight on to one foot.

'Oswin has given Aidan land on the banks of the River Wear and would begin a convent there. Our bishop and abbot asks for your help, Hilda. It is why I am here.'

The two sisters looked at each other and smiled.

'Were you eavesdropping on our conversations these last two weeks, Utta?'

Hilda chided him, laughing, 'Where I might go has been central to our prayers and to our chatter for these last weekss: and seemingly I also was inclined to be an itinerant, for we were inclining to Chelles.'

'Your people in Deira need you. It is Aidan's message. He does not want to see you to go abroad. You are needed in your homeland.'

There was no beating about the bush with Utta. His transparent conviction was difficult to resist. Aidan had chosen his messenger well again. Was Utta to take two princesses from Kent to the North, Hereswid had asked? Had he not already taken Eanfled from them? He did simply state, when so accused, that he was simply returning them to their rightful home. Hilda did not like to give in too quickly, but she did feel a definite sense of relief. Was this what a calling was really like? Had she really been waiting for this to happen? In her wondering and wandering was this finally the right path? Of course, it did occur to her that her young cousin Eanfled had gone northwards before her, which Hereswid was quick to observe.

So it came about that plans were made to return northwards. Bassus and Aldwin had remained with Aldwulf during Hilda's visit, generally making themselves useful, delaying their own original planned journey to go north. But now they needed no persuasion to join Hilda in her journey. Aldwulf had offered Aldwin land to become a thegn on his estate. Bassus, pursed his lips, saying that it was Aldwin's choice. But Aldwin felt that his greater allegiance was to his father in his homeward journey and he was also intrigued to meet his original family in Northumbria. Bassus was mightily relieved, clasping him on his shoulders with,

■■■■■■■■■■■■■■■■■■■■■■■■■■■■■■■■■■■■■■■

'Then I shall have to put up with you a little longer,' and Hilda smiled with quiet pleasure at them both.

With Utta to accompany them it augered well for the journey. Hereswid and Hilda hugged; and did not voice the thought that this might be their last meeting.

'God speed.'

'God be with you: and write!' were their respective farewells.

It would be the last time that the sisters were together.

For this final northward journey a small ship would suffice; although Utta had vivid memories of his near catastrophic sailing on these seas but two years ago with Eanfled; and this time he had no precious oil from Aidan to calm the waters. However, the balm of midsummer was upon them, and they were escorted by the crying of the gulls as the sailors trawled for fish on their journey. Since the weather held they decided that they would be very bold and sail even up to the mouth of the Wear. They had a steady force four from the south west that carried them overnight up to the beginning of the Deira coast, but then the wind dropped so that Bassus and Aldwin had to help with the oars to get them to the nearest cove. The cliffs rose high on the

203

east coast as they moved further northwards. But they saw the roman ruins of a lighthouse at an entrance where the cliffs ended to give way to a sandy bay. As the tide was running in they decided that they would overnight there. It was home territory and for sure there would be habitation with welcoming countrymen which Hilda dimly remembered from a previous visit long ago.

A cluster of men had gathered on the shore at the sight of an unknown boat, for piracy was not unknown on these seas. But Bassus had his old shield from his days in the north, and was recognized. Nevertheless a few of the locals had taken to their coracles with bows, arrows, and spears, in case they were being deceived. But when Hilda stood up in the boat all arms were rested. No pirates carried such a distinctive lady. The locals guided their coracles, signalling where the sandbanks were to be avoided, making a small escorting flotilla for a royal visitor as they approached the wooden pier round which the water swirled in the rising tide.

'What is the name of this pleasing harbour. I do remember it ' Hilda asked Bassus.

'My father's land lies not ten miles north. It goes by the name of Streanthlecsh. The fishing is good and there is silver in the hills, with a black stone that is favoured by the makers of swords and shields,' was Bassus' reply.

'And favoured for ladies' brooches and rings,' was Aldwin's addition, with an impish grin. He had heard his father talk of his homelands many a time.

'It would seem to be a good spot for a foundation,' mused Hilda as she was escorted off the gently rocking boat. 'Is there a good supply of fresh water?'

'I think I remember a spring up on the cliff on the south side. Mind this wood; it is slippy,' he offered a hand as Hilda clambered off the rocking boat.

'Thank you. I am stiff from all that cramped sitting in the boat. It would have done me good to take a turn at the oars,' she murmured. Bassus raised an eyebrow but said nothing.

'You would have been welcome to take mine for a while,' offered Aldwin, feeling distinctly chirpy at being back on land. Hilda smiled affectionately.

Hilda looked up at the cliffs and saw the framework of roman buildings

'Trust the Romans to find a good site. We have much to learn from them. I hope that the mouth of the Wear is as well set.'

'You will find that it has more sand banks than this. You'd best get a local to get you in there. There's plenty got marooned there, thinking they could just go with the current.' This was Aelred who seemed to be in charge of the welcoming party.

'Then perhaps we had better stay here for a while to sort things out,' Hilda had suggested with a smile.

Stay they did for a few days. This gave Bassus time to ride north with his son and introduce him to his homestead. Bassus arrived to find that his mother was widowed, while his younger brother, Hewen, married with two daughters and a son, was running the estate. They all rejoiced. So much catching up to do. So much the same; yet so much changed: so many stories to tell. And Aldric was especially feasted; he over the moon at finding that he had three young cousins, suddenly feeling the fact that he had no brothers and sisters; but now it was as if he had three ready made. He was reluctant to think of returning to Streantlesch, but Bassus, loyal to the last, declared that he had promised to see Hilda to Wearmouth, so he would do that and then return to his homelands. So he thought.

He saw that his estates were in good hands. If he went away for a while it also gave the brothers time to see what the new order might be between them on his return. Their mother pondered, overjoyed to have her eldest son returned, and with a lively new grandson. She prayed for peace. Too often had she seen strife between brothers and cousins. Her thanks were for the return of her son in her old age, and the addition of a lovely young grandson. But she did so hope that there would be no conflict between her sons. For Bassus was the rightful heir.

Hilda was pleased to welcome him back to Streantlesch, and nodded when he reported that Aldric had decided to stay with his new found family for at least another week.

'You have been a mainstay, Bassus. I know not how Tata and I would have survived without you all these years. It is a blessing that you have returned to find your family well and thriving.'

'It was something not to have seen my father again. But Hewen looks after mother and the estate well. I have not gone short of anything while I was with the Queen: and it was my promise to the King, to look after her.'

'He had no more loyal subject; nor did she, Bassus. You have more than paid your dues.'

Bassus smiled and shuffled his big feet.

'You will not get rid of me so easily. I have yet to see you safely installed at Wearmouth; and who knows there may be some building needs doing?'

Hilda smiled.

'Let us sail with the tide in three days' time. I do not wish for a hasty decision on your part. Wearmouth will not disappear overnight.' She paused.

'Of course, Wearmouth will only be two days ride from your homestead?' she added.

'Nay, princess, you'd have to have a horse that could fly to do it in two days,' he paused.

'Tis true you could sail it in a day with a good north easterly behind you. But I'm not given to more time at sea than is necessary,' and they both nodded ruefully in agreement.

'I am sure you are right, Bassus. But I think that we might pass the Isle of the Hart on our way to Wearmouth? We could anchor there to see Heiu?'

'Aye we could do that, princess. But we should let these fellows who brought us from Dunwich return. I'm sure that Aelred will be pleased to lend us a boat, with men who know the local waters. For I remember all the sand banks at the mouth of the Wear; how they shift with the seasons and the tides. Its local knowledge that we'll be wanting.'

'I am in your hands again. So be it. But no rush as to your decision to see this through.'

By which very means she bound him more closely in his loyalty.

The visit to the Isle of the Hart was a mixed experience. It was more than ten years since Hilda and Heiu had that memorable year on Iona together, followed by a short time, for Hilda, at Lindisfarne. Heiu was still recognizable, but obviously not well, even as she was delighted to see Hilda, Utta, and Bassus.

Heiu saw that Hilda had grown into something more self-assured and gently confident. The abbess noticed how both Bassus and Utta deferred to her without any sense of servitude yet waiting in precisely that mode. Heiu found the same thing happening to herself and had an inward smile of the memories of Iona. Had not the seed of this role always been there between the three of them, Hilda, Ebba, and Heiu?

For the few days that the party stayed on Hartlepool it was as if the days rolled back to more carefree times. Friendship renewed worked its therapy on Heiu.

Hilda admired the work that Heiu had managed on this headland, battling against the eastern winds. They had a wooden chapel now and were well on the way with several stone buildings, using the stonework of the abandoned roman lighthouse. But the limestone headland was a hard crust with a thin layer of soil, so that turf and wicker buildings still housed much of the community. However, the location did provide much in the way of fish and fowl.

Hilda was most impressed by the beautiful work that Heiu was overseeing in the small scriptorium. Hilda had forgotten how gifted Heiu had been in her drawing, even when they had those lazy summer days by the pool where the bright blue dragon flies hovered , where the three rowan trees were mirror-imaged in the stillness of the pool, with their reflections seeming to come alive in the ripples caused by the surfacing of a brown trout, and in the reality of a summer breeze blowing across the moorland and whispering in the leaves. It seemed so long ago. Yet here on the pages was that loveliness and vitality of nature brought alive in the interweaving of animal figures amongst curling vegetation, all in bright colours, with curious quirks of humour, of faces from rustic shepherds, of geese chasing a fox, of a rabbit flashing a white tail to a giant crow. Hilda's enthusiastic appreciation lifted Heiu's spirits even more. The abbess knew that she was fortunate to have her willing and able young sisters and Aidan was always so supportive when he visited. But the eye of Hilda appreciated different things from her bishop's that warmed Heiu in this brief visit.

They feasted on sheep's cheese, crab, and goose, with young beans and herbs from the sheltered garden. Bassus and Aldric inspected the farm on the mainland across the sea marsh, and Bassus commented that he would have built the monastery on higher land than Heiu had chosen. He thought that the low cliffs were too vulnerable to the sea. Hilda agreed but chose not to pass this information on to Heiu.

Having heard of the complexities of the sandbanks at Wearmouth, and with Bassus having his family land south of Hartlepool, the party decided that they would complete the rest of the journey on horses. Utta sought a very staid cob on which to plod. Aldric rode ahead to warn his grandmother and uncle that the party would stay overnight. So, they again feasted well and with two more days riding, at Utta's pace, arrived on the south bank of the Wear where the river curved before opening into the sea through its shifting sandbanks. From their land approach they could see across the river to what was the remains of a settlement while, not far away, what looked like the remains of yet another roman lighthouse. Bassus knew the area sufficiently well to know that once there had been a ferry crossing here, and that it still was easiest and safest to make this crossing when the turning of the tide balanced the outflow of the river. So they waited; crossing with their horses and luggage when it was safe to do so. They did all get somewhat wet, with Utta clinging on to the mane of his sturdy little mare. Hilda, enjoying the challenge as much as Bassus, was concerned for them all, shouting encouragement to Utta, knowing that the little mare would swim between the sand banks better than the larger horses if need be.

On arrival there were but a few tents, along with turf and wicker houses, and one wooden longhall in the making on the northern slope rising up from the river. As the arriving party clambered out of the muddy bank they saw the figure of Aidan emerge from one of the tents. He went straight to Utta and embraced him.

'You have travelled well, Utta. Thankyou. You bring great riches with you.'

Utta blinked and grimaced somewhat, slightly shivering in his wet garb.

'Go in, change and warm up.'

Aidan turned to Hilda and she received one of his open smiles.

'Princess, Hilda, you have come back. You are most welcome. Thankyou for answering our call; it is an answer to our prayers. You look well. I think Heiu must have treated you well?'

'I think that the journey has invigorated me, Aidan. Bassus always seems to take good care of me, while his Aldwin does seem to impart me of some of his young energy. So I cannot be other than well, even as I had forgotten how invigorating the northern air is.' They continued to smile in different modes. Time slid and oscillated between past and present. Hilda continued,

'Thankyou for calling me back to my homeland. It was so good to stay and catch up with Heiu,' here she hesitated, 'even as it was difficult to leave dear Hereswid and my nephew.' But she continued.

'Heiu's art work is extraordinary and she seems well organized at Hartlepool. Yet she is not well in herself I think?'

'Princess, it is an answer to our prayers that you have arrived and here you are already worrying about others.' Aidan turned to pick up some of their baggage.

'There is not much organized here yet. But we can get all of you dry and concentrate on preparing a meal. Then there will be time for discussions.'

And so it was.

■■■■■■■■■■■■■■■■■■■■■■■■■■■■■■■■■■■■■■■

The long evenings of midsummer were beginning to shorten. But it did not seem to diminish the activity of the midges by the river shore. Yet it did mean that the few farmers round the holding at Wearmouth were busy scything the harvest with the women and children all out in the fields gathering up sheaths, tying them with ropes of dried grass and stooking them so that they would be safe from any rain, ready to be transported to the threshing circle at a later date. It was all hands into the fields, with Bassus, Aldwin, and even Utta, lending a hand. The blackberries had set green and were turning red, with some of the small trees bearing early crab apples. As they ripened the pigs would avidly crunch those that were allowed to fall. So the women and children would often pick them from the trees late into the evening. The children delighting in being given a hand to scramble in the trees, throwing the fruit down onto blankets spread beneath the canopy.

This whole estate had belonged to Hrothgar, one of Oswald's old thegns. But he and his wife had died childless, so the estate had reverted to the King. Aidan had been able to persuade King Oswin to give the land to a new foundation; and now he had successfully persuaded Hilda to lead the community.

Aidan remembered the three exiled princesses from their year on Iona, more than fifteen years ago, when he was a monk there, how this had subsequently translated to the three young ladies becoming resident guests at Lindisfarne, with Heiu and Ebba seeking a vocation, while Hilda eventually had withdrawn to honour her promises to Eanfled and Tata, to be with her family in Kent. Even then Aidan had noticed the quiet detachment of Hilda, her considered manner, and her overiding loyalty to Tata and Eanfled which had taken her to stay with them.

At Wearmouth, over the next week he heard of her times in Kent. While Aidan could update Hilda on the marriage of Eanfled and Oswy. He also reported on the steady growth of the foundations both at Lindisfarne and at Coldingham where Ebba was abbess.

But most of their days in that week were spent in planning the layout of the new monastery at Wearmouth. Aidan was experienced from both Iona and his own efforts in building at Lindisfarne. But in Hilda he quickly realized that he had a well-informed match as she had the experience of the formation and running of monasteries at both Folkestone and Lyminge to her credit, with the trump card of the loyal Bassus at her side and his local knowledge, both of the land and the making buildings happen. Utta frequently smiled to himself as he heard Aidan's suggestions subjected to, 'Yes, that is a good suggestion, but perhaps….?', until Aidan would advance an amendment and trail off with, 'but perhaps you have other considerations?' Quietly, he gave thanks that he had been able to persuade such a capable force to return to her native land. He would leave with his heart uplifted and keen to encourage the King to make a visit as soon as she was moderately established, encouraging Oswin to bring gifts that would help the foundation find its feet.

Bassus and Aldwin could not resist the challenge of a new building project; the first plan etched out in a thin bed of wax, with the marks brushed over with fine charcoal so that they stood out clearly. They would make a wooden chapel and longhall first, while tents and turf huts would see them through the first winter. Aldwin was allowed a week's ride to their estates to tell Ursula, his grandmother, and his uncle Hewen of their plans and hopefully to elicit gifts and manpower from the estate.

His grandmother gave thanks that they were all safe, but mostly thankful of the promise that her two sons were well reunited and living in peace. God be praised indeed! She promised that, even with her rheumatism, she would travel north to see the new site as soon as they could promise her a rain proof tent and a comfortable bed.

'These old bones will still travel, Aldwin. But they do need some nursing through the night, or I am no good for anything the next day.'

'You can bring your down pillows with you, and we'll sling you between two willow trees to gently rock in the wind,' was Aldwin's grinning reply. She waved the broom stick, on which she was leaning, at him.

'Be off with you. And make sure that you give my love to your father; and to Hilda. And mind your manners with her too.' She quipped, trying to hide her smile.

It was well that they had Bassus and Aldwin, along with two serfs from Ursula's estate to make good progress with the building. For that winter was early to set; and to set hard for three long months. Hilda was reminded that she had softened amongst the vineyards of Kent. The snow fell thickly and regularly, sometimes blown in blizzard winds from the east that drifted the snow in deceptive banks. To the west the river froze so that they could cross on sledges or skates. The men had hacked down much of the small, wind-shaped, thorn trees to make enclosures for the sheep and cattte;

for the wolves could be heard howling in the dark hours of the night. Wood had been stocked and dried for fires that were needed at all hours of the day, while the children would go out and collect more fallen branches in the short hours of daylight. The women would help the shepherd to milk the sheep and goats in the enclosures; spending their evenings spinning and weaving, while the cauldron simmered in the longhall. The small group of sisters shared a dormitory where they took hot stones from the embers of the fire, wrapped in hessian to help to ward off the freezing cold of the night and even carried them into the early hours for matins.

But the days did eventually get longer and the watery sun beamed out more strength in its rays, reflecting brightly off the glittering carpet of snow. The ice on the river began to thin, even to crack, just as the tips of icicles on the branches began to drip translucent drops of water, refracting the bright sunlight, then falling to make small holes in the underlying snow. Only for it all to refreeze as the sun sank and the wind blew again.

But change was in the air. The change grew into two good summers and the community grew, enriched by Ursula visiting and deciding to take up residence with her eldest son and grandson; while King Oswin visited several times. But most special were the visits of Eanfled, as soon as she could slip away from the court at Yeavering or Bamburgh, secretly sending gifts in between visits. She had given thanks that Hilda had returned to her homeland.

All these visits reinvigorated Hilda, so that she knew that it had been a fullfillment that this had been the direction of her calling. Thank goodness that Aidan had sent Utta to her again! Surely an inspired mission?

King Oswin reminded her of Oswald, who she remembered from Iona. Like Oswald he was of a tall, broad build, useful on the battlefield; yet he also was capable of a gentle disposition, so that while he was brusque enough with his warrior thegns, yet he was quietly courteous to Aidan and to his womenfolk. He was pleased to have this new monastery in his kingdom, to see the buildings progressing, to be impressed by the quiet authority of Hilda. He brought skins for parchment with him, but lost Ossi, one of his young warriors, who was so taken by the tranquility of the household that he decided that he would stay to help with the building.

Of course, for Hilda the reunion with Eanfled was something else.

'How welcome you are, Hilda. You have been so much in my prayers. I am ever grateful that you nursed mother.' She had paused to look around.

'You already seem to have done so much here, and so much is afoot. It is almost like mother at Lyminge all over again!'

'I think nothing quite so grand, nor hardly begun. But how well queenhood and motherhood becomes you Eanfled. It seems this marriage was well ordained. I hear that it was well celebrated, and with Aidan officiating.'

'It was an occasion. It seems some time ago already. Oswy certainly keeps me on my toes. He is something of a challenge.' She hesitated. 'But generous in his ways with me, even in our differences. I had been so used to the only man in my life being Bassus, who I could tell what to do, even if he quietly modified it. It is no longer so.' Eanfled sighed, pursing her lips, quizzically raising her eyebrows. Hilda had returned an appreciative wry smile.

'But there is much to be grateful for and I have enough help that we could make linen and a tapestry to bring to you.' Eanfled concluded and they crossed over to inspect the buildings and to meet Bassus and Aldwin.

So Hilda's first house did flourish.

■■■

But two years later change of a more serious nature was in the air. Aidan visited the growing community in the spring with the sad news that at Hartlepool the convent had suffered a devastating winter with ten of the young sisters all dying of influenza, dying within a week of each other and buried in a row in the convent cemetery. Heiu had survived but was very frail. Aidan worried that she too might succumb.

'Then I must go and see what I can do.' offered Hilda, reading a question into Aidan's visit. She continued,

'We are blessed that Ursula has joined us here. I know that I can leave her in charge while I visit Heiu. Ursula is well founded in her faith and has run her own estates.'

'Then we might make a visit together,' Aidan acknowledged with a gentle smile.

They did make the journey.

Aidan even borrowing a pony in order that they might make haste. A rare event for the good abbot, who usually insisted on travelling everywhere on foot.

They arrived to find a distressing row of ten new graves and Heiu too weak to rise from her bed. The compound was now attended only by two elderly sisters and three lay brothers.

■■■■■■■■■■■■■■■■■■■■■■■■■■■■■■■■■■■■■■■

'Hilda, how good it is of you to come. I hope that you have been spared this illness. I feel that I have failed, and I have no strength at all,' Heiu offered from her bed.

'We are all tested from time to time, Heiu. But first and foremost it is most important that we get you better. Now look at the state that your bed is in,' Hilda gently chided.

So Hilda took to rearranging the drapes on the low lying pallet, noticing how very thin Heiu had become and how it pained her to even move in the bed. She asked if Aidan might bring some warm water from the kitchen that she might try to wash and revive the fading abbess. Wynn, one of the older remaining sisters, overheard and scuttled off to bring the water and a fresh linen cloth. She felt that the convent's depressed feeling of desertion might just be turning. It certainly would be an answer to their prayers.

Aidan sat with the two sisters for the office hours and helped with the clearing of the dishes after the frugal evening meal. Hilda busied herself making some broth from left-over scraps to take to Heiu.

The following day it was a misty sunrise spreading over the island; the hazy grey shroud of waking night giving way to a spreading gentle light. No wind this day, so that it was as if the gloom was drawn up by invisible hands to reveal a resting landscape and a sea that did but lap the shore as a fawning dog, rather than its usual pounding as if to break the firmament.

The community seemed to breath a sigh of relief, even if still in shock and mourning for the ten young sisters.

'I think that I need to stay for a while, good father,' Hilda offered to Aidan after the office of Terce. 'I even wonder if Heiu might need to go away to recuperate? I fear that this has all been too much for her.'

Aidan nodded in agreement, quietly delighted to hear of Hilda's offer.

'But what will happen at Wearmouth in your absence, Hilda?'

'There is no problem there, Aidan. Ursula ran her estate for a decade when she was widowed, with Hewen well trained to take over. She is now reunited with her eldest son and grandson at Wearmouth. It could not be in safer hands. And you know that they have Utta with them, who will make sure that all the traditions are maintained. You trained him well.'

'I was fortunate that he was called. He has always been a blessing. But I think that you will miss them, even as they will miss you?'

::

Hilda smiled. How good it was to spend time with Aidan. How he saw to the heart of the matter instantly.

'Do you know where Heiu might go? I think this dream of trying to recreate Iona has not worked for her constitution. She might recover better in a more sheltered place?' Hilda tried to move the conversation on, for she knew that Aidan had been right, that she would miss her community of friends and family at Wearmouth.

'Heiu's family lands are in Bernicia, in the north west. But it was those that she left behind. So, I think that is not a solution at any level. If I remember rightly, she has a distant cousin in the vale of York who stayed here for a while as a would-be novice. I think that her name is Ingrid, and that she did return to make a small house of her own, with her widowed aunt.' Aidan paused. Then, with raised eyebrows, went on,

'We might explore that option; with Heiu; and with Ingrid; and in our prayers?'

Hilda nodded in agreement.

'Indeed: all three. But I think that Heiu will receive that news, and direction, most readily from you, Bishop?'

'That I will undertake. But I imagine that it will be your advice that she also seeks.'

224

'She is as my sister, she has always been part of family since childhood, and my every hope is for her well-being.'

Hilda bowed her head with many memories of Heiu at Edwin's court; and they were both silent; even as they were both resolved. Aidan again silently giving thanks that Hilda had responded positively to his call when she was in East Anglia. How he saw that her natural disposition was to be wise, with the tangible calm that true wisdom brings.

Heiu's initial shock at their advice to her moderated into a feeling of acceptance and relief.

It was some three weeks before the news came from Ingrid that Heiu would be most welcome, and in that time Hilda had brought about a quiet transformation at Hartlepool, not only in Heiu.

Aidan had left after a week to return to Lindisfarne with the caveat that if Heiu were to go to Tadcaster, then he would like to see her safely installed and would escort her there.

But the word spread in the surrounding countryside, that the princess Hilda was now in charge at Hartlepool: that good things were happening again after the influenza had run its course. Young men came to work the farm as lay brothers, while there were four new supplicants for noviciates: two young ladies and two widows, one of the latter with land to add to the monastery estates.

The migrating geese and wigeon had winged northwards for their summer grounds. But the resident wildfowl were busy nesting and incubating eggs. There were even some early, fluffy mallard ducklings scuttling among the marsh reeds inland. While the vegetation shot sentinel green shoots from the warming earth, and the weatherproof cases of buds began to give way to the crumpled green leaves, swelling them apart. It was as if the dormant landscape suddenly breathed in and woke from its winter sleep, throwing off the shroud of winter.

Hilda had been at Hartlepool but a month when a familiar figure appeared in the longhall.

'I just wanted to see that all was safe and sound,' bowed Bassus when he had dismounted. He continued,

'The building at Wearmouth is all under the control of Aldwin and watched over by his grandmother. They have your plans. I felt redundant!' he grinned somewhat sheepishly.

'My dear Bassus, you are irreproachable; even as you are always welcome. Did I ever deserve such a loyal friend?'

■■

'It was our good Queen who bid me that I must look after you, once her daughter had come north.'

'She is ever with us Bassus, even as Eanfled has visited us at Wearmouth. I think that you must be part of this family, Bassus.'

The slightly embarrassed Bassus rapidly changed the direction of the conversation.

'I have a feeling that there might be some more building that needs tackling here? This present housing seems to be mightily near to the cliffs. And they are not of good stone to stand the thrashing by the winter seas.'

'Bassus you have scarcely set your foot inside and you are planning new buildings; and I have much nursing to do at the moment.'

'Mother, I am in no rush. It was just an observation.'

'And a valid one too. We would be safer further up the hill,' Hilda acquiesced.

'But see to your horse and then let me introduce you to Jefri who organizes the menfolk here. Heiu is resting. You will meet her later. She is much changed from when you last saw her. If we can restore her strength a little, we hope to retire her to her cousin at Tadcaster. She has burnt herself out here.'

■■■

'It is good to have you with us, Bassus', Hilda concluded with a warm smile.

It was two months before Aidan came to take Heiu to her new home. Bassus had worked with the local wheelwright to make a small cart in which she might sit, for she was no longer mobile enough to ride, or even walk for any great distance. Aidan promised to lead the oxen on foot, but Bassus and Hilda did persuade him that it would be quicker and kinder to Heiu if he actually got on board and let Jefri drive the very steady oxen that the brothers had provided. The brothers would have to make do without their full quota of oxen for ploughing while he was away. So, this finally convinced him that he needed to make good speed: the corn must be sown: so he too became a passenger.

Heiu's departure was an emotional parting for those few brothers and sisters who had been with her since the beginning of the foundation. Sister Frigyth had asked if she might travel with her to Tadcaster to take care of her.

'My heart says yes, Frigyth. But my head says no. It is here that you are now needed, and here that your vows were made. Mother Hilda is now your abbess and she will need your knowledge of this place and our fragile community. You and Jefri are the heart of the community. Always, you will all be in my prayers. I am sure that Ingrid will be quite capable of looking after me, and I am so much improved over these last few weeks. Please look to Mother Hilda and your new sisters for my sake; even as I thank you and shall miss you.'

So the first chapter of the monastery at Hartlepool ended: and a new one began.

A shift in the Northern Kingdoms

The shrewd observations of Bassus had been predictive, while Hilda, with all her previous experience, soon set to with plans for new buildings further up the hill of Hartlepool, away from the cliff's edge. Hilda's visit to Hartlepool turned into a decade of rebuilding. Heiu's old foundation was left behind, but honoured as a memorial to her and her founding sisters, hoping that there would be no further urgent additions to the young sisters' graveyard.

King Oswin, often brought calf skins to the renewed house as he had heard of the enthusiasm of Hilda to extend the work that Heiu had begun and had so beautifully illustrated, even during her illness. It was the King's first meeting with Hilda. He had heard much of her, knowing that she was closer by birth to Edwin than he; that she was a true princess of Deira. He was impressed. There was such order and due deference to her in her community. Also, there was none of the hassle of the Witan, or requests for judgement on this that and the other. He found himself discussing his problems of the kingdom with her as someone who was related to both himself and even more closely to Oswy; with whom there was the rivalry of Kingship. For Oswy had made it plain that he had seen himself as the successor to both kingdoms after Oswald's death. Hilda had listened and nodded.

'It seems to be ever so. Brothers, cousins, nephews, uncles always striving against each other. Not seeking to live in peace even with their kin as we are taught; and try to teach by our way of life,' came her mild reprimand.

'I do see what you have achieved. I can feel the consolation that such peace brings. But I have my people to protect,' was returned as a parry.

'That seems to go with Kingship. Yet I would see that the greater threat to both your kingdoms lies still from Mercia. It is Penda who has taken both Edwin and Oswald. He still plunders both our lands. You must know that Oswy has tried to placate him by marrying a daughter and a son into his household, seemingly well received on both sides. Now I hear from Eanfled that he might offer Egfrid, her first born, to Penda's household, whether for safe keeping or as a hostage it is hard to tell. I think that I know how Eanfled must feel, as would any mother.' Hilda paused before continuing.

'I can see that Penda will rejoice in any divisions between you and Oswy; even seek to exploit them. I am no warrior, but if the Northern Kingdoms do not seek to live peacefully it is to Penda's advantage. You must decide on your priorities.'

'Wise words, good Mother. In the calm of this place I hear their wisdom. But I cannot see me conveying them to my thegns in the Witan.'

Tondhere, Oswin's righ- hand thegn, whose loyalty came above his own life, nodded his head in agreement with his king.

This place was not where the power struggle really lay; even if Hilda's analysis had a frightening truth about it, he thought.

Hilda felt a distinct sadness when the King left. Oswin did remind her of the gifts and stature that she had seen in the young Oswald on Iona those many years ago. She wondered if the gentle perceptive side to his nature which, while making him a more attractive personality, might well be his undoing in the ruthless world of the warrior- king.

So she mused, even as she prayed for peace between the two Kingdoms.

Oswin would think on these matters and of the haven of Hartlepool on his return to York, making sure that more gifts were sent to the monastery. He did rank Hilda's good counsel highly, but, as Trondhere had predicted, persuading the Witan or, equally importantly, Oswy was another matter.

A letter from Eanfled did nothing to reassure Hilda.

Dear Hilda

I would so like to be able to spend some time with you in the peace of Hartlepool. Oswy is away northwards checking on his nephew, Talorcan, in Gododdin under the guise of some good hunting. So, I am left with placating and adjudicating the petitions of the court: not my favourite pastime; but necessary.

I am also with child again and morning sickness drains me of energy so that the thought of travelling is quite beyond me. But please pray for the infant in your prayers. Losing a child before its birth does take me down so, and that has happened before.

■■

232

But it is not just of myself that I write. I am so worried about the friction between our two northern Kingdoms. I plead with Oswy that we might live in peace to face Penda, who is an ever present threat, but Oswy argues that he needs the army of both kingdoms if he is to beat Penda as his brother Oswald did. His brother is forever a shadow for Oswy to match up to. I fear that my King's strategy will be to take on Oswin as a step towards facing Penda. Meanwhile you must know that he has bartered Alhflaed and Aldfrith in marriage to Penda's offspring, trying to buy time and political allegiance. I did try to advise each of them as well as I could.

How I am reminded of my own naivety when I came here; even as my mother's words and your advice still echo in my mind when I was a young innocent in Kent. Now my stepchildren are cast upon more doubtful waters by their marriages, even as we pray for their safety daily. I am forever reminded how protected I was from the ways of men, being brought up in the safety of Lyminge.

The worst is that Penda, who I think laughs at our predicament, has now asked for Egfrid, my first born, as a token of our trust in him! I think that when Oswy returns I shall lose my dear son to the Mercian court. There I can only trust that his stepsister will keep him from harm and remind him of his real family. He is a somewhat tempestuous child, rather like his father. This way and that. None of this is what I would have wished; but nor do I wish to see our land and people ravaged again.

How I look back on those idyllic years in Lyminge, with you and mother, and the delight of Eanswith and Sexburg. What untapped wisdom there was in grandma Bertha. What journeys she had made!?

My love to you Hilda in all your good works.

Do please pray for us all at this time.

We do need your prayers so: and your wise counsel.

Eanfled

The high rocks of Bamburgh were wrapped in a rolling sea mist; so common at that time of the year. It lay as a shroud on the land, the light of the sun so heavily blocked that only an uneasy, dim flicker, of light pervaded the gloom.

Then, seemingly out of nowhere, an hundredfold of geese flew low in everchanging spearheads; mostly in an eerie silence, yet somehow carrying their grey shadows across the sullen seas, silent silhouettes, noiseless wings stirring the mist. Occasionally a solitary voice would honk an encouragement, and the order of flight would seamlessly change.

Eanfled and Jessica stood with their heads lifted.

'They say, in the old ways, that it is as our ancestor's souls do travel. In and out of time, from where, to where we know not: but forever journeying.'

'It is a powerful symbol; and it so defines the time of year. Thank goodness that they are going north, heralding the coming of spring as do these buds of the white blossom of the blackthorn,' was Eanfled's reply to Jessica's rather gloomy remarks.

The young queen had Jessica with her, while Oswy again was away northwards in Gododdin. Eanfled had left the business of the court behind. It was a breath of fresh air in more ways than one to escape the politics of the court for a while with Jessica. Oswy had tended to cope with the traumas of her miscarriages by making himself very busy with hunting sorties, working himself into schemes against Oswin in Deira. Eanfled was still adjusting to the outcomes of the destruction of war; of husbands not returning, or with ghastly wounds that would all too often be infected, which, even with the dressings of cobwebs and herbal potions, only led to a lingering death. How now she understood Hilda's constant prayers that there might be peace between kingdoms.

They had experienced a real threat when Penda and his thegns pillaged their way up to Oswy's fortress on the coast, trying to burn them out of their rocky fortress in the sand dunes. But it was said that the prayers of Aidan had prevailed and the wind had changed to turn the flames onto Penda and his camp; although there were sailors from the coastal hamlets amongst the Bernicians who said that it showed what land- lubbers these marauding Mercians were. For any coastal man knew that, just as the morning wind blew west from land into the sea, helping their fire; so, in the late afternoon, the wind halted, then turned to blow as a easterly from the sea back to the land. These Mercians knew not how to respect the rules of creation; and God's vengeance was turned upon them.

Meanwhile the buildings grew, higher up the hill, at Hartlepool.

When Penda's troops had plundered the north, the community on the would-be island of the convent had been saved by the marshes and the tides. But the house at Wearmouth had not been so well protected and had been ravaged. Three of the community had escaped but Ursula had died in the fire that burnt down the small chapel, too immobile to defend herself or escape the flames. There was no news of Aldwin. The three that had escaped, a lay brother who knew the fields and woods well, along with two sisters who were out helping with the sheep, had hidden in the woods until the invaders moved on. Then they made their way by sea in a small sailing boat, which the Mercians had missed, as it had been kept hidden, downstream from the monastery. Their arrival at Hartlepool was a mixture of joy and sadness; the happiness that they had survived, yet mourning the loss of the innocent: for there had been little wealth to plunder at the young monastery: a wanton desolation. Hilda had rested them as guests for a few days, then gently introduced them into her rotas: to be busy was one way of coping with loss: while reconciliation came in the routine of the services, in the petitions of thanksgiving and remembrance in their prayers of those who had died.

While the seasons unfurled and intertwined with human peace and man-made strife the complex at Hartlepool grew. But it was a further letter from Eanfled that saddened and shocked Hilda most.

    She related that Oswy had murdered his distant cousin Oswin, not in battle, but treacherously by betrayal of a pledged truce. Oswy had secretly bought off Hunwald, a Deiran thegn, well trusted by Oswin. Oswin had disbanded his own men, seeing that they were greatly outnumbered by Oswy's troops and, trustingly, offered to negotiate a peace with Oswy, taking only his loyal Tondhere with him. Too trustingly, they had agreed to meet in Hunwald's longhall for the negotiations.

Ethelwin, Oswy's trusted general, and a cohort of Bernician thegns, had master- minded the betrayal, first killing Tondhere, so that minutes after Oswin was also overpowered and slain. In true fashion, Oswy had then arranged for the death of his own general, Ethelwin, thereby denying all kingly responsibility for the betrayal.

But nobody was deceived.

Hilda was in deep sadness. Had she not advised Oswin to seek peace? Had not Aidan advised him to seek peace? Oswin had been martyred. Her cousin, Oswy, was dishonourable and an abomination. To die in warfare was an honourable death, but a scheming, cold blooded, murder ran against all codes of conduct: and was an offence punishable by law. Hilda understood Eanfled's anger and despair:

' To what am I married, that he behaves in this treacherous, despicable way?' she wrote in her letter, ' by the law of the land there should be payment by blood or retribution in atonement for this deed. I shall do my utmost to uphold it and pray for your support. He is your cousin and does respect your counsel. I have written also to Aidan for his counsel. I can only begin to imagine Aidan's distress, for he dearly loved Oswin.'

Hilda had prayed and waited for twenty-four hours before replying. She needed to calm her shock and despair. For not only was it the murder of the noble Oswin, but it echoed the treacherous murder of her own father all those years ago when he had thought that he was in safe keeping.

Having struggled, but tempered her personal distress, Hilda anticipated that now Oswy would be all contrition, even as he had achieved his objective. She saw that, as he was the King, it was unlikely that his own blood would be the justified retribution as it would have been for a lesser personage. But Hilda did write to him directly, not mincing her words, recommending that the very least he could do was to pray for forgiveness, even found a monastery on the traitor Hunwald's estate [for he had also been killed by Ethelwin!], and that it might be overseen by Trumhere, a relation of Oswin who was presently with Hilda at Hartleypool.

Their mission at the new monastery would be to pray in perpetuity for the souls of the murdered Oswin and the loyal Trondhere. But equally to pray for the repentance and forgiveness of Oswy and the other perpetrators of the murders. Both living and dead.

And so it was.

Oswy now heeded his wife and his cousin's indignation, trying to buy peace.

But within twelve days of Oswin's murder the saintly Aidan died in his church, kneeling in prayer, with his arm resting against a wooden pillar of the chapel. Had this foul betrayal been as a fatal blow from afar off for so saintly a soul? How he had loved and nurtured Oswin in his faith: and his death the outcome? Was all his work to be in vain? It had surely seemed too much to bear.

While Lindisfarne and Hartlepool were in deep mourning, Oswy astutely moved to appoint Aethelwald, thegn, nephew, and son of Oswald as the new subking of Deira: and half apologized to his wife, saying, in the end it might save them from the Mercians.

The muddy waters of the seven kingdoms swirled, murky, and darkly. Oswy sought allegiance from East Anglia and the East Saxons. But Penda picked them off, one by one. The King of the East Saxons was dispatched. Hilda was further saddened to hear that Ana, puppet king of East Anglia for many years, had his life and his army taken at the battle of Narborough before Oswy could muster troops to help him: even though his brother, Ethelwald, had ridden north to seek help.

Hilda remembered her childhood days on the East Anglian beaches: what innocent days! She now feared for her sister, Hereswid and her nephew Adwulf. But she heard that Penda had simply appointed another puppet king, Ethelhere, brother to Ana. At least the Mercians had not ravaged the countryside. Her sister and nephew might still be safe? She prayed.

Oswy predicted that Penda had not ravaged East Anglia because he had greater plans which, in spite of marriages and the holding of a son and possible heir, would seek total subjugation of the northern kingdoms as a final goal. As a bartering position Oswy offered the trappings of gold, silver, jewels, and whatever glittered, petitioning for time to collect them. But made little secret of marshalling what troops they had. This time he had Aethelwald from Deira in the south and Ahlfrid, his eldest son, with troops. They moved southwards from the plain of York and into the valleys of the Pennine hills. He also had the value of Ethelwald and his cohort of thegns from East Anglia whose mission had been to seek assistance from Oswy before the slaughter of their kinsfolk at Narborough. The Anglians could scarcely contain their desire to assist in vengeance.

In this weave of intrigue, it served Oswy well to have two feisty married daughters in the Mercian court. Details of the widespread allegiances that Penda was demanding, from the Welsh and the East Anglians, filtered through to the Northumbrian court.

Oswy and Ahlfrid decided that they must be proactive. They chose a hill site on the river Winead as a meeting place, in a season of wet and windy weather.

How the rain fell, soaking man, beast, and land already sodden; sapping morale even as it bogged down the entourage of a major battle. It was good to be on a hill.

Penda had perhaps tried too hard to marshal forces, with the greater numbers simply becoming unwieldy. They lacked the core loyalty that Oswy held. Their numbers created a quagmire of a camp.

Alchfled, daughter of Oswy, drugged her husband, Penda's eldest son and heir, so that he was unfit to lead his Mercian troops. This was the first omission.

■■■■■■■■■■■■■■■■■■■■■■■■■■■■■■■■■■■■

Biscop, Oswy's trusted thegn, had successfully bought off the Welsh Cadafael and his troops by offering him the treasures that Penda had so scorned as inadequate. It had sapped morale when Penda saw the Welsh troops disappear over the horizon. Then, hoping that he saw them returning, had seen that it was a Northumbrian flag returning with Biscop leading his warriors to attack the Mercians on their western flank.

How the rain fell.

Aethelwald of Deira had feigned allegiance to Penda, only to hold back and then attack him from the south side of the river as the tide of the battle turned.

How the rain fell.

Ethelhere, puppet king of Anglia with his few thegns, seeing his brother Ethelwald leading the Anglian flank on the northern hill, deserted Penda, and rallied to the flag of his country. It cost him his life via one of the Mercian's arrows, but most of his thegns became reinforcements for Oswy.

How the rain fell.

The swollen river began to burst its banks.

In the chaos that ensued Penda's horse was speared, fell, and the king was pinned to the ground. His head, soon severed from his body, was jubilantly mounted on the same spear, which for years to come was mounted in the longhall of

Yeavering, and referenced in many a merry evening of song.

The cry on the battlefield went up: the battle was lost: the ruthless plunder began. The river Winead ran a muddied red of floating corpses, men and horses: and still the rain fell.

In the north the relentless wetness that autumn meant that there was much liver fluke in the sheep. Even wool could not hide the thinness of the flock. There was also more rot in their feet even as the blacksmith attempted to trim the smelling hooves. There would not be much meat on the lambs harvested as the fall descended on them.

But at least there was peace in the country.

There were other unexpected positives in these turbulent times.

Oswy's trusted thegn, Biscop, who had been so instrumental in diverting the Welsh and successfully leading a flanking attack, was rewarded with land. He had chosen the vanquished site of Wearmouth. Weary of the violence and destructiveness of the warrior's life he transformed to dedicate his life to God, hoping to restore at Wearmouth what Hilda had started. The lands he soon put in order, leaving Midrek to supervise them, while he submitted himself to Hilda's monastery for his noviciate, with his contributions to the scriptorium being immediately welcomed, both practically and educationally. He assumed the name of Benedict, after the founder of the order that Hilda had followed, even as she married his rules with the Celtic rhythms of the church calendar.

It was to be a turning point for Wearmouth, even as the small graveyard of the martyred Ursula and her household were reverently preserved. Hilda felt in some way that some of her prayers were answered. Even more so when Eanfled, a year later, visited Hilda at Hartlepool with her freshly weaned daughter, Aelffled.

'Hilda, I have Egfrid returned to me after the battle. But my new daughter I will not have taken from me. So I will ask you to take her into your care. I did tell this to Oswy before he went to war: and he did promise that it might be so if all went well. I cannot think of anything that would give me more pleasure than to know that she is safe with you; and that she will receive some of the care that you gave to me throughout my childhood.'

Hilda, deeply moved, had taken the child in her arms.

'And it will give me an excuse to visit you more often!' Eanfled concluded, lightening the emotion that they both felt.

'I see that I shall really have to be a mother now,' acknowledged Hilda. 'It is a great and delightful gift. I hope that you will be able to stay awhile and instruct me in the ways of motherhood!?'

So it was.

A tent was made in the community for the queen and her child.

The arival of children reminded Hilda of her time spent with Eanswith on the cliffs of Folkestone; remembering how the young princess had fostered children from the coastal village. She remembered the wise words of Gertrude in setting up a small school for the children within her monastery. Hilda resolved to follow in their footsteps. It was as if Eanswith and Gertrude spoke to them through the years. Another seed had been planted.

The two cousins, Mother Abbess and Mother Queen, were taken back in unspoken smiles to their palace at Lyminge, as well as to the cliffs of Folkestone.

Inevitably the word spread; a steady trickle of orphans and widowed mothers sought to join the monastery.

It was sister Gyseld that Hilda appointed to be in charge of the young girls, while their mothers were integrated according to their skills: some to spin, some to weave; some to cook, some to wash;

some to make pots, some to write and to paint. All were taught to pray and to recite the psalms. The wooden school room had the name of Abbess Eanswith carved above its door, even as the scriptorium had the name of Abbess Heiu; for they ever remembered their founder's work on this Island of the Hart.

So through the Queen's gift of her daughter to the monastery grew; and by her petition a larger settlement of land was made.

A New Home

    The cliffs of Whitby had reawoken Hilda's imagination on her memorable journey northwards in her answer to Aidan's call. The image of the bay with the high cliffs and the roman lighthouse had stayed with her for the twelve years that had passed.

    The land had been owned by Dryad, a thegn of Oswy, who had been one of the Northumbrian casualties at the bloody battle of Winead. His widow had sought to join Hilda at Hartlepool, which prompted Oswy, to whom the land reverted, to make over the ten hides of land for Hilda's new home. After all it was also a suitable estate for his daughter, now happily in Hilda's care!

    In true fashion, now that Oswy felt secure with Penda out of the way, he created more monasteries, which some read as a recurring attempt to appease the murder of Oswin; but it served equally well as a strategy for bringing peace between the Deirans and the Bernicians. Yet within his family he worried more about the aspirations of his son Aldfrith at York than of his other children. However, for a while he was well pleased, even if as restless as ever.

■■

Aelred had long been the head man, under Dryad, at the coastal hamlet of Whitby, where the collection of houses survived on fishing and sea trade as much as by farming. But it was higher up on the southern cliffs, where there was a spring, that Hilda and Bassus decided to start to build.

Bassus was now using a staff to get around. He was so grateful that when Wearmouth had been sacked by the Mercians, many years ago, Aldwin had been out hunting with Cedric and two deerhounds. It was while the young men were on their chase, stopping to look for another set of recent, cloven hoof imprints, that they had seen great clouds of smoke curling into the sky, rising from the estuary. They looked at each other and, without a word, had turned their horses homewards, moving with considerable caution. For the heavy cloud of smoke spoke to them of already being too late. At the edge of the wood they had muzzled the dogs so that their bark would not give them away. They tied their horses in the shrubbery so that they could quickly release them if they needed to flee and sneaked cautiously towards the smoking ruins of the enclosure. A plethora of hoof marks heading north suggested that the invaders had already left.

They had found a desolation.

■■■■■■■■■■■■■■■■■■■■■■■■■■■■■■■■■■■■■■

Some of the poultry and geese had escaped, and the sheep had been out away on pastures. But the oxen had been slaughtered and the corn store spilt to feed the invader's horses. The Mercians had wantonly put the villagers to the sword or spear, while there was a collection of charred bodies in the smoking ruins of the monastery chapel, mainly women and children, suffocated by the smoke before being consumed by the flames. The two young men had silently wept.

It had taken them a week to dig sufficient graves, making one long trench for the several children, for they could no longer recognise who was who. However, Aldwin had recognized his grandmother by the charred rings and cross that she had still been wearing, missed by the invaders. He had buried them with her.

Cedric found his parents' farmhouse similarly plundered and, after more burials, the two of them, their work completed, resolved to leave the ruins and travel south to see how Aldwin's uncle had survived: or not.

They had been relieved to see but a single controlled column of smoke arising through the autumn sky as they approached his uncle's hamlet. But, as they entered the clearing they saw that the buildings were in ruins and that the single fire was from a new build of turf and saplings, covered in bracken and moss. Initially they had been greeted with spears and swords but put away and changed to hugs and celebrations when they realized who the new arrivals were.

Before Penda had arrived, his uncle had heard that trouble was on its way and had posted young folk on the southern and western paths into the village. Hidden in the high trees they all imitated the howl of the vixen in heat, which carried so well, to let the households know the state of play. One cry meant that all was well. But two or three meant gather your things and disappear, some into the woods, and some quickly to the coast to hide in the caves of the cliffs. When several howls were heard the men snatched only weapons, although the women had scooped the weights from the loom and a caldron from the doorway. No welcoming water for these mercenaries!

The strategy had saved their lives even though the village had been torched. Enough livestock had been recovered for them to regroup and to begin to rebuild, albeit in the temporary shelter of tents and turf walls.

The two young men had stayed for three months to assist in the rebuilding; replenishing the caldron with hare and venison in their time off, for their two dogs were well trained. But come the onset of winter they had seen enough meat dressed

251

and smoked for the short dark months to keep the small community going and had travelled further south to Hartlepool to see if the monastery, with Aldwin's father there, had been spared.

Their arrival had been met with astonishment and great celebration. For the news of the devastation of the house at Wearmouth had been received in Hartlepool some months ago. Prayers had been offered for all who had been taken, which had included Aldwin. The two young men decided that they would become lay brothers to the household; Cedric in honour to his parents, and Aldwin to his grandmother. Besides which Aldwin could see the tide turning; that now he could do things that his father could no longer manage.

Hilda had given thanks for these new recruits.

It was to them that she now looked to lead the building of her new home on the high heights of the southern cliffs at Whitby. Bassus, pushing on his staff to get up the steep incline, had pointed out that the roman lighthouse was now close to falling into the sea; that it would make sense to build away from the cliff as even the houses of earlier settlements were being eroded.

'You are right, as ever, Bassus,' was Hilda's reply. 'But we must also find the right distance from the spring, so that it is both convenient, but not easily contaminated: and the right shelter from the east winds, as Aelred has advised. We do not all want to catch your rheumatism yet.'

'Mother, my rheumatism came not with the east wind, but with old age,' sighed Bassus, with the banter that many years of devotion had fostered.

Hilda did not take all her household to Whitby. She left the house at Hartlepool under the care of Wynn, but she did take Frigyth with her. She left some of her precious books, but took most of her scriptorium with her, aiming to give priority to new works for both houses, while the established house at Lindisfarne were generous in their gifts for the new monastery on the cliffs. It fell naturally for Benedict initially to take charge of the scriptorium, while Eanfled sent a new young courtier, by the name of Wilfrid, with a fresh supply of calf skins to be cured and scraped. A meeting of minds and a long friendship was to lie between these two recent recruits. Some of which Hilda would approve; some of which she would not.

The roman stone from the old lighthouse was taken as a foundation, following the experience of Eanswith at Folkestone and Bassus at Lyminge. Now Bassus would but sit and direct while Cedric and Aldwin cut wood for scaffolding and a team of ten brothers sought to tackle the larger beams that would give the framework of the new church. The landscape slowly began to change.

The wind blew freshly across the sea and onto the cliffs, so that as Hilda walked she could almost lean into the wind. A slightly dangerous attitude as the drop into the sea was considerable. It had recently rained and droplets of rain still clung to the angular gorse, catching the spring sunshine and glistening small beads of dancing, sparkling light. The occasional yellow bud had burst into flower, while below the gnarled stems of the tough old gorse some bright sea pinks, their pin cushion heads buffeted in the wind, rose from the dense tufted green of their foliage, growing in even the bravest of places. The gulls and kittiwakes were well on in their nesting, providing a constant cacophony of cries, a whirling of wings to land on impossibly small ledges, an elegant glide to take them back out to sea on the everlasting quest for food, with the cries becoming even louder and more indignant when some of the lay brothers lowered ropes over the edge of the cliffs down which they scarily dared to clamber to fill woven baskets with stolen eggs.

But today Hilda was alone, walking, pondering, celebrating the coming of spring and the growth of her new community. But also treasuring these moments alone. How she now understood why Aidan had sometimes disappeared on retreats, and she meditated on the example in the scriptures of the good Lord taking time out in the wilderness. She greatly missed the wise company of Aidan but heard good things of the twelve young boys that he had started on their calling at Lindisfarne: another small school that would bear much fruit. Hilda wondered when she might feel able to make a journey there for some respite; but, at the moment, there seemed too much to organize here at Whitby. As she turned to make her way back to the compound, a single black headed tern rose up into the sun and seemed to call to her. She stopped and saw its cruciform silhouette pasted in the palest of blue skies: it seemed to be a suspended moment; as if her heart rose to soar in flight with it. Then she caught her breath and turned homewards. But for some reason, at the same time, she had thought of her sister, Hereswid,, quite vividly brought to mind; and she knew not why. For although her dear sister was always in her prayers, this had almost seemed as if her sister was calling to her. 'how strange the mind does catch us,' she murmured to herself as she retraced her footsteps.

    Meanwhile Hereswid was praying that she might soon be spared, 'Oh to have the feel of the good earth beneath my feet, to walk on dry land

255

again,' she moaned. For she was literally at sea, nor was the sea being kind to her as she and her companions headed for the French coast.

She had been in a state of indecision for some months. Her son, Aldwulf, had taken over the running of the estate in Anglia and, while he still respected his mother's wishes, there was considerable conflict between his wife and his mother. Having two strong ladies in a household gave more than a sporting chance of conflict! Cynwise was a princess in her own right from the East Saxon household: a useful political marriage, and in its own rights a successful one. But less so with a resident mother- in- law.

Hereswid struggled with feeling displaced after all those years of widowhood, bringing up Adwulf, losing a daughter, Tamolin, in infancy. Throughout this time her neighbours, the family of Eredith and Ana, had been a considerable consolation and support. The loss of Eredith in childbirth to a stillborn son, after five delightful daughters, had been a great loss to the community, and a catastrophe for Ana and his daughters. The following months had been particularly dark and hollow for him. But he had survived; while the later marriage to Mathilde, from the same village in France as Eredith, had gone a long way to restoring the family unit. The naming of Mathilde's first daughter Hereswid reflected the closeness of the two families, with the elder Hereswid godmother to the youngest in what was to become a notable line of daughters.

So it was not really very surprising that it was with this family that Hereswid now had found a comforting escape from her own household. The whole of the East Anglian kingdom had shuddered at the loss of Ana and his troops in the massacre at Narborough; non more so than his new young wife, Mathilde. The four remaining stepdaughters had by this time all dispersed; two were wed; two had taken orders in their mother's homeland.

Mathilde had debated and discussed with the older Hereswid, who was by now a close confidante, as to whether the three of them, including the young Hereswid, might make the voyage to France, to retire to Chelles and join Eredith's other daughters in France.

It was putting this decision into action that was the cause of Hereswid's present sea sickness.

But they did arrive safely on dry land. With a mule, a donkey and a pony, under the guidance of Trondhere, a wily guide, they did take the journey to the abbey of Chelles via Mathilde's former home. While this visit had been a matter of great rejoicing, meeting her sister, not seen for many years, and introducing the young Hereswid to cousins that she had never met, it was also incident to Mathilde fatally contracting the plague. So that it was only two new novices that enrolled at the abbey in the fertile and substantial hectares on the curve of the river Auberin. And it was Ethelburga, the middle daughter of Ana and Eredith who welcomed them as Abbess.

Hilda heard about this some months later when a letter arrived with some travelling merchants. She had received it with some trepidation, fearing some sad news. So she carefully set it aside that she might read it in private.

My dear Hilda,

I could not discuss all these events with you, as I would have dearly liked. But I would that you might read my version.

Although first, I am so full of admiration for what I hear of your work in our old homelands. Each house that you are drawn to seems to grow and flourish. You truly seem to have found your vocation. Not that I am surprised; but I do give thanks each day for you and your safety.

It is my confession that I was not drawn to return to the north, even as it has also been my sadness that I felt it better to leave my dear Adwulf to his estates and his new wife. But the good Lord gave me the friendship of Ana and Eredith, even sharing all their awful traumas. From all these rose the friendship of Mathilde. She was so supportive. Even more by the kindness of making her firstborn as a namesake to me, almost as a replacement for Tamolin for me. It is as if you and I have both become godmothers to precious daughters. For I hear that Eanfled has placed her daughter in your care. I think that being a godmother is so enriching for each of us.

The sadness of Mathilde's passing with the curse of the plague so reminded me of the loss of our own dear mother when we were so young; and could scarcely comprehend. I saw the same bewilderment in my god daughter; losing her mother when so young. I could but hug her in her consolation. How life seems to go in circles, each returning enlarging our own understanding, bringing new insights to this temporary space that we inhabit. I think that only you can know how much Mathilde's passing moved me in so many ways.

But now, here in the convent, Chelles does seem a rightful resolution. My god daughter is flowering, as am I. Ethelburga has allowed me to be a cook, mercifully shedding all the responsibilities of running the estate. The smell of baking bread,is even as incense to my old nose. And at lent, when

259

we eschew red meat, I am amazed at what miracles can be made with fresh watercress from the streams, chopped finely with a portion of the large onions from the fields, then sprinkled into copious sliced cabbage, still wet with dew; finished with a dash of salt. Served with the fresh bread it is a treat, even if I do so boast.

So, dear Hilda, things are well. And from traumas, life has resolved into a cadence of blessings here at Chelles.

I send my love and my prayers; and know that you will understand my situation so well.

In His Name,

Hereswid.

Hilda was moved; relieved that Hereswid seemed both safe and resolved. How fortunate she had been with the friendship of Ana's family. How clear a vocation Ethelburga had always had, reminding Hilda of the uncluttered certainty of Eanswith at Folkestone, whereas she felt that she herself had waited on circumstance, on the call of Aidan. Yet Hilda did distinctly feel that she had been led, all in good time! How they all journeyed: variously. She wondered how the younger daughters of Ana had fared, Etheldreda and Witburga. She knew that Etheldreda had married the widowed Prince of the Fens, a partly political marriage from all accounts which seemed to have worked well even against the age differences. But she had also heard that there had been some crisis with the younger daughter, with some hint of a tragic breakdown. They were both on her list of prayers.

Her thoughts were brought to an abrupt halt as she retraced her footsteps to the monastery enclosure. Gyseld, sister in charge of the school, met her just as she had crossed the large ditch by the bridged gateway. Gyseld was worried about four of the girls; they had fevers. They were all coughing and had sore, reddened, eyes. Two of them also seemed to have reddish brown rashes.

'It does sound like measles Gyseld? How are the other girls?'

'Well, at the moment. But you know how excited they can become when something like this happens.'

'I do indeed. And I know how it can spread so quickly.' She remembered to herself the devastating outbreak of diptheria in Eanswith's convent at Folkestone when so many had succumbed. But she said nothing of this. She continued,

261

'I remember that Hereswid and I did recover from it when we were in East Anglia, and we were their age. But we must be careful. I seem to remember crushed garlic and honey; and do see if there are any dried olive leaves from Kent. We had olive trees from the roman villas at Lyminge, and Gertrude taught me that they were useful against measles. But the olive trees do not seem to like these northern lands.'

Gyseld had nodded, turning away to carry out the abbess's instructions after adding,

'I think that they have lost two children in the village, and they thought it might be the pox.'

'Chicken pox and measles can be difficult to tell apart at the fever stage. I will come shortly to have a look.'

Hilda pondered again.

This time wondering whether she should let the Queen know of the outbreak of measles in her small school, her daughter under threat.

It was not long before nine of the ten children had fevers, and the young princess Aelffledd, her precious godchild, was one of the nine. How now Hilda also recollected that Tata had sent her two boys away to the safety of France, only to lose them to scarlet fever. Was there to be no end to these worries!

■■■■■■■■■■■■■■■■■■■■■■■■■■■■■■■■■■■■■■■

A Visitor from East Anglia

Amongst these worries, Hilda received a letter via one of the travelling merchants. It was from Etheldreda, daughter of Ana of the East Anglians, whom she had not seen since attending Hereswid's wedding so many years ago. How all those memories now seemed like a perpetual summertime. But perhaps that was the kindness of memory?

Hilda had heard that the young princess had grown into a very eligible young lady and was much respected for her learning. Hilda had heard that her husband, Tonberg, had died and that the kingdom was in a state of flux. The letter brought her up to date and the dilemma of her present situation.

Dear Mother Abbess

I write from the calm of the fens with its great skyscapes where I have had years of happiness and peace with my dear Tonberg, as wife and companion in his old age; and from whom I learnt so much and treasured so dearly.

■■

263

It seems an age away from the lovely memories of the marriage of Hereswid and Aldwulf when you were last with us.

You will probably know that first I lost Tonberg, through the pain of a crippling illness. Then the dreaded Mercians took my father, uncle and cousins at the disastrous battle at Narborough before the Northumbrians could come to our help. In many ways we are still struggling to recover from that loss. But the people of the Fens are resilient and loyal. My heart's inclination is to stay with them; even to found an abbey in the fens in memory of those who have lost their lives for us.

But Uncle Aethelwald now heads the Witan and, as I think you might know, Oswy has sought to bind our two kingdoms more closely, and I the subject of that binding by a marriage to your young nephew. It is not my inclination, the more so, if I may say so confidentially, as my would-be spouse is but fourteen years of age and my age twice that. But I am persuaded to put the safety of our kingdoms above my own wishes. Political compromise seems to be a system above our own apsirations. I am sure that you must appreciate the quandary of my situation!

So, I am already preparing to travel north with Frishere and Aldhelm as escorts. I do so hope that we may visit you and rest a while before travelling on to the court? I shall so value your advice and the time spent with you. For I hear nothing but good things about your foundations.

My regards to you,

Etheldreda

Hilda nodded, and sighed.

Indeed, she had heard from Eanfled of Oswy's plans for his son. It seemed that no sooner had the boy been recovered from his exile in Mercia than Oswy was again using his son as a pawn on the chess board. Eanfled had confided in another letter,

'My supplication was that my son is still far too young to marry. He scarcely sports a beard and has all the oscillations of adolescence still upon him.

But I hardly need to tell you how set in his ways Oswy is once he has decided on something. As we know to our sad cost, nothing will then stand in his way. He will listen to discussions and pleas, but only to see if there is something that he can use to his own advantage. How we are driven to prayer. How even when he is praying I can see that he is also scheming!

Please remember us in your prayers; and pray for this Anglian princess. How we all must feel for her. I do not know how I would have handled such a proposition! For all the difficulties in our marriage we do have a family and the consolation of children!

My love and prayers,

Eanfled

As ever, Hilda and Eanfled were of a mind. But Hilda anticipated that she must consider her advice to her visitor with some delicacy and flexibility. It was indeed a quandary for Etheldreda.

Hilda made some preparations for the visit, feeling sure that the entourage of Etheldreda would come prepared with their own accommodation as they must be travelling over several days, if not weeks, to make their northward journey.

So it was. Fortunately, by then the outbreak of measles was over. They had sadly lost two of the children, but the young princess Aelffled had survived: amongst all the grieving there was much to be thankful for. Eanfled had been spared the worry of the outbreak and was but to raise her eyebrows when eventually told, and add,

'The Lord has indeed been merciful.'

She too remembered losing her two brothers, albeit to 'Scarlet Fever', when the boys had scarcely reached double figures.

But the arrival of Etheldreda did create some excitement in the monastery at Whitby. Gyseld was supervising the children while they played leapfrog in a break from their lessons when some of the children cried out.

'See there is a stag coming up the hill with a procession.'

It was Aldhelm carrying the Anglian flag of the leaping stag that headed the guests. Gyseld had herded the children back into the small hut where they were taught and hastened to inform the mother Abbess. Hilda had risen from going through her accounts with Cedric and asked Gyseld to inform the kitchens; to inform Sewera that they may need to make room in the dormitory; and to inform young Aldwin to be on hand to show the retinue where they might make their base and marshal whatever other lay brothers he might need to help them put up their tents.

Hilda would not have recognized Etheldreda. This tall, elegant figure bore no resemblance to the rather gangly adolescent girl that she remembered from so many years ago.

■■■■■■■■■■■■■■■■■■■■■■■■■■■■■■■■■■■■■■■

267

'No wonder that my dear sister had been drawn to Ana and Eredith's family if there were daughters like this,' Hilda thought to herself.

Etheldreda was looking quite flushed from all the exercise of her travels. She rode well but had dismounted to walk her horse up the steep incline to the abbey, which had brought an extra colouring to her cheeks, even as it left her slightly breathless. The whole journey had helped to temporarily alleviate her from the seriousness of her quest. Her whole adult life had so far been spent on the flat plains of East Anglia and the marshy wildness of the fens. Once the Humber had been crossed and they had rested at Beverley, the land had started to rise up to the moors which were beginning to break from winter's hold, with primroses and celandines bright by babbling brooks. Hidden vales had dancing catkins in the copses of hazel. There was a new energy in the gentle breezes. Birch and willow sported bright green bursting buds of fragile leaves, pushing off winter's scales to breath in the spring sunlight. The height of the cliffs at the end of the moors was exhilarating. Here the wind blew more strongly. The seabirds made a cacophony of harsh calling amidst a whirl of wings that was electrifying to the uninitiated, while the precipitous downward views had made Etheldreda giddy, so that she had to step back quickly, even as she felt the world begin to spin around her.

However, they had decided to approach Hilda's monastery from the valley, having followed the river Esk from the hamlet of Sleights, with Etheldreda stopping briefly in the riverside village of Whitby to refresh and compose herself after a longish ride. However, as she had underestimated the steepness of the walk up to the monastery, it left her just as flushed as she had been after the morning's ride.

She, for her part, would not have recognized Hilda either. As a young adlolescent she had seen Hilda as this slightly taller, kind, figure who was always interested in her and her studies. Now the Anglian princess was considerably taller than her Mother Abbess, even as perhaps the mother abbess was perhaps a little more substantial in her figure. But in the cool appraisal that she received, within the scope of the warm welcome, Etheldreda recognized why Hilda had the reputation and respect that went before her. Etheldreda, having been in charge of the Fenlands after Tonberg's death, had sufficient experience to grasp that she was entering a considerable household where all was in order!

The entourage was soon settled. Aldhelm and Frishere saw the opportunity to try some hunting while their Princess conferred with the Mother Abbess. The attendant serfs in the visiting retinue were commandeered by Aldwin to help with the continuous building programme that Hilda had instituted: although two of them rapidly defected to help with the spring ploughing, claiming to be experts with the oxen; and one, known for his love of sowing the oats with a fiddle, was also rapidly adapted into the needs of the monastery. All were expected to attend the services at the beginning and the end of the day in the long nave of the chapel, even though it was but a tented shell at the moment.

' I shall greatly value all that you can tell me about Oswy and his family, so that I can in some measure be prepared for this new chapter in my life,' was Etheldreda's opening when she and Hilda made time to confer in the late afternoon between None and Vespers.

Hilda nodded in agreement.

'It is as well to start with my cousin Oswy. He is head of the household, even the Kingdom. He is somewhat volatile and headstrong. Once he has decided he will use any means necessary to achieve it: and is then quite capable of a seemingly genuine repentance after some reprehensible actions. You would do well to have him on your side.' Here Hilda smiled to herself. She did not doubt that this princess from the fens was more than capable of achieving this.

Etheldreda probed.

'Is it true that he has been married three times, and seems to have so many children: some closer to my age; and, I think, already married?'

'That is true; and you will meet Eanfled, his present queen, who is my niece, and has been as a younger sister to me for many years,' Hilda paused. 'She will be your closest ally in the court and you may learn much from her.'

Hilda continued,

'I never met either of his previous wives,' a pause before continuing.

'Oswy has never spoken of Fina, the liaison of his youth, I think. We do not know how or when she died. But he is very fond of Aldfrith,, his first born, their son and heir. Some say that she died in childbirth; but that is only hearsay. I hear that Aldfrith earned his sub kingship in the battle at Winead and resides at York, so you will not meet him at court. But he is devout and of a more even keel than his father. Yet not without ambition from what I hear.'

Hilda shifted a little.

271

'Rheimelt, his second princess was, by all accounts, a fiery and striking beauty and the daughter of the King of Rheged, which lies to the west of our countries. It seems to have been a successful marriage, with two children, each of which Oswy has now married into Penda's family. I need not to explain the ins and outs of that to you. But I think that each of them played hidden roles in the victory over the Mercians at Winead.'

Hilda merely raised her eyebrows and continued,

'It is not known for sure what happened to Rheinfelt. But there are stories that she returned to Rheged to attend her father's funeral. It is said that in her journey both she and her horse fell. She was a competitive, even an aggressive, rider. The story goes that both were injured in the fall. The rumours say that both she and the horse developed the rigour that comes with tetanus. Rheinfelt died and the horse was killed. Somehow, it seems so implausible that both horse and rider were affected that it might just be true.'

Another pause.

'But again their children have done well.'

Hilda looked out at the spring sunlight before bringing this history to its conclusion.

'Eanfled has made her marriage work. She has borne Oswy many children,' more raised eyebrows from Hilda, 'She has her first daughter, Aelffled, safe here in my house, my delightful goddaughter, who you will shortly meet. While Aelffled and Egfrid also have Osthryth and Alfwine as younger sister and brother. You do indeed enter a new family Ette!'

They both half-smiled and raised their eyebrows.

They heard the bell for vespers and rose together.

Aldhelm returned from the hunt with but rabbits and hares for he did not know the real lie of the land in this new territory. However he was able to report to his Princess that there was a fine smithy in the port of Whitby, who had some fine swords, and who shared his furnace with a silversmith who wrought some ' impressive stuff' as the bluff warrior described it.

Hilda had smiled at his description and confirmed that silver was mined from the local hills, along with an unusual black stone that did look quite dramatic when polished and set in silver. Etheldreda saw an excuse to prolong her stay, to visit the silversmith and the sword maker, as well as hunt for the polishers of the black jetstone. This sounded like an ideal source of gifts for the royal family that she was about to encompass. It would

273

show that she was already acquainted with the privileges and customs of her new kingdoms. The gold medallion, inlaid with cloissone and garnet, that she had brought as a gift for Egfrid, might happily transfer to the Queen. Ette, with her own collection of fine jewelry, knew that she would have been delighted had someone brought it to her as a gift!

Hilda had quietly noticed her tasteful decorations.

The blacksmith and silversmith had advised that Ette's commission would take at least a fortnight to complete, giving her the excuse to prolong her stay even further. She spent much of the time absorbing the lay out and the running of the abbey as well as managing regular discourses with Hilda; which prompted Hilda to draft an urgent letter to the queen.

Dear Eanfled,

I trust this finds you, your family and the court well.

I write to petition you for the care of Etheldreda, who is pledged to your son. You are unlikely to remember, and certainly would not recognize her. She is as the royal white swan from the fenlands. She would grace the courts of any of the kingdoms: and her learning and devotions do

274

match her elegance. So much so that I do worry about a marriage to your young son. I know that you would have left him to work through his adolescence before marriage. But I equally know that, even as this is Oswy's scheming, nobody is more experienced than yourself at working round, and defending Egfrid from the obstinacy of Oswy !

I am the more worried because, while I think that Ette is well able to defend herself, I think that her true calling might be to the sisterhood, and to a life of prayer. But, putting the peace of her people before her own wishes, she has agreed to this marriage. With her high principles, she wishes it to be a purely political contract, and a celibate marriage: which is where I begin to worry.

She was fortunate that this was the case with her much older Tonberg, where she was more a companion to him and as sister to his sons. But I fear that this may be a more difficult proposition when Egfrid comes to his manhood. I really do not read Oswy's intentions in all this. Is he becoming worried about the authority of Aldfrith at York? Is he trying, ahead of time, to put Egfrid in a stronger position as a successor? Or is he recognizing the impetuousness of his own early liaisons, and trying to prevent his son learning from similar misadventures? If so, it does seem to be a hazardous liaison for both parties.

Etheldreda will need all your advice and support. I do most earnestly commend her to your care my dear Eanfled, even as you are always in our prayers.

By His Grace,

Hilda

With the arrival of the finely-worked torc and bracelet, each with woven motifs of intertwining serpents, accompanied by a sword that had Aldhelm and Frishere full of admiration, Ette realized that she had no more excuse but to complete the final stage of her journey.

Yet this sojourn at Whitby had unknowingly strengthened her appreciation of her true calling, of an impressively ordered double community, of a devotion to religious observance, away from the politics and gossip of the royal households. It was so different from the small community that she had at Ely, and even more impressive than Felix's monastery at Dunwich. Here in the north, she had been introduced to the school of young girls and met Aelffled, who, like all the other pupils, called Hilda 'Mother'. But as the daughter of the Queen was certainly given greater care and attention, even as she was nominally, 'treated equally', as part of her training. Ette could not but wonder how she would have responded had she had such an upbringing, much as she loved all her own sisters and the relative freedom that they had lived at Exning and Dunwich.

Ette also had the privilege in the chapel of hearing the shepherd, Caedmon, expound the scriptures of the day. Hilda had recounted that he was a great gift to her and to the community, coming as a lay brother to help look after the sheep. He was as an innocent; seemingly happiest when talking or singing to his animals, and not at all learned in reading or writing; a seemingly natural recluse who had a private world of his own dreams. To him it was as if the fine grey rain, so frequent, was a source of amazement, while if the sun broke through he was transfixed, as if it was the first time that he had seen it. Yet, previously reticent in company, he had been gifted to translate the stories of the scriptures, told to him by the learned brothers, into spontaneous utterances of lyrical poetry. Hilda confessed that she was not sure that he fully understood his declarations, for his stare was so far away. Yet from his mouth the words poured like some reflected echoes from another place. Even so, he humbly told his Mother Abbess that he was told these words by the vision of an angel each night.

'He has the gift of tongues; even as he has the true gift of innocence. He reminds me that I must be ever humble to have such a brother in my midst. I do try to persuade him to stay with the other brothers; but I know that he sneaks out to be with his sheep; and how they know him!'

Hilda shook her head with a gentle smile. And paused.

'To know someone who is regularly so transparently granted visions is an inspiration to us all.' Again, a pause,

'I think that we all have dreams: and that half waking dreams are often confused with possible visions. So, we are more half hoping, half wondering in our uncertainty. But in Caedmon is there no confusion. I do dream. But I know that I do not have his visions.'

Yet another pause.

'I think that sometimes I did see such transport in Aidan when he celebrated mass at Lindisfarne. But to see these things are but our privileges.' She concluded.

Ette could but nod in agreement. She remembered her father telling his young daughters of the visions of Fursa, the Irish monk, when Ana and King Sigbert had visited Fursa's outpost cluster of stone huts in the Roman ruins of the fortress of Burgh on the exposed east coast of Anglia. But they were visions of prophecy: and the prophecy of destruction. So Etheldreda said nothing. For her own experience of Caedmon's uplifting inspiration was still with her.

Etheldreda stirred in her tent. She heard the bell for Lauds ringing. She had slept through the early Matins again! Thank goodness the days were getting longer! Here was the frailty of dawn pushing the dark of night away. She stretched, and quickly wrapped herself in her outer garments and a voluminous dark, woollen cloak that might prevail against the cool of the morning air and the damp that was somewhere between mist and fine rain. Having but slid her bare feet into open sandals, she felt the fresh cool of the dew with a slight shiver of delight, mixed with chill. In the damp grass, gossamer spider's webs shone with the captured dew.

Entering the long chapel, the dawn chorus of birdsong was replaced by the fabric of silence; Ette feeling almost intrusive as she slipped onto the end of one of the benches, puncturing the membrane of stillness that held the community together in the silent prayer of waiting.

Another bell rang, and three of the sisters began the opening line of the hymn.

'As light of dawn makes darkness yield
So Christ has conquered death and sin...'
In the nave, behind the screen, the brother's voices joined and the unison ran for the three verses, filling the cavernous space of the chapel. The reading of the psalms followed, with the Mother Abbess leading the sisters in the first verse; the brothers responding with alternate verses. Those lay brothers and sisters that attended sat further down the nave on opposite sides. But they were not many, for many of them were already about their work. They would make an effort to attend the shorter office of Prime.

Ette realized that she would sorely miss this rhythm to the day, now that she knew that she had extended her stay as long as possible. The court at Yeavering awaited her arrival.

The weather was threatening as her entourage left the abbey. The clouds scowled in a surly, bowling, grey; pushed by a driving wind that kept the curlews and shrikes hidden in the heather, while small plovers scuttled out of the way of the horses hooves, not daring to take flight in the brazen wind, that might, most unkindly, dash them to the stony ground. The group of riders kept their heads well down and bound their robes about them as closely as they could to counteract the billowing force of the wind. The sturdy shrubs of bristly heather had their branches pushed into the ground in rippling waves by the buffeting wind. Such was the traveller's battle with the elements for most of the first day.

But the next day, once they descended from the height of the moorland, it was the sun that reigned, and gentle spring breezes were restored. Villagers came out to view the arrival of this new Princess and her followers. Some in the hamlets attending their daily chores: some in the fields as they completed the harrowing of the soil before sowing the summer corn: others were out in the woods as they herded the pigs to feed on late acorns. All of them waving to this fine princess on her white mare with her considerable entourage. A pageant indeed!

Hilda had not attended Etheldreda's wedding. But she did eventually receive an account from Eanfled.

Dear Hilda
How time rushes by!
But so many thanks for your timely letter some months ago.

■■

We do indeed have a new presence with us. Etheldreda certainly needed little instruction from me. I might even have learnt some strategies for handling Oswy from her! But I did advise her as best I could. She does indeed grace the court, even as I do worry about the long-term liaison with my Egfrid. He seems more like a nephew to her than a spouse. It may well be a sustainable relationship to his benefit for a few years. She so obviously exceeds him in learning that he devotes himself even more enthusiastically to the challenges of the warrior, working off his frustrated energies. I do wonder if this might have been part of Oswy's design?

But Etheldreda does manage the King well too. She has some fine hides of land at Hexham from him as a wedding gift. Somebody had done some homework?

The wedding was a splendid feast at York. I think that Oswy had arranged it so that he might keep an eye on Alchfrid, even as there is always this two-sided dynamic of loyalty and competition between them; father and son; and heir. Their dialogue is forever one of hidden manoeuvers, covered by jocular bonhomie.

I was surprised and touched that Abbess Ebba came from Coldingham. It was a long journey for her.

She was good counsel for Ette and chose to give the bride away. I think that only Oswy's sister could have brought that off! Etheldreda and Ebba just seemed to gel. I think that Ebba shared all your apprehensions about the marriage and Ette's real vocation.

But the more interesting unspoken interaction was that between Wilfrid and Ette. When you saw them together they matched in height and elegance; and probably equally matched in intelligence, although I was not party to their conversation. Whereas my dear Egfrid, scarcely reaching up to her shoulder, did look rather more like a page boy than a spouse! But I fear that he will grow, in more ways than one!

I think that all our prayers are needed: and for all parties.

At least we do seem to have the blessing of peace between the kingdoms at the moment. For which we all constantly give thanks.

I do so hope that I might soon find time to visit you and Aelffled. I do wonder if she will recognize me, I am so rare a visitor; even as I am so grateful that, even as you care for her, you do persuade her to write to me. Her small tapestry is by my bedside, the more appreciated that she worked it with one of her sisters. It is a treasure.

My love and thanks, as ever,

Eanfled

■■■■■■■■■■■■■■■■■■■■■■■■■■■■■■■■■■■■■■■

A Meeting

The seasons ran into years. For a time the seven kingdoms were at peace. Some of those years were good and the corn was plentiful, as were supplicants for the monastery at Whitby. But some of the years had hard winters and very wet summers when the corn was not so plentiful. Yet Hilda's wise management saw all her growing flock through these times too.

However, there were other battles that were encountered. These miasmas seemed to come on the wind out of nowhere. The seasonal illnesses of colds and hay fever were well borne; and wound infections and toothache depended on fortitude, the blacksmith [for tooth extraction!], and the herbal remedies of the wise women. But the dread was always of the plague, casting its shadow across the land, running as a relentless cloud, blotting out the sun, visibly moving across the landscape, silencing the birdsong; filling the graves.

■■

285

Its advance was unstoppable.

It was in such a year, which included a wet summer and a poor harvest, when, in early May, the moon had fully eclipsed the sun, casting day into the shadow of night, an omen seen with foreboding by the villagers of Whitby, that the plague did indeed come upon them. Yet Oswy chose this ill-fated year to sort out for once and for all where Easter should fall in the calendar year. He was tired and vexed by his queen still being in Lent while he, with his upbringing from Iona and the teachings of Aidan, still held to the Celtic calculation of Easter.

Hilda had sighed in her monastery on the cliffs. Did Oswy really have to bring this domestic issue to a head in a year of the plague? Had they not all lived peacefully for many years, charitably recognizing their differences between the Roman and the Celtic? She wondered further, had it been Oswy and his entourage, returning north from the monastery at Peterborough, that had brought the miasma with them?

Hilda knew that Eanfled had adhered to her Roman instruction, maintained by her mother in Lyminge: and to all the details of ritual thereby laid down. Hilda also knew that the Eanfled favoured a sometimes much delayed date for Easter, as it gave her an excuse to distance herself from the attention's of Oswy for a while. She was a faithful spouse and had known no other man. Yet, while the robust, vigorous, bedding by her king had certainly produced the required children, in her imagination it was certainly lacking in the tender courtship of which she had once dreamt. She had borne it all stoically; but some respite was welcome.

Hilda was well aware of the differences and the arguments on both sides for the calculation of the dates for Easter. Had she not also been instructed by Paulinus and Romanus? Yet had she not also had the idyll of a year with the Celtic brothers on the island of Iona? It was there that she had first met the gentle Aidan, then unaware that this was to be such an important life- long friendship for her. There, the unadorned simplicity, even frugality, of the brother's lives, within a framework of discipline, had spoken more clearly to her than the adorned rituals of Paulinus, with his love of beautiful things. It was true that both schools revered the sacredness of the written word, devoting much of their time and income to it. But where Paulinus would accumulate fine robes and land, Aidan dressed very plainly and was almost too prone to giving to the poor. Hilda had learnt from both, striving for a middle way in her monastery, seeking to marry the best of each, and always welcoming either party. But her heart leant towards

287

the transparent simplicity of the brothers at Iona and Lindisfarne

However, her cousin, the King, had decreed that there should be a meeting in the autumn at which he would adjudicate. It did cross Hilda's mind to question his secular authority over these matters, but she kept this to herself. She consulted with Bishop Colman and began to implement the logistics of accommodating such a distinguished gathering. The royal party would come with their own tents, but she would have to provide for the travelling clergy.

Many accounts have been written of how the devout and solid Colman, now abbot and bishop of the Celtic community at Lindisfarne, had clearly laid out how they followed the teaching of the beloved John, who was surely the closest to the Lord? How this had been countered, not by Agilbert, the French speaking protagonist for the Roman Easter, but by the younger Wilfrid, a Paulinus prototype; tall, charismatic, and erudite; extolling the more widely accepted authority of 'Peter, the rock, who verily held the keys to heaven.'

Hilda had watched the rather bemused expression on her cousin's face as the King listened to these learned expositions on the authority of the scriptures. She wondered exactly what process was going on in his scheming brain, even as she made her own prayers. She did not fail to notice that as Wilfrid dramatically gestured,

'….and it is he who verily holds the keys to the gates of heaven.!' that Oswy's face lit up. The King had seen a simple solution, even if it reneged on all his previous Celtic upbringing. Machiavelli was yet to come, but here, in Oswy, was one of his precursors.

He raised his hand. He had heard enough of the discourse.

'Then if it is true, and agreed by all,' here an attempt to be inclusive, Hilda noted, ' that as it is St Peter, the very rock of the church, who holds the keys to Heaven, then it is him who we should follow. For it is my dearest wish that we might all attain this future meeting place.'

Hilda saw Eanfled raise her eyebrows: even as she did not raise her eyes.

Hilda had felt her own heart sink. This had not been the answer to the petition of her prayers.

In her mild indignation she had longed to ask whether it was not true that the same St Peter had denied his Lord thrice on the very eve of his crucifixion; and was it not blessed John and his mother who were at the foot of his cross in the last hour; moreover did the good Lord not entrust the care of his mother to John, not to the absent Peter? And, more to the point, if Peter did hold the keys, would not Peter surely let in anybody who loved and followed his brother, John?

But the good Mother Abbess took a deep breath; praying for peace and charity in the gathering. She remembered the goals that they all shared; the spirit of love that she had known both with the Celtic Aidan and his brothers; and with Tata and Eanswith in their Roman Kent. She saw how divisive interpreting the letter of the law could be.

'Beware ye teachers!' ran through her mind. 'How the church politic can divide rather than unite?' was as a murmured echo in her thoughts.

She was saddened, but checked these thoughts, moving to see that all the arrangements were in place for a final service.

But bishop Colman had already left with his Celtic contingent.

It was another forty-eight hours before all the company dispersed, which felt something like several days to Hilda. For there was much bidding and promising to accomplish with such an extensive gathering.

■■

'I am sorry that it had to come to this,' was Eanfled's parting brief, continuing,

'I do leave Aelffled, our precious daughter, here with you. She is a delight: and I hope that you will continue to receive me whenever I can escape?'

Hilda managed a wan smile.

'My dear Eanfled, you know that you are always welcome, and that this has not been of your doing. I am so saddened if we lose the brothers at Lindisfarne; and I fear that the plague may be seen as a visitation upon us all. God speed; may you all travel safely and stay well. I shall hope to see you again, soon,' was Hilda's final assurance and blessing.

Hilda would look back and consider it something of a miracle that her house was not cursed by the serious outbreak of the plague at the time of the meeting.

But her thoughts were also prophetic inasmuch as Colman did leave his monastery at Lindisfarne, taking brothers and books with him. First, they headed for Iona: to return to their home, where their Celtic ways were still sacrosanct. Then they would form a new community on the west coast of Ireland at Innesboffin. A last sanctuary in the west!

But even worse news was to follow.

Abbot Cedd, who had attended the meeting at Whitby, also representing the Celtic faction, had returned to his monastery deep in the nearby moors at Lastingham, only to develop the wheals of the plague, and to die transmitting them to his monks, so that several also died. This news grieved Hilda more than any other. Had she not known Cedd and his brothers Chad and Caelin, from so many years as part of the original twelve brought up by Aidan at Lindisfarne? Had she not followed their ascendency, heard favourably of them all as much-travelled bearers of the faith, about whose good works a book might well be written; such models of humility and kindness: so loved wherever they went? At least it was Cedd's gentle brother, Chad, who would now become Abbott at Lastingham.

Losing Colman and Cedd made it a dark chapter in Hilda's life.

And the Mother Abbess still had the threat of the plague to cope with at home.

The conference over at last Hilda found a space in her days to walk on her own along the cliffs. She noticed how the incessant pounding of the sea was eating into the fabric of these craggy eastern boundaries. How the striking Roman ruins of the light house had almost all crumbled and fallen into the sea. It somehow served to remind her of the temporary nature of worldly achievements; of the vanity of man. It brought some strange element of consolation, the perception of the frailty of human endeavour that had gone before: even as there was an element of admiration for the Roman's successes: their love of order.

The sea birds, herring gulls, kittiwakes, and terns, drifted and glided, idly calling to each other as she stood on the very edge of the cliffs, looking down at the thudding, pounding, waters. It was that time of year and that time of day, when the year's brood had flown, and the time was late in the afternoon; the hour of the day for play and socializing. Hilda stood, quite alone on the cliff, admiring the grace and ease with which these windborne small forms seemed to glide, soar, and tumble; and glide again: so carefree. So happily seeming to call to each other and enjoy their hour of play.

Her spirit rose toward them, momentarily unfettered; even as she felt her feet firmly planted on the ground. A deep breath of the coastal wind seemed to cleanse body and soul: reinvigorating, healing, restoring.

It was with some reluctance that she turned to retrace her steps.

293

Yet even more grief was to come. It was but two weeks later that the news came that Acha had also died of the plague as it had moved inexorably northwards.

Acha's passing caught Hilda totally by surprise. She had been so engrossed with the symposium and the death of Cedd, that she had forgotten Acha, her aunt, the King's mother; and Ebba's mother too. She must write to both of them.

What a sustaining figure Acha had been to them all, so quietly strong in her care of them when Edwin reigned, even more so when Edwin fell: her life so central to all of theirs?

For no reason that she knew, Hilda found silent tears running down her face. Perhaps it was a release of all the stress that she had borne this dreadful year? Perhaps it was a deeper, unrecognized understanding that her aunt was the last connection of a generation that had moulded and informed Hilda's younger life. Finally, there was no other wiser, older support. Did she finally recognize that now the mantle fell full square on her shoulders?

But she accepted her tears as tears of affection for somebody she had so taken for granted without realizing how much she had been given and how much it was an unspoken, deep seated, love. Hilda wished she had been able to be with her, to tell her this; even as she remembered how healing that had been for herself caring for Tata in her last illness. Healing for them both: a resolution, meet and right. Now she could only mourn and express her gratitude in prayer.

As the year drew to a close, Hilda felt that the plague had been as a war. In some ways worse than a warrior's conflict. A straightforward battle between men would take out a group of warriors, creating widows and orphans, true. But, providing pillaging did not follow, [and the Mercians had been the worst for this], widows, orphans and the serfs of the land were remarkably resilient; stoically recovering if the crops were good. But the plague did not discriminate between age, sex, or rank. It would ravage them all; even the crops might die in the fields, unharvested, and the fields remained unploughed for at least a season.

The final blow from the plague that year was that the King lost Alhfrith, his son and heir, at York. His first born to his Irish Princess. It took him down; and the whole court mourned.

But, by the onset of winter, this present devastation of the plague had died out. The fragile remainers creaked through the cold months, bitterly awaiting the sun to strengthen and lengthen, to nurse the shoots of spring, to encourage their blood to pulse more strongly. For time might slowly, slowly heal them all.

The services in the monastery at Whitby had their own poignancy in these austere times.

'Let my cry come unto Thee,' came from the very heart of their prayers:

'Out of the deep have I cried to Thee,' echoed round the chapel walls.

A Celebration and a Change

Dear Eanfled

I trust that you are safely arrived home, and that the plague has not visited you there. You are all much in our prayers.

I was mortified to learn that we lost Cedd along with so many of his brothers at Lastingham. But in some ways it struck my heart more deeply to hear that aunt Acha had died on her estate, also by the merciless plague.

I think that Oswy will have many memories that will resurface, for I know that she actively cared for all her brood.

It is not just the loss of one so dearly loved, but the memories of her that now flood our minds, that moves us to mourn her more deeply.

She is much in our prayers.

How long the list has become!

I do wish that I might make the journey to her funeral, but I judge it more important to be with my community at this time. Should you be able to attend I know that you will take our prayers with you.

Here, Aelffled, and indeed all the school, are an inspiration to us. Their innocence of death makes them appear so resilient and brings us joy in our sadness.

My love and prayers be with you,

Hilda

The Queen mused on receiving this letter from Hilda. Oswy had disappeared south on one of his outings to the Kingdom of Mercia to see that all was well, to visit his daughter and son-in-law and the foundation of the monastery at Peterborough that was some reparation for all the dreadful deeds that had gone before.

Eanfled decided that, in his absence, she would attend the funeral of her mother-in-law. It was seemly that her family should be represented. She would take Osryth, her youngest daughter with her. It might be that Ethelberga and Egfrid would attend. It would be good for her son to represent his father.

■■

There was less of the plague. It should be safe to travel.

The whole of Acha's estate turned out for the funeral, along with the families of the neighbouring estates. She had been well loved. The small wooden chapel was packed, with the windows and the door left open so that the crowd outside might hear the service.

Hilda need not have worried that she could not be there for in addition to Eanfled, with Etheldreda, Egfrid , and Osryth, they were delighted to meet Aethelwald, Acha's other remaining son. But Eanfled was most pleased that Abbess Ebba from Coldingham also had arrived with the escort of two of her lay brothers.

It was no surprise, to those that had known Acha well, that it was the monks from the nearby monastery at Melrose on the river Tweed who came to take the service. Acha had long been a supporter of their house. So, it was fitting, even as an acknowledgement of respect, that it was Eata, the present Prior, who came to lead the proceedings. Moreover, he was helped by his young, impressive deputy, who went by the name of Cuthbert. Their monastery had suffered an early visitation of the plague a year before, which had taken Boisil, who had been as a father to the young Cuthbert, but both Eata and Cuthbert, although ill, had recovered.

The service was solemn, but with a strong element of the celebration of an exemplary life, that was as an encouragement to them all: an element of rejoicing that she had deservedly gone on to a better place.

It was also inevitable that with such a gathering there was much catching up and reparation to achieve.

Aethelwald and Egfrid decided that after the funeral they might spend a few days exercising Acha's falcons, for she had been famous for her expertise with them. It also seemed that the restrained practice of falconry might be more appropriate than the rumbustiousness of hunting the boar or deer.

Although they were uncle and nephew, they were close enough in years to be of a peer group and, at this time, on the periphery of the royal household. Eanfled was pleased to see that there was a ready fraternizing between the young princes: as was Etheldreda. It did give the royal ladies time to confer.

Etheldreda was even more delighted to have the opportunity to catch up with Ebba, who had been such a support for her at her wedding amidst all the new Northumbrian court. That had been nearly five years ago; and Ebba saw the changes.

'Your prince is no longer an adolescent, Ette. He has become a young man I think?' the abbess began, when they had time for a private walk along the wooded riverbanks.

Etheldreda nodded,

'Yes, he has come of age,' a pause. 'He spends much of his time training with the thegns; and I think Oswy is well pleased with him.' Here she pursed her lips, but continued,

'I think that I do see that my original optimism of a purely political marriage was too idealistic: perhaps, unrealistic. I was so fortunate with Tonberg. He did, at his age, really only wish for a companion. His sons were as my brothers; and I think that I loved them as such.' They walked a little further and Ebba held her peace.

'I pray and I live from day to day,' Etheldreda continued. 'I am fortunate that the King gave me the lands at Hexham. I have my own house there and am so fortunate to have brought Astral with me. Our time there, copying and making new writings, are my happiest times. But it is not what is expected of a Princess of the Court.'

They turned to wander back via another pathway, Ette leading and pushing some of the offending brambles out of the way. They reached a small clearing where the sun came through. A fallen trunk seemed like a natural seat. Ebba signalled that perhaps they might sit a while; she still holding her peace.

'Eanfled is very kind,' Etheldreda continued. 'She manages to hold neutral ground, which is most considerate, as Egfrid is her son; and I think most mothers look to enjoy grandchildren. She does have enough of those already, but I don't think that stops the expectation.' Here a wry smile from the Princess, which was echoed by the Abbess.

Etheldreda continued, plucking at a sprouting, fragile, twig that was seemingly trying to revive the fallen tree on which they were sitting.

'I think that he has his pleasures elsewhere from time to time: on which I muse. It was not a problem that I had with dear Tonberg. I think that I recognize it as inevitable here. I know not how I shall resolve it as days turn into years.'

Here Etheldreda finally turned to look at the Abbess directly, as if hoping for some answer, or at least some consolation: or perhaps not.

Ebba nodded.

'It is not unexpected, Ette. We all pray that you may be guided. But the final decision can only be made between you and Egfrid.' The Abbess continued,

'You do know that in the event of any crisis you will always be most welcome at Coldingham. The King is my brother, your Prince my nephew. I think that they both will respect my small Kingdom.' Ebba raised her eyebrows and placed a cool hand on Ette's hands, which were still twisting the twig.

Etheldreda felt calmed, and let the twig go, brushing it aside.

As they proceeded to wander back Etheldreda volunteered,

'I do value the company and advice of Wilfrid. But he is not here?'

A smile crossed Ebba's face as she stared at her sandaled feet.

'No, he is not here.' She paused. ' He is tall and charismatic,' she offered, answering a hidden component of the Princess's comments, 'and it was Eanfled who found him, and nurtured him, even encouraging him to stay with Aidan at Lindisfarne for a while; which he did with good grace; even also with Hilda. But he always aspired for greater things: had the abilities and intelligence to achieve them: and his father's wealth; rather to his stepmother's displeasure. But that is another story.'

The Abbess stopped to shake out a small stone that had caught in her sandal. This achieved, she continued.

303

'I understand that he is presently in France; and has been gone some time. I understand that he seeks to be initiated to the rank of bishop by three properly consecrated bishops. We of the Celtic disposition seemingly do not qualify. You will have gathered that he is a stickler for the law, and doubtless have heard how he swung the argument at Hilda's meeting.' She paused.

'You do well to have him as an adversary. He seems to have persuaded my brother with his arguments and is much in favour at court I gather, having always had the support of the Queen.' Another pause.

'Although, in Wilfrid's absence, I think that Eanfled is already cultivating the young Cuthbert. She definitely has a good eye.'

Etheldreda could not but think that the eye of the abbess seemed to miss very little. But she held her peace.

'Do I hear that Eata might move to Lindisfarne now that Colman and most of his monks have left?' Etheldreda tried, thinking it time to move away from the topic of Wilfrid.

'I had heard the same. It would not surprise me if these matters were being discussed at this very time and in this very place. I might even go as far as saying that it would not surprise me were Cuthbert to replace Eata as Prior at Melrose.'

Eyebrows were raised and knowing smiles exchanged.

So did the Abbess prophesy: and so it came about.

Aethelwald and Egfrid returned with their two falcons, and with a catch of three leverets and two rabbits.

'Acha had trained her falcons well,' they acknowledged.

The company could but agree; and that indeed it was the celebration of a good life in its many dimensions.

The congregation eventually dispersed, wiser for having met, enriched for having celebrated. There was much debate as to where Acha should be finally buried.

The people of her estate sought to keep her near her chapel by the river. The monks thought that perhaps she should be taken to their abbey at Melrose. But Eanfled, after consulting with Ebba, inclined towards the coffin travelling back to lie with her brother Edwin at Whitby. They agreed that for the time being she might remain in the monastery in Melrose, to which her followers might make pilgrimage,

305

Oswy, returning to his kingdom from his southern visits, was pleased that his wife had represented him at his mother's funeral, and interested to hear those items of information that she chose to pass on to him, including her coffin translating to Melrose.

The king was changing as he aged. He was not so restless, still suspicious, but not quite so devious, or so ruthless. Recognised as Bretwalda of the seven Kingdoms he was more confident of his diplomatic manoeuvres. The shadow of his older brother had almost faded. Oswy had not ever expected to exceed him in his achievements. But here he was. The highest in the land.

However, the shadow of some of the things that he had done on the way to achieving his present position did still hang over him, did haunt his versatile memory. He had created a monastery at Gilling in wergeld for the calculated murder of Oswin. But this monastery, under Trumhere, served as much to remind him of his crime rather than to absolve him.

Wilfrid, who was sympathetic to this hidden guilt, began to be a bigger influence in his life, having been the definitively persuasive advocate at the meeting at Whitby. Oswy knew that the outcome had not pleased Hilda, even though she had accepted the decision: yet shown her opinion by continuing her traditional rituals at Whitby.

But Wilfrid saw a bigger canvass. He, and Biscop at Wearmouth, were of a mindset. Both, wealthy and accomplished, had travelled to Rome, taking their time to journey and acquire many delightful objects in the form of books and vestments; admiring and making contacts with the masons and glass makers of the fine churches that had been built in France and Italy. The fruits of these explorations now were to be seen in Biscop's monastery at Wearmouth. What had been Hilda's firs modest house was presently being rebuilt with stone and fine glass, and with the makings of an impressive library. While Wilfrid had similar ambitions at both York and Ripon. Moreover, at York, Wilfrid had been much encouraged by Alchfrid, the king's son and heir; that is until the plague had taken him.

So, the building at York remained half finished. Wilfrid was still away seeking, indulging in, his consecration as a bishop, extending his travels for more than three years. But Oswy, awaiting his return, mourning the loss of his son and heir, was also missing Wilfrid's advice.

However, Wilfrid's advice was not missed by his younger son, Egfrid, now promoted into the position of son and heir, with his princess

Etheldreda now a potential Queen for the second time. Wilfrid had consistently been a supporter of Etheldreda's vows of chastity within her marriage: these increasingly irksome to the young Prince, a would be King who needed heirs.

The clouds of a storm were brewing; and the fickle wind could easily chop and change.

The new archbishop, Theodore, at Canterbury, hearing that Wilfrid was finally returning from France, having been both magnificently consecrated as a bishop, and even temporarily imprisoned by a feisty princess, anticipated that there might be more problems in the north on his return.

In this he was right. For in Wilfrid's absence the diocese of York had been filled by the gentle Chad, who saw his calling to help the poor as more important than completion of the building of the cathedral that Wilfrid had begun.

Of course, on his return Wilfrid now demanded to be reinstated as bishop at York. Theodore, a benevolent and astute patrician of the English church, thought it best to visit Chad in person, for he had approved his appointment at York. He was delighted and surprised when Chad was graciously pleased to be relieved from his post and pleaded to retire to his brother's monastery at

Lastingham on the remote moors of Deira. Moved by his gentle charity, Theodore, agreed to Chad's wishes; but after a little reflection, and hearing all the good accounts from his congregation, appointed him bishop of a new See at Lichfield.

Wilfrid was reinstated as bishop at York.

Sometime later, Theodore chose to reduce the size of the diocese.

The chess board was reconfigured.

However Oswy was pleased to have Wilfrid back, and the King, having seen the fine buildings that were being made at Peterborough and at Wearmouth, was pleased to support Wilfrid's progress in completing the cathedral at York with masonry and fine glass. Moreover, the king was also beguiled by Wilfrid's accounts of his visits to Rome, as was his Queen. Now that his kingdom was at peace, it occurred to Oswy that he might make a visit to Rome himself. Who better to organize it than Wilfrid?

But it was not to be.

For Oswy began to waste. Through the long drab winter his weight fell even as the leaves of autumn had been shed, matched by a loss of energy and drive; exacerbated by an incessant thirst.

Some of his medical advisors subjected him to bleeding by leeches, which only seemed to make him worse; distinctly weaker. Others plied him with

309

tinctures of hemlock, or verbena. But to no avail. He became a frail shadow of his former self. In the month of February, when all the world is at its lowest ebb, he knew that he had only one thing to do. He formally nominated Egfrid as his successor; this least of his sons, whom he had bartered to the Mercians, who he had challenged with this uneven marriage, was now turning into a possible Bretwalda?

The Queen was constantly tending her King. Urgent letters were sent to his sister at Coldingham and to Hilda at Whitby, to Trumhere at Gilling, so that the welfare of the King might be at the forefront of their prayers and petitions.

But he died at Bamborough in this coldest of months; only dreaming of Rome.

Wilfrid came to conduct the funeral with great ceremony, as befitted the Bretwalda of the seven kingdoms. But the bishop recognized that he would not find such favour with the new king.

Eanfled was in mourning. It had not been an easy marriage, but now that he had gone, it was the good things and her children that she remembered.

It was indeed a new chapter.

Eanfled felt bound to stay to see her son accepted by the council of the Witan as their new leader, and for the formal enthronement. The news had travelled quickly to the other kingdoms, so

Egfrid followed his dying father's advice and, after his enthronement, set off almost immediately with a considerable group of his thegns to establish his position as Bretwalda of the southern kingdoms.

His Queen retired to her household at Hexham to await his return.

Eanfeld was left to run the household at Bamborough, feeling somewhat exhausted after the protracted worry of nursing Oswy, followed by the responsibility of organising her husband's funeral: and the obligatory attendance at the enthronement.

The summer came and passed into autumn.

On a cool autumnal day Eanfled found time to stroll alone on the wide beaches of Bamborough from which, as she turned to head northwards, she could see the island of Lindisfarne, sitting serenely on a glittering sea that was a mixture of textured blues with sparkles of silver, coming and going like the flight of mayflies on a summer's evening: a cloudless, azure sky. She knew that Eata and his community of monks were there. She felt an overriding calm welling up, pushing out her anxieties, gently restoring a surge of energy.

The next day a letter was despatched.

311

Dear Hilda

I feel that I have turned a corner.

You must know the trials and tribulations that I have gone through these last months. I have been quite exhausted.

But my eyes, quite literally, turned to Lindisfarne yesterday when I managed some time on my own. It did seem like an inspiration. Today it is translating into this letter to you asking if I might come to stay with you?

I think that my time at court is done. I feel that I do at least deserve an escape and some solace.

There are several things that trouble me, but I will not solve them here.

Egfrid has taken Osfryth, my youngest, with him to Mercia to marry into their court. So, it is only my dearest Aelffled that I have left; she so safely with you at Whitby. I can think of no better company than the two of you with the consolation of your peaceful way of life. I wonder if you might accept me as a guest novice? You cannot know how the prospect gives me the delight of shedding my responsibilities here of running the court. Even how it seems to echo my mother's life at Lyminge.

One of my worries is that we have a new princess from Kent in our northern court, [how often this seems to have happened!]. She is

312

Eormenburga, quite capable of taking over the court: young and vivacious: also ambitious.

I fear for Etheldreda, who has simply retired to her estate at Hexham while the king is away. But these matters I might discuss further with you shortly.

I think that few marriages are perfect, but I do miss Oswy. My fears only grow for Egfrid and Etheldreda and the scheming of Eormemburga.

I so look forward to hearing from you: and have started preparing myself.

All my hope and my love

Eanfled

So it was. The widowed queen made her journey south, with but two of her servants, within the week. Each day of the journey Eanfled's spirits rose. Never before had she so enjoyed the autumn colours: the dark greens of the conifers setting off the haloed yellows of the beeches with their silver trunks. How moving from a wood of conifers to a wood of beeches was as if moving between two worlds; from one of enclosed shade to one of opening light where the gentle autumn sun cast its spell; as if emerging from a tunnel into light.

313

Then the treeless, purple of the open moorland stretched before them, busy with bees collecting their autumn honey from the heather, and the air carrying the freshness of sea breezes from the coast. Even the laconic call of the curlew, echoing across the landscape, seemed to suit their mood.

They finally descended on narrow paths, through waist-high bracken, to Sleights; thence following the river Esk, lined with its weeping willows, now elegant with this year's crop of shoots; then downwards towards the hamlet of Whitby, welcoming the coolness of the river walk, before climbing up to the nestling monastery: rejoicing at seeing the harvest being made; of the steady rhythms of the men scything, of the following of women and children, binding and stooking the corn.

.Eanfled found herself reciting,
'I am filled with love when He listens
To the sound of my prayer:
when He bends down to hear me
as I call…..'

As they arrived at the monastery entrance, Joseph, the gate keeper, rang the bell three times, as he had been instructed. Hilda and Aenfledda, hearing the three tones, downed their pen and ink, exchanged smiles of anticipation, and hastened to meet this special homecoming.

Resolutions.

It was a whole season of rejoicing.
The festival of St Michael and All Angels fell but three days after their arrival.

Eanfled and her accompanying travellers soon had discarded their travelling outfits and assumed the robes of the monastery: plain tunics, their hair cropped and heads covered in linen caps. They were instantly familiar with their rooms, the dormitory, the chapel, and the refectory. But by this time Hilda had a community that was larger than the original fishing hamlet down by the mouth of the river. The ten hides that Oswy had given Hilda had doubled, mainly from widows joining the community, so that there was a considerable estate to manage outside the confines of the monastery. A large ditch marked the boundary of the enclosure itself, but immediately outside this were the houses for the lay brothers and sisters, who also ran the smithy, the glass foundry, the timber yard, and the mason's yard. While hardly a stone's throw away the farming began with the dairy, and the stables.

For some reason they also included the wood cutters and the osiers. The weaving, the scriptorium, and the main kitchen were found inside the compound since many of the sisters ran these as part of their duties between the services.

But the feast of St Michael and All Angels made it a holiday for all, so that the kitchens were the busiest places. Since the feast day also fell on a Friday in this year, the village fishermen had been petitioned in advance, so that paniers of herrings, crab and lobster came up on the backs of patient doe-eyed donkeys, brought up for the celebrations in and outside the monastery. As many of the lay brothers and sisters that could be accommodated shared the refectory. Eanfled was delighted to be told that it was no longer her duty to see that the guests had their beakers filled with wine and beer; that fell to the Mother Abbess: and was in moderation. The queen felt that she had never quite so enjoyed a celebration of St Michael and All Angels. It was the first of many, but one that she would always treasure.

Towards the end of the day there was time for Eanfled and Hilda to relax together in private.

'How many years since we were in mother's palace at Lyminge. I, itching to be in charge, and you forever your wise self,' began Eanfled. 'It

317

seems so many, many years ago. And how headstrong I was then.'

'I think that you would not have done so well had you not had considerable strength in that head of yours,' and both smiled at how Hilda had turned the phrase, and how it seemed to reflect and re-establish their long standing roles, in the way that some deep friendships are easily and instantly restored outside the distances of time, as if conversation was simply resumed.

'But now I am more than pleased to acquiesce and recognize the Mother of this house. I shall appreciate shedding the responsibilities of decision making more than you can know.'

Hilda nodded in acknowledgement.

'It is a delight, long awaited, to have you here. But everybody brings their own talents, and I shall always value your advice as ever. You will meet Elle who is the sister in charge of the weaving. I think you will like her and I remember your skills of old?'

'It sounds more than I deserve: I shall be as a bee in a field of flowering clover.'

The Mother Abbess paused.

'The greater adjustment might be with Aelffled. She has now come of age. She even does remind me of your good self at Lyminge. I feel her wings flapping on the edge of the nest! Not that I

318

think she might fly away. But I do encourage her to fly around the estate. I increasingly look to delegate things to her and am as rewarded as I am relieved. I think only you can know how much your gift has meant to me over these years. But you are her mother too; and I wonder if motherhood ever stops?'

'There is motherhood and motherhood, Hilda. It is one thing of which I have considerable experience; with quite diverse ones in my brood.'

Here Eanfled paused, with an easy silence following between the two of them, sitting outside in a small courtyard which caught the late September sun. There was the tinge of early autumn yellows in some of the small leaves of the few thorn trees that struggled in the shelter of the headland winds. Eanfled picked up the conversation again.

'I hope you will not have to worry on that score. Aelffled is in many ways the most precious of my children, if I am allowed to have favourites; which I think every mother does, however hard she tries. I still think that finding her a home here was one of the best things that I did; even as much as it was a particular circumstance where I could effectively lean on Oswy. She has been no worry and but a joy: even as I am not surprised.' Here they both smiled without exchanging glances.

The queen continued.

'I think, as most mothers do, that my present anxieties lie mostly with my youngest, dear Osthryth, who Egfrid has married into the Mercian household. We have such a chequered history there that I can but worry. Alhflaed, my eldest stepdaughter was singularly spirited. I think that she never quite accepted me as her stepmother. But she was feisty and a match for Peada. Dear Osthryth is of a gentler mold: even if there is a hidden determination. And so far away in Mercia that I can do little but worry and pray!'

Another silence followed. Hilda was waiting for the queen to find the right space. At last she began.

'We have not mentioned Egfrid and his Queen. But I know that they are in your prayers. I think that on this feast day we might defer this story, which I fear I cannot influence, even as it is another reason why it is good for me to be here under the care of yourself and my dear daughter. I think the hour for vespers approaches.'

Hilda nodded in acquiescence to all her comments.

Now there would be many more days of being together again.

320

The autumn turned to winter and there was less business on the estate. They all hunkered down. The days were shorter and colder.

The Abbess and the Queen had their conversation about the state of the Northumbrian court, with Eanfled confirming it as part of her reason to seek an escape to the tranquility of the monastery hiding in the dip behind the cliffs.

The marriage of Egfrid and Etheldreda had been a political challenge from the very beginning, with little doubt that the Anglian princess had held the upper hand initially. But ten years later the pendulum had swung; and the advent of the Princess from Kent pushed it to swing further. Eanfled had never been quite sure who had invited Eormenburga. But it had certainly divided the household, and pushed the marriage into an unstable, fluctuating dynamic.

There was no pretence that Egfrid enjoyed the pleasures of his new visitor, although they managed not to be too public. Etheldreda could but muster a restrained, dignified, silence; much as Eormenburga tried to goad her. But Etheldreda's years at the Anglian court had versed her well in parrying and deflecting the sharp thrusts: even retreating, when deemed necessary, to the tranquillity of her estate at Hexham; where she did make it quite clear that Eormenburga was not

321

welcome: but , of course, the King might visit as he wished.

Such exits would leave Eormenburga fuming.

But the very heart of the new relationship between Egfrid and Eormenburga seemed to thrive on rows and reconciliations.

It had been this endless occurrence of confrontations in public that had finally persuaded Eanfled to seek to retire to Whitby.

'Oswy and I did have our differences. But they were not sorted out in public. They were privately considered; and I always had the good counsel of Romanus; and even the young Wilfrid when he was with us.' Eanfled picked at a thread, then deftly sewed it into the weave of the fabric. She continued,

'Eormenburga never seems to think of counsel. She speaks immediately from her head, without much processing; and, inevitably, gets back the same from Egfrid. It is most unseemly.'

She picked at another thread in the tapestry.

'I did initially try to moderate. But came to respect Etheldreda's strategy of avoiding the battle. 'An eye for an eye, and a tooth for a tooth' was very much Eormenburga's game. I think that she would be quite ruthless on the battlefield: and perhaps that is what Egfrid likes in her!'

Eanfled shook her head. Hilda held her peace. They continued with their needlework for a while. Then the Mother Abbess ventured,

'We can only commend them all in our prayers,' and continued,

'I think that it would be useful for you to write to Ebba at Coldingham with your appreciation of the situation. I think that she should be made aware of how the wind is blowing. She is both the King's aunt and has always been a hands- on supporter of Etheldreda. I will always offer Ette what support I can. But I think that dear Ebba can be even more forthright than I!' Here Hilda had smiled wryly, drawing the same from the queen.

The letter was duly written and delivered: and Abbess Ebba did make preparations.

The coldness of winter brought snow and ice. But the monastery was well prepared. The wood and peat, carefully stored in the summer months, crackled and sparkled in many hearths on the dark evenings, while the monks and nuns were allowed heated stones in clay holders, or wrapped in linen, to fend off the cold of the dormitories. Some days had the brilliance of the low sun dazzling as it was reflected from the carpets of drifted snow, glistening where it had collected on the curved branches of the trees. The few overwintered stock

323

were sometimes let out of their thorn enclosures to see what they could forage, but carefully herded back as the sun set, for the wolves could be heard howling in the nearby woods.

But as the thaw came and the brave shoots of winter barley were seen again, the monastery did have a visit from the royal household.

The King's mistress had overstepped the mark. She had been banished from the court; even as she declared that it was impossible to stay in such an unwelcome place. So, in a moment of reparation Egfrid thought it appropriate to take his lawful wife to Whitby to visit his mother and the sister, of whom he had seen so little. His visit made him realise that he had missed the quiet, considered, counsel of his mother: so much drowned out by his confrontational mistress. He was even more impressed by his sister. The initial thought of, 'How could she be so wasted in this place?', was reinforced by an appreciation of how smoothly the household functioned, and she an integral part, 'even as one of my chief thegns', he thought. It did not stop him thinking that she might have been more useful to him married to a Mercian Prince. But the triumvirate of the Mother Abbess, his mother, and his sister, by their very glances directed that he kept such thoughts to himself.

He decided that he would explore the estates: giving Etheldreda time to confer with the Mother Abbess.

'It is a relief not to have Eormemburga around. I think that she has but retired to her sister in the west, hoping and scheming to return. The court is more civilized and easier to run without her. None of my day to day decisions are any longer contradicted or sabotaged. But I can see that it still leaves Egfrid restless. My energies seem dissipated in placating him inasmuch as I can.'

Etheldreda sighed, gazed wistfully out of the window, but continued.

'I think that the Witan enjoyed Eormenburga's company in the longhall. She thrived on the male banter, giving as good as she got. It was a more rumbustious occasion when she carried the flagon round the hall, topping up their drinks.

When I am at a distance, alone at Hexham, I feel that she is more suited, both by age and disposition to take on the role tending to Egfrid; and to provide him with heirs.

I do feel that the seven kingdoms now seem to be at ease: that my heart is still with my people in East Anglia: where I dream that I might have a house such as this, but in the fens where my lands still lie, amongst all my friends, cared for by Ovin.'

325

Etheldreda paused.

'Not that I have not had so much constant kindness from Eanfled, while you and Ebbe have been an inspiration: and Romanus and Wilfrid a consolation.'

Hilda nodded and they sat together silently for a while.

'You have always been in our prayers, Ette. You chose a difficult path for reasons which were laudable. Times do change and have changed. Marriage is a sacrament. I do not approve of the way Eormemburga and Egfrid behave: but that is as another matter.' She paused.

'A true vocation may arise variously. I have seen so many. Eanfled and Aelffled might illustrate the beginning and the end of such occasions. The one early, the other late,' she smiled.

She rested a while.

'I would speak on your behalf with Egfrid if I thought it would achieve much. I think that it will not. Yet I might be able to prepare the ground,' she mused and continued,

'Wilfrid is probably your best advocate. He is not my favourite bishop. But he is an intelligent and zealous brother of the church. It does go with a self confidence that could be read as arrogance. He comprehends enough to work at humility; but modesty is not his natural metier. He definitely puts righteousness above a little humility, and much energy into his righteousness', she paused, 'whereas the humility of Aidan brought him his unquestioned righteousness.'

Here Hilda broke off, staring out of the open porch, wishing that she had the wisdom of Aidan to consult at this time. How she missed him.

Then she added,

'I think that Egfrid might expect to receive the news of your vows from Wilfrid. You could not have a more fearless advocate; even as I think you genuinely have his sympathy.'

Here the meeting ended, each with their own thoughts.

Egfrid returned from his inspection of the estates, impressed by the order of things, but unaware of the conversation that had taken place.

Eanfled had entered the gentlest phase of her life. She was free to celebrate and be thankful for every day: to have no greater worry than how good this year's crop of flax might be; how well the shorn wool would wash before the spinning began; how well would the dyes take to the wool? How many sisters could she train in spinning? Such quandaries before they could think of setting up the looms and beginning the weaving!

■■

She enjoyed the freedom of going outside the enclosure on her own, unhindered by courtiers or servants, always knowing that she could quietly return to the safety of the enclosure. Crossing the ditch assumed a psychological frisson; freedom going out; security on returning. And the delights of the company of her daughter and Hilda were a constant reassurance.

But it was not so tranquil for Etheldreda. It was only a few months later that the abbey heard that, while Egfrid was away visiting his northern kingdoms, Wilfrid had heard Ette take her religious vows at Hexham along with her companions, Astral and Sewara. On his return the King had been outraged. After the show down, Wilfrid had escorted the three novices to the abbey at Coldingham under Abbess Ebba's protection, while the King stormed off to his court at Bamborough.

Within a fortnight Eormemburga was reinstated back at the court, restored from exile with her sister at Carlisle.

By the autumn the harvest festival was celebrated by the church, yet was synonymous with the Baer fest, the bloody slaughter of the livestock that would not overwinter. It was a time of much consumption, both meat and ale. It was a time when the King, goaded by Eormemburga, rode north to finally assert the rights of marriage from his Queen. But the beacons that Abbess Ebba had prepared along the coast transmitted the news of his intentions faster than his horses could travel. So Etheldreda, along with Sewara and Sewenna, aided by Ashar, had escaped from the headland abbey in a flimsy coracle: battered by the heaving waves and carried out by the wind and the tide into a cloaking sea mist. The King, sobered by his long ride, seeing them fragile in the tumultuous seas, and well away from the goading of Eormemburga, finally realized that he had lost his Queen: his first love. He held his men back from the pursuit.

At Whitby they had heard of the vows taken. They had also been told of the beacons burning on the headlands and feared the worst.

Their prayers and thoughts were constant for the safety of Etheldreda and her sisters.

It was scarcely a week later that an unknown boat sailed into Whitby bay and beached itself, with two men leaping into the shallow water to drag the fishing boat onto the sandy beach. They were helped by the small group of fishermen who had spotted the approaching sail and come down to the shore, half armed, as it was not one of their boats.

329

But the sight of women aboard had assured them that all was safe, it was not pirates; so that their mode had changed to one of welcoming hospitality for the travellers; the more so when they recognized the monastic garb of the three sisters, with one so tall and graceful.

Word was quickly sent up to the abbey.

Hilda was ill in bed with a fever that seemed to have established itself, recurrently waxing and waning as it pleased. But which she bore with characteristic fortitude. Aelffled, quietly deputizing and supporting Hilda, looked to Eanfled with hope in her glance.

'I shall go down, mother. Will you arrange to send three ponies down. If it is as I think they will be exhausted.'

She called on Aldwin to accompany her and they made a nimble-footed descent down to the hamlet. Aelffled was full of hope that it might be Etheldreda and her companions. Arriving at the riverside, she saw the three women in their cloaks sitting on a bench, nursing warm cups of broth. They rose to greet her, and her elation and enthusiasm was tempered by the appearance of Ette. Still tall and slender, but to the point of gaunt, Aelffled could see on her face the stresses and strains that the last few weeks had demanded. She

330

looked exhausted. Aelffled moved to hold her hands, gently.

'My dear Ette, it is so good to see you: that you are safely arrived. Do please finish your broth. We have some ponies coming down to take you up to the abbey; there is no rush. You have been in our prayers. We scarcely dared to prepare rooms, but our small hospital will be at your disposal.'

'You can only begin to imagine how glad I am to be safe on land again, and in this haven. Ebba said that I might be safe here for a while.' Etheldreda turned to introduce the two sisters.

'Sewara and Sewenna have saved my life seven times over. I would have been lost at sea several times had they not plied their skills as if it was their natural calling.'

The sisters smiled.

'We are a fisherman's daughters. Our father taught us well. And it is my uncle and cousin who brought us safely here. Your villagers have welcomed us as well as we would do at home,' Sewenna offered.

Etheldreda added,

'I can vouch that is some compliment. For their villagers did rescue us all from a memorable night at sea that I shall never forget: and did restore us to our right minds with their hospitality.' Etheldreda drew another breath, almost a sigh. 'But

Sewenna also was my mainstay in the scriptorium at Hexham for several years. I did not know that she had these other talents.'

Aelffled nodded, with a smile.

'You shall tell us all. I see that you will all bring considerable skills to our abbey even as you are most welcome. I know that Hilda awaits you and welcomes you.' Aelffled paused.

'I think I see the ponies arriving. When you are ready we will make the last stage of your journey, where you will all be very welcome.'

So it was that the three travellers were absorbed into the life of the abbey. A new stability restored to the visitor's lives.

The winter came and Ette stayed. At last she felt secure; even as her thoughts and dreams repeatedly had images of the open skies of the fenlands. Yet she absorbed much, as she had at Coldingham, of the way in which a double monastery was organized.

While the court at Bamborough realigned itself, with Eormemburga now back in favour, even as Queen apparent. It was also true that the church politic had not stood still. The willfullness of Wilfrid had ranged further than his patronage of Etheldreda.

■■

Archbishop Theodore had arranged a synod of bishops with a scarcely disguised agenda of moderating the activities of this northern bishop. Eormemburga and Egfrid had some input into the reasoning. They sought to curtail the power of Wilfrid. Egfrid had finally accepted Etheldreda's vocation, but greatly resented Wilfrid's interference, his feelings fuelled by Eormemburga's own antagonism to the bishop as well as to Etheldreda.

It was notable that while the majority of the other bishops attended the synod at Hertford in person, Wilfrid chose only to send his representative. The outcome of the synod was to restrict bishops to their diocese and not to interfere with the running of monasteries. Moreover, the northern diocese, currently under Wilfrid's jurisdiction, was to be divided into four parts, with Bosa, educated at Whitby, to be the new bishop of York. Almost inevitably Wilfrid reacted by disappearing on another journey to Rome with a papal submission in his right hand.

It was a hard winter on the headlands. The thorn trees bowed, grimly and stiffly, with their bare branches all beaten to the west by the eastern winds, as if they had flexed in the wind and then been frozen in their form, forever bent. There were the bright days of sparkling diamonds of frost on the carpets of glistening snow. There were even the occasional magic green lights of the aurora, dancing in the night sky as if it were an overspill of the heavenly host, yet eerily silent; making the awed, earthbound, viewers feel so small. But the earth was cold and shut down. There was no grazing for the stock, nor any hunting with the hounds; only the craft of the traps and snares managed to keep the pots boiling with fresh meat, seasoned with the dried herbs of the summer months.

It was a time for telling tales, for weaving and spinning in the short daylight hours, then, as the sunlight disappeared, by the soft light of the tallow. Cold fingers in the scriptorium; raw knuckles and chilblains as the vellum was stretched and scraped.

Spring did come. The tough thorn trees pushed tight buds to a bursting lively green. The stock men no longer had to break the ice and carry water to their penned stock. The stocky ewes began to lamb and soon they would all be out in the fields, leaping and cavorting for the simple reason that they could and that it was exhilarating.

Etheldreda knew that it was time for her to return to her fenlands. Hilda nodded and smiled gently.

■■

'It does seem meet and right Ette. You have done more than your duty for your people in East Anglia and you have brought much to my people. I know that Ebba and I have always been grateful to you for your time with Egfrid. It was a courageous journey. You have earned your freedom and I thank you for spending some of your new vocation here with us'. A pause followed.

'I know that both Eanfled, and now Aelffled, for she has come of age, are both grateful for your time with Egfrid,' here the Mother Abbess paused again, but then continued,

'I hope you will let me know how you reflect on it; and see how you managed him from adolescence to manhood when you are at a distance. Oswy was more fortunate in his choice of you as his son's bride than I think he could have known.

I think that your abbey in the fens will be well received, both by your sisters and by my nephew Aldwulf, who I think is now your king? How we have all become one family!

You will always be in our prayers.

Once you are settled please do let us know what we can send to help your new foundation. My blessing goes with you Ette.'

Here Etheldreda rose to kneel by her bed to receive a blessing. For Hilda was not well again and Etheldreda could see that the conversation had

335

exhausted her, even as Etheldreda would remember every word: even as they would be the last that she shared with Hilda.

It was Aelffled, who had first welcomed her to the abbey, who now saw that Etheldreda was suitably provided for her southwards journey. She and Eanfled did indeed thank her for her perseverance with their brother and son, the King. Eanfled knew all too well how much this had cost the East Anglian Princess.

The group travelled with four cob ponies and a mule to carry the baggage. Sewara and Sewenna had decided that they were in service to their Queen, while Aelred was a trusted lay brother from the abbey who knew the lie of the land as well as being well versed in managing ponies. He had two hounds with him who knew how to hunt and scrounge, whose noses and ears were also more perceptive than their master's when travelling over new ground.

'God Speed!' was chorused from the abbey gates as the party began its southwards journey: and even Hilda's fever subsided for a while. Yet her thoughts ran southwards with Ette. Hilda remembering her own visits to East Anglia. Her first memories being when she had attended her sister's marriage to the young prince Aethelric. How the sun had seemed to shine all that summer!

Then there was that crossroad in her life when her years at Lyminge had come to an end with the death of Tata, and Eanfled already married to Oswy here in Deira. It had been that, as always, she had looked to Hereswid, then widowed, but still in East Anglia with young Adwulf. How different life might have been if they had both retired to Chelles in France, joining the daughters of Ana and Eredith? How different if dear Aidan had not sent Utta to call her back to her homeland. Now the young Adwulf was king; with good reports of his kingship. How proud Hereswid would have been.

  How strange our journeys, Hilda mused; and dozed: even as dozing was its own blessing in those days of her illness.

Home to rest

How easily the rhythm of the seasons filled life when the world was at peace; neither plagued by illness nor the consequences of the striving ambitions of warrior- kings. How the serious matters became celebrating and worrying about the crops, the thriving of the stock, the harvesting of the wild fruits of summer, the departing and arrival of the migrating birds, which so boosted their cooking pots and provided a year's stock of quills for the scribes.

But peace also gave space to plan for buildings; to spin, to weave new tapestries and clothes; to build and throw new pots; to make new wooden buckets and barrels, even new lyres and tambourines. The smiths would beat out more caldrons than weapons, while the more refined furnaces might produce works of silver and gold for jewelry or for the rims of leather cups. Even where, in the latest addition to the furnaces, glass was made into beakers and bowls, nothing was wasted; for even the spared droplets were made into necklaces or brooches.

■■

The summer meadows would run full of the white stars of ox eye daisies in great swathes among the feather seeding grasses, punctuated with the bright blues of cornflowers, scattered with lilac and white scabious heads, forever busy with bees. While bright red poppies helped to pepper the shimmering green of the pastures with splashes of scarlet. Butterflies of various hues and sizes fluttered; paused with open wings to maximise the heat the summer sun so generously bestowed, then sought yet another source of nectar or a safe place to neatly lay their rows of tiny white eggs.

All was well upon the land.
But Hilda was thinking.
Her illness now confined her to bed for days, which had the unexpected outcome of giving her time apart: to reassess. She mused that it was almost as if she had become a victim of the abbey's success. It was now so large that she scarcely knew some of the supplicants. She had no problem delegating and had the joy of Aelffled and Eanfled to readily take on that role. But it gave her time to look back at the smaller, tightly knit, communities that she previously had formed or taken over, at Wearmouth and at Hartlepool; where she had known everybody in her household. She was also

339

aware that perhaps, like Heiu, her own health would not allow her to continue as she always had done. She could see that the Queen and her daughter would succeed her; but she also felt that Frigyth of Hartlepool, who had been such a pillar in her life, should be recognized.

The Mother Abbess decided that she would discuss it with Eanfled.

'I cannot think of you not being with us: of you not being here for me to discuss my woes and wherefores, Hilda. You have been such a mainstay in my life; as an older sister, always such wise advice, even if I did not always heed it.'

This gently said by Eanfled. Hilda had smiled.

'You gild the lily somewhat, Eanfled. But I thank you. It seems some kind of resolution in this journey that we have shared for so long, that we might be reunited here as a family once again. But I fear that this place has become too large?

In some ways I do rejoice and am thankful. Yet I am reminded of other days, of simpler houses: of Aidan's house on Lindisfarne with his twelve young monks: of the brothers on Iona: of dear Eanswith with her small house of children at Folkestone. Indeed, of our Lord with his twelve disciples. I wonder if it is not time to make a smaller house?'

Eanfled nodded.

'You do well to remind me of Eanswith. It does take me back to distant times: and of mother and her small house at Lyminge.'

Hilda continued.

'We have certainly seen the fruits of Aidan's house. Aidan was a saint in the making if ever there was one, as it has been our privilege to experience.' She mused. 'Cuthbert has his luminous innocence. While Cedd, Chad, and Cynibil have been three extraordinary brothers in the church.' Eanfled nodded and anticipated the drift of the conversation.

'But, dear Hilda, I think that I know you well enough to think that this is no idle question that you ask. Perhaps you have in mind to start another house?'

And Eanfled raised her eyebrows, as if to emphasise her question, as she went back to her embroidery.

Hilda eased in her pallet, smiled, and nodded.

'It is so. And I feel that Frigyth would be advantaged to lead a new house. But I wonder where as yet?'Eanfled nodded.

'I agree. You have been so fortunate to have someone so able with you all these years. I would have loved to have had her in my court. I was always in admiration for your striving in those

341

smaller houses at Wearmouth and Hartlepool, while I think this abbey is more smoothly run than my household at the courts of Yeavering and Bamborough, for there I never quite knew how or when Oswy might come or go. But let us think of where this new house might be. We might discuss it with Frigyth? I think that we have the means and the resources?'

Eanfled sewed for a while in silence, with the space between the two easy through their long years of friendship. It was Eanfled who reopened their conversation.

'It does occur to me that I might suggest the matter to Egfrid. Finally, he is to wed Eormemburga. She has her way at last. The founding of a new house to celebrate their marriage might become them both?'

This last sentence a hybrid between a statement and a question. Hilda nodded.

'Yes, I had heard that their relationship was to be blessed by the Church at last. And no surprise that Wilfrid will not be called on to officiate at the marriage. I think that they both agreed on Trumhere. Egfrid had a genuine fondness for the abbot of Gilling from his father in his younger days: and Eormemburga was pleased because it is not Wilfrid I think'

Eanfled smiled into her needlework.

■■

342

'The same might be said of Egfrid. Wilfrid is never afraid of ruffling feathers, Hilda.'

'That is true. He never is, nor I think ever will be. I never saw eye to eye with him over several things. But he was key to helping Etheldreda in her troubled journey. And for that I am always grateful.'

A bout of pain from her illness passed over the Hilda's face. As the pain subsided she continued.

'But thank you for the thought of asking the newlyweds for a new foundation. I think that they might need, even deserve, our prayers.'

They both smiled in agreement.

The bell of the gatehouse rang out, three clear sounds. Hilda and Eanfled looked at each other.

'We have a visitor. Martin would not ring at this hour,' Hilda murmured to herself.

'I will go and deal with it, Mother. You must rest.'

The Mother Abbess nodded in acquiescence, with the consolation that increasingly she was aware that her infirmity was leading to her quietly being taken over by the Queen and their daughter. It was a blessing, even as it seemed meet and right. She must not fight it. She must accept it with the grace with which it was given, she told herself;

343

smiling at herself, giving herself advice that she had so often given to others in their vocational training.

Eanfled gathered herself to go down the steps to the abbey gate. As she approached the wooden gatehouse she could see that there was a plainly dressed figure who could well be a fellow sister, accompanied by a youngish fellow. They were both being very careful with the load on an accompanying mule, suggesting that it was not just the trappings of their travel. It was when Eanfled drew close and the sister turned towards her that she was as surprised as delighted.

'Why, Astral. What a surprise! How welcome you are; and Frishere. I had not expected to see you again. You have come from Coldingham, from Mother Ebba? She has let you go!'

This last exclamation with raised eyebrows and a smile. For Eanfled remembered that Astral originally had accompanied Etheldreda when she had come north, being her right hand and companion in the scriptorium at Hexham. Ever loyal, she had taken her vows with her queen under Wilfrid's benediction and moved with her into the care of Ebba at Coldingham: and how excellent her work with the quill was appreciated there. But only the two sisters, Sewera and Sewenna, had helped her queen escape when King Egfrid had ridden north to assert his marital rights. Astral had been left at Coldingham.

Astral now turned to Eanfled somewhat pleadingly.

'I have stayed with Ebba. But there is no French spoken at Coldingham and I so missed Ette. We heard that she is now safely returned to her fenlands and has set up a house there. Mother Ebba has so kindly allowed me to take the books that we made at Hexham, They are safely stored on this mule, and, God willing, we will take them to Ely and Etheldreda.'

Astral smiled in anticipation of her thoughts, but with her head still bowed.

'Mother Ebba instructed me that I should call at your house to seek refuge: and to convey the warmest greetings to Mother Hilda; and to you all.'

Eanfled greeted her warmly and, without thinking, continued in French.

'You are both very welcome. You will bring joy to Mother Hilda, especially with your greetings from Ebba. I am so pleased to see you, and so well. Let us get you sorted and then you can share all your news. I know that you will be welcome for as long as you wish to stay, but I should warn you that Mother Hilda does struggle with a recurring illness, so that your times with her may be short. She can get exhausted very quickly.'

■■■■■■■■■■■■■■■■■■■■■■■■■■■■■■■■■■■■■■■

345

They discoursed further as they ascended the hill. Frishere took their mounts to the stables to unload, to water and to feed; and to make sure that the precious books in their protective wrappings were taken to store in the library attached to the church.

Eanfled had known Astral well when Etheldreda was at court. She knew how close Etheldreda and she had been, and how she had brought her French influences with her, which only served to remind Eanfled of her own life at Lyminge where she and Tata had often lapsed into French, and where a young Hilda was also a fluent conversationalist.

Hilda's French now felt rather rusty when she finally met Astral, who she had scarcely met previously. But she was keen to hear of Ebba and the abbey of Coldingham: even as she tired quickly, as Eanfled had warned.

At Whitby the scriptorium was just finishing a book of the psalms. Hilda suggested that Astral might wait until it was bound in stronger leather. Then it might be added to Astral's collection to take to Ely as the abbey's gift, along with a small, silver, chalice that they had already had made by their silversmith. Astral could not but remember that when they first passed through the hamlet of Whitby Ette had ordered a sword and a torc to be made by the same smith. There was some poetic resolution that now she left bearing a chalice for her mistress by the same silver smith: her mission completed.

They debated whether she and Frishere would make the whole journey by land or possibly by sea. Astral was wary of the sea but saw that it might shorten the time. They would have to further seal the books in waxed cloth to keep them dry. They were so precious. In the end Frishere did persuade her, and Aelred and Casper from the hamlet at the mouth of the Esk were delighted, and well rewarded, for carrying them to the south bank of the river Humber, where they would leave Deira and make for the small abbey at Fixborough. There Astral might recover from the sea journey. Thence again by pony, this time accompanied by two donkeys, to Ely where Etheldreda, at last an Abbess in the fens, could scarcely believe that Astral had made the journey, bearing such gifts, even as they also were treasured memories of their time together at Hexham, when the scriptorium had been such a consolation to her. Additionally, gifts from Ebba and Hilda, and Eanfled and Aelffled. How blessed Etheldreda's life in the fens now felt, with the restoration of Astral to her house the most comforting of all the gifts.

347

Meanwhile, Eanfled and Aelffled had conferred with Egfrid, resulting in ten hides of land being given for a new convent at Hackness, on the Beck of Whisper Dale. Frigyth and twelve sisters were chosen, or volunteered, to form a daughter house. Hilda felt cadences were moving through a final sequence in her life. Despite her infirmity she determined to go to see the new house in the first spring of its life. Eanfled proposed that she would travel with her and that they might well leave Aelffled in charge at Whitby for a month. Eanfled argued that, while she would manage to ride a steady roan cob, the Mother Abbess should travel in a sling between two of the ploughing oxen who were used to being yoked together. With her arthritis the gentle swing of the sling was kinder than the unsprung bumps that she might have experienced in the haycart that had been suggested.

Even so the Mother Abbess was somewhat exhausted by the two-day journey. However, she soon revived, as much by the tranquility of the setting as by the gentle hospitality of her sisters. It was a comfort and a fulfillment to see Frigyth in her element. The constrained size of the place was a consolation, awaking memories of Lyminge, of Folkestone, of early days at Wearmouth, of the desperation at Hartlepool where she had first met Frigyth

Hilda was somewhat restored by the tranquility of the site. The quiet flowing waters of Lowdale Beck before it wound down the dale to join the swell of the river Derwent, enclosed in the wooded hills of the sheltered vale, now spoke comfortingly to her older years. Whereas the younger Hilda had loved the bracing challenge of her coastal settings, the older Mother Abbess was thankful that creating this secluded house had been a right decision. She found time to write to Egfrid and Eormemburga to thank them; inviting them to visit if they could find time and assuring them that they would be remembered there in their daily prayers.

Her fever abated for a while. She was even able to make short walks by the beck with Eanfled or Frigyth. The latter full of gentle plans and still seeking the advice of her Mother Abbess: even as Hilda knew full well that her new prioress was quite capable of the appropriate decisions. It was more a formal expression of the bond that they had developed over the years. Each not addressing the hidden thought that, even as this was a fulfillment, it might also be the the last time that they might be together.

When the two placid oxen were re-yoked to take Hilda back, Frigyth had knelt for her Mother Abbess's blessing. Frigyth remained kneeling as the oxen stopped chewing their cud and began to roll their way forward and homeward. When Frigyth finally looked up, as Hilda disappeared, she found that all her sisters were also kneeling. But as she rose, so did they: and silently went back to their work. The services that day did have a tangible resonance of thanksgiving above their usual level.

The two royal ladies were duly welcomed home, refreshed by their short sabbatical. They found all to be in order, with the lay brothers bowing, kneeling, or making the sign of the cross, as the entourage passed through the outer fields of the estate. The brothers were busy sowing the last of the spring corn on the tilled fields; and were just as pleased also to see two of their most reliable oxen returning to the fold!

It was some days later that Eanfled ventured to raise another matter with Hilda.

'It is a great consolation for me to have the grave of Oswy here at the abbey, Hilda. I do find that here I reflect on my good fortune and the family that I have had, none more so than here with you and Aelffled. But I wonder if we might join Oswy's grave with that of his mother, Acha. Even with Edwin? That they may be even more tangibly present in our prayers?'

■■

She left her supplication hanging in the air. It was followed by a nod, merely indicating that the question had been heard, and a period of silence while the Mother Abbess deliberated.

'I do understand the sentiment Eanfled. I am forever full of remorse that when I was so busy with Oswy making us choose between our differences over the dates of Easter that I missed the deaths of Cedd and Acha during that dreaded outbreak of the plague.' Another pause.

'Even as I think our aunt has forgiven me, I also would feel some strange consolation in having her here. It is strange, yet real, the consolation that we receive from our prayers at the graveside. Although we know the soul has left its earthly frame, how we are consoled by our remembrances at the graveside? It is so often as if we are with them again.'

Another silence.

'Edwin is even as close to me as he was to you. Perhaps more so, for he rescued Hereswid and me, and mother, from the treacherous Cerdic. Edwin and Tata did bring us up as their family. We were even baptized at the same time.'

Hilda smiled, slightly lost in reverie of good things, blocking out the final brutal assassination and dismembering of her uncle.

'It is a delicate matter. For each community will treasure these graves: but you have my support. However, do tread carefully. You might make a gentle proposition to the heads of the communities, while also asking the advice of Egfrid?'

Eanfled nodded.

So, it came about that a royal enclosure began around the grave of Oswy in an area to the east of the main church at Whitby. A plot that was destined to become the resting place of several of the present company; a royal graveyard.

It was some months later when, after delicate negotiations and the support of the King, that the coffins of Acha and Edwin, sister and brother, were re-interred in the royal enclosure on the cliffs.

Eanfled, while sitting with Hilda, ventured, half musing,

'It is only mother that is missing.'

There was a silence from Hilda: but it lay easily between them. Each with their remembrances of Tata. It was Hilda who broke the silence.

'Your mother lies in peace at Lyminge. It is her foundation and her home. It seems right and meet. Her community rightly treasure her presence. I would not have it otherwise, and, I think, nor would she. But I think that I have a confession Eanfled.'

Hilda sat herself up.

'Eanfled, will you please reach down that small wooden box next to my books from the shelf please?'

Eanfled did as she was bid and moved across the small cell with its square open window looking across the graveyard towards the cliffs and the sea. A light breeze rustled in the grass.

Hilda, for a moment, simply laid her hand on the lid, as if offering a blessing; as if receiving a blessing. Then she opened it.

'Oh,' was all Eanfled managed. For in the box, on a small square of white linen, shone a ring of a single sapphire.

'I had quite forgotten mother's ring. It is so beautiful,' managed Eanfled.

'Yes, it is. She always had exquisite taste. She gave it to me when I was caring for her.' A pause while the two of them simply admired the ring; each with their own memories.

'You know that I never wear a ring but that of my vocation, nor had I fully found my vocation when your mother gave me this. But I have always kept and treasured this. I had always hoped to pass it on to you and Aelffled. But now I wonder if this box and its contents might not lie as a commemoration to your mother within Edwin's grave that we may all remember her; and them.'

Eanfled bowed her head, deeply moved.

'Let it be so,' Hilda eventually offered.

And so it was: and as if the whole family became re- united in the royal enclosure on the cliffs: where the wind would blow from the east and the cry of the whirling sea birds would drift across the standing stones. Haunting cries forever evoking distant memories.

The recurrent bouts of fever that Hilda bore with fortitude did not only bind her to her pallet but ate at her physical condition: and she wasted, even as her mind was as sharp and as clear as ever. The community knew that they would not have her with them for much longer. So each service that she managed to attend became particularly special.

Hilda knew that her earthly time was coming to an end. Sleep was a precious time with her fevered illness. Much of the time that was allowed for sleep was half in half out of consciousness; fitful. It made her more aware of the many dreams that occupy our sleeping time. How time and people appear and disappear, how places form and change, morphing seamlessly into another place. How things unimagined can be frequented by those who are known, and how the known can be confusingly mixed in time and place. It was such a strange land of turmoil, sometimes so serene, sometimes so dark. Often her dreams would take her back to Edwin's reign; of when she, Hereswid and Heiu would escape to the pool where the three rowan trees grew between the rocks of the waterfall. Where the blue dragonflies hovered. Or were they now the smaller blue damsel flies, but lasting for a day?

Sometimes it was a young Tata who sat on the bank as they splashed in the water, the small trout scuttling into the shady water. Sometimes their mother, Breguswith would appear; she sometimes young and sprightly; sometimes wan and pale. So strange that she would seem only to chat with Tata, only smiling at the young maidens splashing in the pool. Then she would be gone, and the water on the pool still, but for the ripples caused by the breeze. It was all so strange.

There were dreams of Lyminge. Dreams of journeying, often between the palace at Lyminge and Eanswith's abbey on the cliffs at Folkestone, with the clouds billowing and the sea birds calling. But such confusion in the journeys. Sometimes they would end up at Canterbury, sometimes on the beach at Withernsea. Sometimes the turnstones would fly around her: sometimes there were tents rather than buildings. Sometimes Bassus was with her, sometimes not. It was all so strange.

Yet when she finally knew that her time had come, she took the viaticum; called her sisters in two and threes and took her leave. Her final images were of the pool; the three trees were now as thorn trees, flowering with white petals, which fell like confetti on the surface of the water. The sisters with her saw the stresses of her life disappear from her face. The light behind the trees grew brighter and the Mother Abbess entered the vision of the final peace that passes understanding.

Epilogue

A lone black-headed tern uttered its call from the cliffs. The rest of the flock had migrated south. It would soon follow. The wind blew keenly as the funeral procession approached the royal enclosure. Aelffled led the procession behind the coffin, the wind buffeting her robes, the coffin borne by six of the monks. Aelffled had been elected as Hilda's successor; Eanfled an ever-supporting figure.

The wind rattled the bent thorn trees, a few remaining leaves scattering, falling vicariously.

A handful of chosen sisters, both at Hackness and at Whitby, also had seen the light that Hilda had perceived on the night of her dying. Their reports gave an added poignancy to the funeral.

The Mother Abbess was interred in the royal enclosure.

It would be a significant span of years before Eanfled and Aelffled joined Hilda. Aelffled, the new abbess, had continued the work of Hilda, building the community, even bridging the differences between Egfrid and Wilfrid. Even, more remarkably, Eormenburga finally repented of her ways.

The seasons would come and go. The cliffs would continue to crumble, taking some of the buildings with them. The Vikings would plunder the abbey and its riches. But the sea birds always would continue to return to the newly exposed crags in the cliffs. In time a new abbey would be built, further back from the ceaseless beating of the sea and its ruins stand to this day. For the light that Hilda had brought was not to be diminished.

Bibliography

■■■

 Several readers of Sisters,Saints and Queens
enquired about sources of reading. I hope the
following are useful for the Family of Hilda.

Bede: A history of the English Church and People.
Penguin Classics. [1984].

Blair J: The church in Anglo-Saxon Society. OUP
[2005]

Blair J: Building Anglo-Saxon England. Princeton
University Press. [2018]

Bright WB: Early English Church History.
Macmillan & Co, London. [1877].

Broadley R: The glass vessels of Anglo-Saxon
England 650-1100. Oxbow books. [2020]

Chadwick N: The Celts. Pelican Books. [1987].

Chadwick H [ed]: Not Angels, but Anglicans. A
History of Christianity in the British Isles.
Canterbury Press. [2000].

Daniels R. Anglo-Saxon Hartlepool and the foundations of English Christianity. Tees Archeology Mongraph. Vol 3. [2007]

Edwards E: St Eanswythe of Folkestone. St Mary & St Eanswythe Folkestone Church. [1980-2012]

Fell C. Women in Anglo-Saxon England. British Museum Publications. [1984]

Hill D: An Atlas of Anglo-Saxon England. Blackwell. [1984]

Hodgkin RH: A History of the Anglo-Saxons. [vol I & II]. Oxford University Press. [1939].

Hope-Taylor B: Yeavering: an Anglo-British Centre of Northumbria. HMSO. [1977]

James E: The Franks. Basil Blackwell. [1988].

Laing L & J: Anglo-Saxon England. Routledge & Kegan Pam. [1979]

Mckerracher M: Farming transformed in Anglo-Saxon England. Oxbow Books. [2018]

Mount T: Medieval Medicine. Amberly. [2015]

Reece R: Excavations in Iona 1964-1974. Institute of Archeology University of London. [1981]

Sawyer PH: From Roman Britain to Norman England. Routledge. [1998].

Stenton F: Anglo-Saxon England. [3rd edition] Oxford University Press. [1971].

Swanton M: The Anglo-Saxon Chronicles. Phoenix Press. [2000]

Thomas G & Knox E : Early Medieval Monasticism in the North Sea [conclusion of the Lyminge excavations 2008-2015]. Oxford University School of Archeology. [2017]

Turner S, Semple S& Turner A: Wearmouth and Jarrow. University of Hertfordshire. [2013]

Warin A: Hilda:the chronicle of a Saint. Marshall Morgan and Scott [1989]

Webb JF: The Age of Bede. Penguin Classics. [1981].

Wilson D: The Anglo-Saxons. Pelican Books. 1986].

Yorke B: Nunneries and the Anglo-Saxon Royal Houses. Continuum. [2003]

Yorke B: Kings and Kingdoms of early Anglo-Saxon England. Routledge. [2013]

Printed in Great Britain
by Amazon

55207141R00206